AWAKEN DREAMER

Awaken Dreamer

SHELLEY CASS

For my beloved ones – my guiding lights.
And for the wonderfully talented and also beloved Kira, who helped
me choose the title of this novel.

Please note, while elements of history, legend and religion are used within these pages, this is a work of fiction.

Copyright © 2020 Shelley Cass
All rights reserved.
Print ISBN: 978-0-6451118-2-8
Ebook: 978-0-6451118-3-5

Enjoy a free taste of the new action-romance series: 'Raze Warfare'
A gritty urban backdrop, gang warfare, a vigilante hero, a corrupt sys-
tem, and a bisexual awakening. Join the action, enjoy the ride.

RECEIVE YOUR EXTRA RAZE WARFARE CHAPTER WHEN YOU SIGN UP FOR SHELLEY CASS' VIP LIST. GET YOUR BONUS HERE:

shelleycass.com/coming-soon-02

LINK TO YOUR FREE VIP READER GIFT

Excerpts from: The Collected Tales of Mythological and Historical Heroes

This is a first edition text, published by the World's third generation of great Leaders. Congratulations – you've purchased one of the last Leader approved hard copy texts!

On the subject of 'religion':

People once practiced ritualistic behaviours, holding spiritual beliefs and faith in 'religions'. These religions focused on the teachings of beings or deities said to guide humanity – 'overseers' of fate and the universe.

*In the earliest primitive times humanity celebrated **the Goddess – a 'Mother Nature'** type figure, for her role as a life giver through birth. She was also known as **Gaea**, the wise woman, **Hecate or Crone**.*

Time shifted and many worshipped pantheons of gods and goddesses overseeing all areas of life – celebration, love, war. Later again there were masculine, all-seeing, yet invisible figures who communicated through prophets, angels, scripture, messengers or human religious leaders.

There were a great many types of religions, and these often brought communities together and provided moral instruction. However, war and division also often resulted from competition between these religions. There were masses killed in crusades to claim holy sites, and there was persecution against 'dissenters'.

So it was decided by the first great Leaders of the modern era that religions should be done away with in all forms. We must count ourselves lucky to have had this danger removed from our World.

| 1 |

– The Dreamer –

"Describe the dream you've been having this time Lili One." A stylus tapped briskly against a screen filled with notes.

"You can see the dream on your screen, doctor," Lili replied dully. Just going through the motions of a mental perfection check.

"Yes," the doctor flicked her stylus across the screen, switching to the scene that she'd downloaded from Lili's memory. "I can see a woman in a cave. But the dreamer always knows much more about what's going on."

Lili's expression was blank as she watched the cave scene from outside of her own mind this time. "The woman in the cave is waiting for something."

The dream woman had Lili's face, but her scalp was shaven, her palms were inked, her furrowed brow was marked and there were crude symbols all over the woman's sun touched skin.

"Do you think the woman in the dream is *you?*" the doctor

probed. "Perhaps you feel you are waiting for something in real life?"

This was a repeat of so many mental perfection checks. Lili often dreamed of herself living in other times that were too ancient for most people to envision as ever having happened.

She was never the hero in these dreams. Usually she was a witch being cast out of villages. People yelled that she was a demoness. And this always prompted the doctor to conclude that Lili, the first lab-bred model of her kind, must be having the dreams because she was feeling 'removed' or 'different'. Though Lili was so full of tech that she hardly felt anything at all. Then the doctor always prescribed a mental update so that they could both move on with their day.

"The woman's markings could be like your skin tech enhancements," the doctor went on. "Her facial features are like yours. And you both definitely sit like Soldiers."

"I *am* a Soldier," Lili replied stiffly, straight backed as ever on the office lounge.

In the dream on the screen the Lili-like woman had a snake tattooed along her own perfectly straight spine, and a screech owl design glared out from beneath her collarbones. As the sky beyond the dream cave's mouth was filled with burning silver starlight, it was also clear that even the rocky walls around the woman were picture covered.

The cave images appeared to tell the dream woman's story, showing her being created from clay, alongside a man. They were pictured as being in a garden at first, before she was drawn running away into a wasteland.

More markings on the cave suggested that she had endured a terrible struggle to survive, until the next lot of figures depicted the woman being saved by what could only be a falling star.

The star had a glowing human shape, and was drawn to be reaching out to the woman as if it had descended from the sky especially to help make the woman's wish for freedom from the garden come true.

"Well this dream version of yourself does not seem to do much," the doctor commented, taking no notice of the cave art.

Lili kept watching the screen. "For two nights in my dreams this woman has been sitting in the decorated cave in perfect meditation."

"As I said," the doctor arched perfectly shaped eyebrows. "She's inactive. Perhaps we can analyse that you're feeling overworked and want to be still and mindless. You should set your Dream-Dictator settings to numb every night."

"No, the woman is waiting. Sending out her thoughts," Lili frowned faintly. "As if she's pushing to be heard by someone, or something."

"Ah," the doctor tapped her stylus. "Classic Soldier case. You're not meant to think and not meant to have your own voice. So you're not feeling appreciated at work."

"I believe the woman in the cave is much older than she looks," Lili went on with a sigh, ready to hear what other work-life problems she could be deemed to have. "And she's near death. But I think she's alone in her final moments because the people in her tribe have shunned her."

The dream woman's image was swiped away and the stylus began moving as notes were jotted down.

"Tribe?" the doctor questioned. "You think your dream is based before the modern era again?"

Lili shrugged one strong shoulder. "These days there are not many real rock caves that can be visited for leisure let alone for dying in."

The doctor pursed her lips. "And why does the 'tribe' shun this primitive woman?"

Lili fidgeted a little. "The dream woman's cave drawings suggest that she and the first man of the World were created together. But when she went her own way she struggled until she was blessed by a saviour from the sky, who gave her freedom and long life. Her rebelliousness and longevity likely set her apart and drew fear from others."

"An outcast woman. Just like the others of your pre-modern era witch dreams," the doctor interjected. "Mhmmmm. Persecution and death. Blessings." The stylus was writing madly again. "And this dream woman has wallowed in that cave in isolation for two nights of your sleep. I think we can analyse that you feel a lack of belonging. Removed and different."

"I actually think," Lili went on. "That this dream woman feels so blessed by the saviour from the sky who once helped her that she wants her spirit to stay in the World for more cycles. She wants to live more lives and to alter her first wish for freedom, to be bigger. She wants freedom not just for herself, but for the heavenly star creature, and for everyone."

The doctor clicked the stylus. "Right. Well ... we'll analyse that you're bored and unappreciated at work, you feel separate, need some meditation, and want to do more with your life as a Soldier," the doctor moved to switch the screen off.

"The dream woman was finally answered by who, or what, she'd been waiting for before I woke up this morning," Lili said. "If that changes your analysis."

"Oh?" the doctor swiped her way through the dream until she gasped at the sudden, blinding appearance of a disc of light. "What in the …"

"The being in the light is something amazing – something that started all life cycles, and it gives the dream woman a warning. Her choice; to make her spirit stay again, *is* possible. Only because of the saviour's blessing that has allowed her to make all of her own decisions freely. But this choice might mean lifetime after lifetime of hardship for her, as her one wish, the first dream of them all, has already been granted and she will have to wait until nearly everyone else has had their turn before she can have another," Lili sat forward slightly in thought. "Despite the warning, she chooses to wait as many lifetimes as it takes until it can be her turn again."

"I see," the doctor replied as at last the light faded from the screen.

The dream woman sank slowly backward until the snake tattooed along her back was pressed against the dirt, and both her eyes and the screech owl's eyes gazed up at the stars beyond the cave. A faint smile spread across the dream woman's darkly stained lips.

"Can we infer anything from all of that?" Lili asked. "Is it normal?"

The doctor shook herself.

"No." The doctor put the screen down. "You need to go to the techies. You're seriously glitching."

Lili sat back. "I have a connection session with my Ordinary buddy tomorrow, but I have an update booked in soon."

"Good. Those dreams need to go."

Excerpts from: The Collected Tales of Mythological and Historical Heroes

This is a first edition text, published by the World's third generation of great Leaders. Congratulations – you've purchased one of the last Leader approved hard copy texts!

On the subject of mythological places:

According to early belief, heaven and the **Elysian Fields** *were supposed to be peaceful realms of the dead, where fulfilled, good spirits came to rest. This can be related to the original garden of paradise, Eden.*

Similarly, **Shangri-La** *was a mythical land supposedly situated in an isolated part of the World that was once known as the Himalayan mountains. Safe and removed, it became a place of health, wisdom and youth. People would find Shangri-La only when they were utterly devoted to a life of peace.*

It was later suggested that rather than being a physical place, Shangri-La was actually a state of mind and a way of being. Only when a person's spirit was truly enlightened or fulfilled could they reach it.

We can all agree that our modern World is more perfect than any such dream, and we have all been made to be as happy as any citizen could ever be.

| 2 |

- The Star -

Blink.

Grey clouds were looming like a surly ceiling above.

Psychedelic street art and signs framed my peripheral vision.

Blink.

Rain was pooling around my body. Absorbing into my denim jacket. Clinging to my silk shirt.

Blink.

There was a face surrounded in fuzzy, dripping afro hair. Looking *so worried*. Her loudly printed bell bottoms would be getting wrecked as she knelt in the puddles beside me. But she was just realising how much she wished she could help me, and that she should ignore social divisions and follow her dream to be that nurse. I had done a good job inspiring her – my unwitting client, just by dramatically getting myself murdered in front of her.

A rose of blood was blooming from my already sexily unbuttoned sixties chest. It had been a shooting death that had got me this time, and I was the perfect muse for a future African American nurse who needed to make a difference in a segregated land.

A new face appeared, blocking out the clouds with a wiry, hippy beard. "Be cool man, hold on …"

His own expression was mighty pinched, like he should be the one to chill. Maybe his skin tight hip huggers had cut off circulation.

"Catch you on the flip side," I grinned bloodily for full dazzling effect. I knew I was getting down to the skinny end of things, after successfully kick starting another truly miraculous revelation.

"No, just hold on," the future nurse said, the life changing desire to be able to save me really written so clearly on her face.

It was another job well done. And sure, it would have given me a real kick to have seen out my whole death and burial just once. But that process was only to help the humans cope, not for my entertainment.

It couldn't be easy to see someone as slick as my sixties self getting gunned down.

Blink.

Waking up again.

Damn. I realised I should have squeezed a 'keep on truckin' suckas' into my final swinging moments. I'd loved that cute saying, and it was ultra-encouraging too.

Blink.

A night sky replaced the rainy one and I wondered what era I was waking up to work in this time.

It was impossible to see the stars with so many flashing city lights.

Blink.

The bitumen ground under my shoulder blades and sharp stones were engraining themselves into the back of my head. Making tiny skin dints to live in.

Blink.

I was lying at the foot of a skyscraper. It rose above like a reflective, black paint strip that had been rollered up the air. Tiny specks of birds circled at the lit up tower pinnacle.

My head wouldn't turn but I could just make out identical buildings on either side. There were banners stretched between the buildings that flashed adverts for great sex and artificial sleep.

They were … the answer came to me. Holograms. Hmmm.

Even though I'd only just shut my eyes on the days of hippies a great deal seemed to have changed.

"Here I am," I groaned to the universe, "shaping history, and you only give me a micro sleep."

The words came out mushily because the mouth I was developing still seemed a bit wobbly.

The poor chap I was currently reinflating had apparently recently suffered quite the drop.

I hoped his dreams would be granted next time round as I sucked at reforming teeth and gums.

The taste of blood and bile from his body was fading and being replaced by the taste of blood and bile from the sticky end I had just come from of my own.

The teeth were starting to feel more like mine too.

A fair bit less shattered by impact that is.

I blinked a few more times to catch up on some missed decades. It was odd that I'd missed a couple of eras this time. Normally I hopped around each decade for a long while, working hard to make an abundance of dreams come true.

But it seemed I'd skipped some seventies discos, the crimpers of the eighties, and fluorescent stockings. I wondered who'd copped that one for the team. I would have loved if Butch had. Butch always got all the glamourous jobs, and stepped way too far into the hero's spotlight if you asked me. We were meant to create and nurture dreams, not steal the show.

Blink.

Oh nice, the internet looked good.

Blink.

Wow, technology actually seemed a bit invasive. I only got a brief flash of something called Brainwave – and its installation into people at birth.

How far into the new millennia was I?

My scalp itched as my own lustrous hair pushed away chunks of ingrained tar from the bald mash that boy-o had rocked out on this body before me.

Cheekbones shifted and my nose angled. I sniffed, welcoming back my features.

Not long now.

Ouch. Skin meshed together over bone baring elbows.

Ouch ouch ouch. Spine reconnected. Floating pieces rejoined.

A puff of breath.

And good to go.

I sat up.

A streetlight not connected by any wires flickered while I adjusted my essence.

I glanced at my scraped fingers.

Empty.

"Ahem?" I implored skyward.

Not empty.

"Better," I grinned, settling now cigarette filled digits in a familiar V over my lips and a long drag filled fresh, unspoiled lungs.

I glanced around at the cracked up road my new body had been broken across a minute before.

Time to hop up.

Stones shifted and scraped as I stepped out of the man-shaped dent.

I flicked my eyes across the road, over the fake green nature strip – of course we hadn't woken up on that – and let them scale the building to the sixty third floor. It had been his home and would now be mine.

His belongings would fast be fading, leaving empty walls and halls. His family would already remember having packed them and farewelling their son.

I rolled my clicky neck and dusted a layer of fine, golden sand from my hands.

"Right mate, what are you doing out here?"

That late night jogger had just come out of *nowhere*. He seemed like the perfect specimen of caveman masculinity brought back to life; rippling and enfolded in burly endorphins.

My blinks had made me think the noughties were all about beer guts and couch potatoes, but he was more military than round. Perhaps he was patrolling rather than jogging, which didn't bode well.

Was that some kind of robotic light flashing in his left eye?

"All good bud," I took one long drag in and then gave him a dazzling smile, dropping the smoke and grinding it into the hole I'd not long died and revived in. "I'm going."

He did seem dazzled, staring at me in fascinated puzzlement when a second before he'd been ready to set down the law, like I shouldn't be innocently standing in a crater on an empty street.

"Ahh. Great…" he managed as I reined my smile into a less enticing grin. "Because you're … meant to be inside."

His left eye kept up its steady blinking light. And that outfit was definitely too snazzy to be a regular jogger's choice. Too uniform.

"Yes, you're right, because it sure is cold out," I agreed pleasantly. "You're a good sport for caring."

"Yeah…"

"Well. See-ya," I kept grinning as he began bouncing off into the night, glancing over his shoulder at me every now and then until he nearly veered off course.

Perhaps I'd been lucky to have run into him while my essence was still so stunningly fresh and unsettled in this body.

"*It sure is cold out,*" I said again with emphasis, appealing to the night sky. Then I rolled my shoulders as they suddenly filled a satisfyingly sleek leather jacket.

My chest was less tight as the memory of being shot faded, the cavity that had been rent open now mostly filled in under my crisp cotton T-shirt.

"I really hope at least a sofa has been left in there," I said conversationally as I envisioned where I would be staying this time. And I made my way toward the neon purple light at the entrance to the high building that this flesh had not long dropped from.

An identity code from my body's past inhabitant automatically flew from my healing fingertips and I pushed the door open as it unsealed with a hiss. But before I could step into the hall, a squeak drew my attention to a huddled figure in the doorway.

Her cheeks were wet with oily black tear drops that had made her platinum blonde, artificially straightened hair sticky, but she managed a smile through smudged baby pink lipstick.

The purple light flickered over our heads as my heart settled.

"Hey Miss Molly," I said easily.

"Mitch," she murmured in relief. Her memory was already filling in a story of how she thought she had known me since my arrival a couple of months before.

"Whatcha been up to?" I asked, crouching beside her as her head tilted to the side to take me in.

"I ... I was wishing," she said unsteadily, with closing eyes.

"Well little doll, this doorway is not where sweet wishes come true. And certainly not sweet dreams."

"I know …" she sighed. She was nineteen. And I could feel how she had been slowly killing herself. Toxins had left dark stains on her young cells like the Nicorette I never lived long enough to drown in. And hurt radiated from every lonely pore under her concealer.

"Hand please," I ordered.

She hiccupped. Then her shiny, little baby pink nails glittered in the light as she reached obediently in my general direction. Her skin was too cold against mine as I pulled her up carefully.

Molly's tiny body barely stood up to my chest despite the platform heels, and she quickly slumped against me. I felt as if that bullet wound had just reopened for a very different reason.

"You are not my assignment, Miss Molly," I told her as I looped an arm under her legs and lifted her. "But I believe in kindness for kindness' sake too, you know."

It felt like I carried a child as she drifted in and out of consciousness for the lift ride. The elevator walls were covered in blue graffiti that glowed in the dark every time the light flickered at my presence. It had a squiggly, juvenile tag from an artist known as 'Boof'.

This century did not seem to be making a return to the classics.

"If only kindness could save me," she murmured.

It was as if the alcohol still danced upon her taste buds, so that I could almost catch the flavour of it.

"Oh, it can really help. Along with a sprinkling of hope to push you in the right direction," I informed her. "I think you once dreamed of being more."

"Mmm. I was going to be much more," she agreed, lolling against me. "But now even my Dream-Dictator's sedated settings can't give me sweet dreams. The World is turning to nothing. Remember … Dom?"

I felt a twitch at the name, and realised Dom must have been the jumper. The person whose body I had used as an anchor for my own.

"He couldn't take it," she said sadly. "Not even the strongest happiness pills of the modern era could have helped him."

I gave her computerised door a stern look until it opened so that I could tuck her into bed.

The apartment felt foreign; dark windows, screens and white shiny surfaces all lit by dim orange lights glowing from numerous hologram posters. Not inviting.

But I stared in disgust at a flashing machine that sat beside her bed. The Dream-Dictator thing's prongs automatically started to extend toward Molly's face as I settled her down. They were mean and sharp, and I quickly pressed the glowing off button that made them retract.

"Now *this* is how good dreams are made," I told her, brushing her forehead gently and leaving a faint line of shimmering golden dust across her skin. "Dream of more, and reach for more my little doll," I said as she fell asleep peacefully.

Her door was much more easily convinced to slide closed behind me as I left, and the stark white, automated door to my own apartment three floors up gave hardly so much attitude.

I stepped inside and found stripped walls, dark rooms and empty halls, but a large black sofa waiting in the living space.

Somehow this alone felt more homely than Molly's up to date apartment.

I stepped over the couch arm and bounced down, stretching long legs out and speculating.

"Another assignment, another dreamer," I told myself, contemplating the city's sprawling lights from the vast window view. "But I'm not sure I recognise the world I've woken up to this time."

Excerpts from: The Collected Tales of Mythological and Historical Heroes

This is a first edition text, published by the World's third generation of great Leaders. Congratulations – you've purchased one of the last Leader approved hard copy texts!

On the subject of 'war' and 'inequality':

*Before our great Leaders put an end to **war** and made us into a one World nation, there were a disturbing number of hate crimes, nationalism fuelled competitions, genocides to wipe out entire races, Stolen Generations, and periods of slavery (one human owning another).*

*Shockingly, there were six **World Wars**. Directly following the 'hot', direct nature of the first two World Wars, the allied victors of the second World War even turned on each other next in a conflict known as **the Cold War**. A war where the opponents' weapons, if used, would have resulted in **MAD** (mutually assured destruction and catastrophic, World ending damage). One then hardly needs mention the level of bloodshed and the kinds of horrors that ensued in World Wars Three to Six, where internal tech, terrorism and biological warfare came into play.*

With such a history of violence, it was of course a glorious day when the first Leaders declared an end to independence and separation for all countries. Country names, tension between different states, and unique cultures and languages were all replaced by the unity of one World.

Everyone speaks World now, and thankfully modern Leaders control all weaponised tech – only keeping powerful weapons for the sake of eliminating natural threats to humanity.

*Yet besides physical warfare, there were also **inequalities** between people that had to be overcome. In the distant past lands were taken from original inhabitants. There were protests by women who, by their gender, were deemed inferior and forced to fight for **suffrage** (the right to vote). There were movements against **segregation** (division and lower quality of life based on skin colour). There were equality movements to end the stigma faced by couples of the same gender. There was a brief Queer Coup in what was once known as the United Nations. There was a resurgence of cannibalism that led to the great Vegan versus People Eater fiasco. And most notably, the riots against IQ based income.*

*So it was also a World changing day when **the new World hierarchy was established: Leaders, Administrators, and All Other People**. This eliminated all inequality and persecution against different groups – as all groups dissolved and simply became people, or World citizens, embraced within the whole.*

As all Leader-loving people belong in the World order, there is now no need for messy, disruptive protest or individual and collective movements or consciousness.

Gender, sexual orientation, appearance and intellect can no longer be used against a person. And if one so decides, these things are easily updateable!

We must also count ourselves fortunate to live in a time where surveillance and data tracking can pick up on any problems, and where Ordinaries are programmed to be unable to hate, unable to harm others, and unable to become corrupt or lawless.

Correction is just a Brainwave update away.

| 3 |

– The Dreamer –

"We were able to detonate the volcano out of existence," Soldier Leader Con growled through his moustache and into the face of the nodding reporter. "The Sciences have not yet found a solution to the quakes, but it won't be long – and the World Soldiers are always minutes away to help anywhere around the globe," he finished.

"So the World is dying?" the pretty reporter, KimLe, pushed, and Lili watched the café newsscreen intently.

"But *we* aren't, and we won't let it." Con folded his arms. "The Leaders will force this World to go on."

"What are Leaders doing to ensure things keep running smoothly and we don't upset the balance? Apart from blowing hazards up?"

"The Leaders are ensuring Soldiers are up to date, and are everywhere, keeping the public and nature in check. It's what they need."

Lili's eyebrow raised as she regarded the screen. Curfews, weapon updates, orders. Saving the World?

She remembered the woman in her dreams wishing for everyone to be free.

"Did you hear what I said? Lili?"

There was the sound of fingernails tapping impatiently on the little café table.

"I'm listening Tiffany," Lili reassured her pouting companion. "I've got tech that helps me hear even the most minute sounds."

"I'm going with 'Tiffie' this week. And it's probably because of all that tech that you were being blank again," Tiffie huffed, and Lili altered her expression to be more receptive.

The young beautician she'd been paired with always found Lili to be too unfeeling, even worse than any other typical Soldier. On the other hand, Lili always found Tiff and all Ordinaries to be erratic and emotional. So it was interesting to observe them.

"I apologise," Lili answered, pulling out her technipen and making an effort to appear relaxed – which was not a natural-feeling stance, even in a civilian skin suit. "Were you discussing the latest observational report we're meant to be writing on each other?"

"Of course not," Tiffie laughed. "You're the brainy one here Lil, I'm happy for you to take charge as usual. This annual buddy report thing is always so ick."

"They say the buddy system, and this compulsory reporting, is designed to make the public understand Soldiers, and to help us be less separate," Lili shrugged.

"Chyeah," Tiff snorted daintily. "Sitting down with the woman covered in fighter design tattoo-tech makes her soo much less intimidating. I'm fully aware that you could jet blast me out of existence. While all I've got, is this," she whipped out her nail laser to perfect her already precise manicure.

"As your life long go-to Soldier, I'd prefer to protect you from jet blasts instead," Lili replied.

"Think about it," Tiff implored. "Out of this partnership, I got the tougher job. How often is a beauty tech going to need saving? Meanwhile keeping *you* grounded and empathetic is getting harder and harder."

Lili said nothing, and her expression was as immovable as ever.

"But anyway," Tiffie shrugged and flicked lemon coloured hair off her shoulder. "More importantly, I was saying it's time for Drew to wake up and realise I'm *perfect* for him."

She launched off about a civvy who sat at each buddy gathering with his antique headphones on to block out any real bonding. Headphones that covered both his ears entirely, and that connected to a tiny tunes device while Drew ignored the Soldier assigned to him.

"I just adore Drew's rebellious style, with his quirky old tech instead of Brainwave. So on trend by being so off trend," Tiff went on. "And after paying so much for my beauty degree chip, my brain is entirely up to date on what's trendy."

Lil twirled her technipen. The energy Tiff put into her crushes was fascinating to Lili, who on the other hand struggled to emote in any situation.

"You are very good at trends," Lili agreed, flipping open a techztbook and using her fingertips to widen its translucent shape into a square on the table top.

She printed the same heading as every other year across

the screen in technipen: 'A connection buddy report – breaching the gap between Soldiers and Regulars.'

Tiff sighed. "Drew would say that even the nouns in the report title, which are common vernacular, point at how vast the gap is between social groups."

The insightfulness of this statement made Lili pause.

"But what would I know?" Tiff went on. "I kind of like us being called 'Regulars' or 'Ordinaries'. It makes me feel predictably safe and comfortable."

Lili returned to editing the glowing page, listing both their full names and codes. She efficiently recorded the different daily routines, beliefs and rules she followed as a Soldier, including any enhancements that had been made to her since the last report. Then she added what she knew of Tiff's life.

"Are there any other interesting developments in our lives that I've missed?" Lili asked. "Anything we've discovered about each other across the year?"

"You were constructed for, and raised as, pure Soldier. You are a Soldier every day in every way. The end," Tiff laughed. "And you can note down for any wealthy Leader who might be reading this that I have become a real guru of the commercial services sector. I am now a *specialist* in tailoring the Biobeauty machine to each unique customer for ultimate statements of individuality or relaxation. I can program the machine to be the best sauna, masseuse, shower, hairdresser, makeup artist, nail technician, tanner, anti-ager, and fashion producer that any client has ever seen. And I could do wonders for Miss Lili One if she would just let me get at her household Biobeauty settings."

Lili shook her head. "My Biobeauty does the basics. Neatening me up for duty. The rest is pointless."

"So *primitive*," Tiffie sniffed.

The statement brought Lili's dream woman to mind, along with a prized book that Lili owned – 'The Collected Tales of Mythological and Historical Heroes'.

A real book with a cover and pages to physically turn, one of the last that the early generations of Leaders had allowed to be printed.

She'd paid dearly for it when her dreams had sparked her curiosity about life before the modern era, and it was about Ordinaries who were able to excel despite their primitive times.

However, the very un-Soldier-like possession was not something Lili had ever wanted to tell Tiff about for their report.

"I don't know how people were ever able to do anything without the advanced tech and programming of the modern era," Tiff mused with her nose crinkling in distaste. "It all would have been so much effort. Such a mess."

"How wild and free it would have been," Lili reflected with an uncharacteristically thoughtful tone.

"How did anyone get anything done with all those decisions and chores to face?" Tiff went on. "Yet despite our luxurious conveniences you willingly allow the most glamourous, helpful settings of your Biobeauty to go to waste."

"I do survive you know. And people in the past managed too. They were strong and capable," Lili remarked, thinking on the things she had learned from her real book. "A man named Da Vinci became very famous for using his own natural talents to forge the way in art and science, for example."

"I'm very naturally talented too," Tiffie announced. "But not everyone is. So ancient times were unfair."

"If it was unfair, there were those who were brave and fought for change, like the women who battled for suffrage."

"See?" Tiff waved her nail laser. "Primitive. In the modern era we don't let anyone go through suffrage."

Lili placed her technipen down on the screen, leaving pixel blots on their list.

"True," she managed at last.

"But thankfully we have no need to dwell on those dark times," Tiff stated contentedly. "Everyone has been totally equal and in no way unique since before I was born and before you were poured into your test tube."

"You're right," Lili intoned. "Everything is fine."

"Fine…" Tiff echoed, suddenly distracted. "Now *he's* fiiine …"

She seemed to be purring.

"Ohh he is a *dreamboat*…"

"Are we talking about Drew again?" Lili frowned.

"Not him," she stopped purring for a second. "He almost seems irrelevant now that I've seen *that*…"

Tiff's eyes appeared to hold less depth than usual, and Lili followed the general direction of her reverie to where a young man was walking past the café window.

"I swear he was looking at us," Tiff whispered, as if he were within earshot.

Lili noticed that the eyes of every other person; male, female, non-binary, digital or otherwise, appeared to also be pinned on the young man.

He strode confidently across the pavement, casually slicing through waves of admiration from surrounding onlookers with one hand hooked in a denim jeans pocket, and the other hand occupied by a cigarette held to his lips.

He lingered by the café door, relishing that cigarette until at last flicking it out as though he were saying goodbye to a dear friend.

"Probably smells like tar," Lili commented, wondering why he would opt to have such a vice when most people had addictive behaviours programmed out of their Brainwave.

He raked his fingers through thick, dark hair, pushing it back from his forehead, and then reached for the café door handle.

Lili noticed he had no visible tech designs, so he couldn't be plain clothed Soldier, but he didn't seem Ordinary. In fact, she found that she couldn't quite look away from the stranger as he opened the door either.

"He's about to be snapped up," Tiff commentated, eyes glued to the window as a girl worked up the courage to accost the dreamboat from outside.

Lili saw the girl jump through a hologram advert about hay fever, distorting an image of new nostril implants.

"Heya!" she chirped so cheerfully that the pitch could be heard through the now ajar door. "I haven't noticed you around here, and would just hate for a newcomer to feel alone! Grab your coffee and come sit with us out here in the fresh filtered air!"

She was super cute and perky.

He gave her a flashing smile and Lili noticed the girl's dimples fade as she took on a dazed countenance.

"You're very kind," he replied. "But I travel a lot, so I'm fine. It's almost like I've been here a million times before."

He made his way inside but she pouted and followed at his heels.

"I can't let you feel like that," she gushed. "I'll show you where the fun is!"

"Actually," he moved to sit at a corner table by the window. "I am expecting someone will be following me shortly. Thanks again."

"Well," she fluttered lilac coloured lashes at him. "Lemme give you my number, in case you do get lonely."

"Sorry," he shrugged. "No phone."

But as he said it, an old-style mobile phone seemed to become noticeable in his hand, as if it had just appeared there, and he paused to scowl at the ceiling for a second. "I mean, no battery."

"Oh, right!" she was losing dignity fast, but she didn't seem to mind. "You know, that's why people communicate via Brainwave," she giggled loudly. "I've only seen phones in museums!"

He raised an eyebrow, as if interested that he had missed something everyone else knew about, but the girl had already scanned the room and was flouncing across to Lili's table.

"You don't mind, do you?" she asked Lili, who didn't have time to answer before the girl had seized her technipen and gone again – ready to brand the gorgeous newcomer with her details.

Lili had to privately admit, he had a strange charismatic

magnetism about him. As if a real rock star from the past had entered the café, filling the room with the kind of gravitational pull that could have drawn crowds of thousands to a stage – before the introduction of virtual concerts.

The café occupants all watched as, in the space of a heartbeat, the girl had imprinted his forearm with a neat line of code, punctuated by a love heart.

"Clever girl," Tiff commented under her breath. "Pixel prints on the skin are a pain to Biobeauty off. He won't be able to forget her."

"Now you know where to find me," the girl beamed encouragingly, and the rock star nodded faintly as a waiter now stepped in front of him, sidelining the girl and appearing ready to ask for some kind of ID code exchange as well.

As soon as the rock star was blocked from Lili's sight she felt suddenly released, as if she had been on high alert since he had first materialised amongst them. Tiff was still craning for a better view while Lili slackened her shoulders and focused back on their unfinished report.

"Tiffan-Tiff-ie," Lili said, frowning at the pixel blots on the techztbook. "I need one of your technipens. Even if it's a glow one."

There was a little gasp from Tiff, and Lili glanced up to find the rock star approaching.

"No need for a new pen," he said, flashing a grin. "Sorry to have stolen this one from you." He placed the technipen on Lili's open palm as she automatically held her hand out, and she unconsciously produced an uncharacteristically warm smile of her own for him before he crossed back to his table.

"Delicious," Tiff breathed. "Absolutely divine."

Lili thoughtfully rolled the warm technipen between her fingertips. Its surface was oddly glittery where he'd held it, as if he'd had shimmer powder on his hands.

"Seriously, he's something else …" Tiff muttered.

People were still watching him at his table, but Lili noticed he had now somehow acquired a digibook – no an old fashioned novel with pages, just like her priceless one – apparently from thin air.

He liked vintage books?

"He's literate too …" Lili joked, while covertly impressed that he'd so tenaciously brought such an item out in public.

"I *know*!" Tiff whispered back intensely.

"But back to this report," Lili returned to business. "Suggestions?"

"Oh I can't go on with this now," Tiff sulked. "We wasted so much time that I have to meet with Davey now."

"What about Drew?" Lili asked.

"I've got to fill in my time waiting for him somehow," she sighed. "You ready to go too?"

Lili shook her head. "I'll finish up here and then head to base."

"Well if you're sure," Tiff said cheerfully, already sweeping out of her chair. "See ya when we have to bond again."

Excerpts from: The Collected Tales of Mythological and Historical Heroes

This is a first edition text, published by the World's third generation of great Leaders. Congratulations – you've purchased one of the last Leader approved hard copy texts!

On the subject of early individuals of note:

**Note, in this section reference is made to geographical places and historical people believed to have existed prior to World unification.*

Herodotus *was an ancient Greek writer known by many as 'the father of history'. He was the first to keep records of general life. However his writing often exaggerated the facts and contained personal opinions.*

Thucydides *was another ancient Greek writer, and a General of early versions of Soldiers. His accounts were the first historical records to appear to be completely clinical and unbiased.*

It is a great relief that our Leaders oversee all media and information to ensure that our records are always consistent and favourable.

| 4 |

– The Dreamer –

Lili tipped a new packet of fizz into her glass and watched the bubbles rise.

She jotted down some more points on Tiff's busy social life, which contrasted to her own Soldier's to do list – fitness course, combat training, patrol, and an up-coming Soldier update with her personal technician, V.

She only glanced up when she felt the mental lurch of Brainwave coming to the foreground of her mind, flashing the time alert. Curfew was approaching, even for off duty Soldiers.

With a blink Lili shrank the time to the edge of her vision, noticing that cleanerbots were already working on the café floors and most of the tables had been cleared.

"This is breaking news," a male news anchor with perfectly trimmed, lime coloured bangs was reporting from the newsscreen. "Leaders have issued statements reporting that a band of Rogues nearly disrupted a recent Leader sanctioned mission to collapse what remained of the Grand Canyon. We have been warned that the Rogues are a growing threat. And since the abduction of our mighty Leading tycoon's heir, Cam Pendragon, it truly is clear that the Rogues are capable of any form of sabotage."

A rotating hologram of the missing Business Empire heir was projected from the screen, showing different angles of Cam Pendragon's blonde curls and a cleanly shaven, noble jaw. But Lili also noticed that the next ultimate Leader had a strangely reluctant, unhappy posture and dull eyes – not projecting a 'knight in shining armour' image even beneath the holographic enhancements.

Nevertheless, Cam's disappearance had thrown Leader ranks into disarray, with lesser Leaders being considered now for the line of complete power, even without the greatest wealth behind them.

"It was only through the intervention of newly updated, indestructible Soldier forces that the mission to eradicate the Grand Canyon was saved," the lime haired reporter continued.

Those were the updates V was going to see Lili about tomorrow. A few more updates and there wouldn't be much left of Lili that could be touchable – she got a little more removed each time, like a good Soldier.

"Thankfully the vast, useless pit is gone at last."

The screen cut to a property corporate representative; a typical Administrator ready to give his opinion on the matter.

"The Grand Canyon was once a defining feature of the part of World that was America. But with wind erosion and sun damage from before the installation of the sun filter, it was crumbling anyway. And now," the corporate man spread his arms benevolently, and gave an overly wide smile. "We've cleared enough land for millions of new apartments!"

The shot returned to the immaculate news anchor. "Leaders have admitted that the Rogues sought to intervene as they feared the land clearance would destabilise the earth further."

"Of course there will be quakes," mister corporate shrugged. "But we can install gravity control in every street to ensure jostling is hardly a problem. There are so many easy fixes, yet the Rogues don't seem to care how much we need the space."

The host had lowered lime green brows, aiming to appear suitably serious when the screen returned to him for a sign off.

"It is for this exact reason that we must obey tightened public controls, must follow our curfew, and must all play a role in surveillance. Every citizen must be on the watch – report anything suspicious and catch those Rogues before they do further harm to World's streamlined society."

As a flow of advertisements rolled out on the newsscreen Lili pushed her fizz glass away and shrank her techztbook closed, standing as a cleanerbot rolled over to get under the table.

Lili noticed that the rock star still sat by the window, leaning back in his chair while another man sat opposite him, speaking intensely; the man's bulky frame straining against his hoodie.

Even with the hood up, it was clear the bulky man was quite beautiful too. His face was oddly cherubic on such a strong body. But the rock star was, as Tiff had put it, *something else.*

Surely he'd had some augmentation work done…

Shaking her head, Lili tore her eyes from the vision of the rock star, stepping out into the crisp, cleaned air, and charitably pretending not to see two abnormally tech covered men who were hiding in the shadows, watching the café.

They were probably Rogues hoping for a free meal, and she was off duty and short on time.

She had a half hour jog from Tiff's glitzy commercial goods and services sector to get to base, so Lili rolled her head to get some Brainwave tunes going, and ignored her surveillance and reporting duties. Another note she would never add to the list for any buddy report.

She skipped across the road through the gaps between the easing automated traffic, and hit the pavement at a paced rhythm, not faltering until she found herself crossing the gardens to her building.

The nightly gardening drones had already come out and were busily restoring every blade of real grass left, as well as polishing every stone in an effort to preserve nature.

When Lili scanned her way into her ninth and tenth floor space, the apartment came alive as if it had missed her.

The fridge unsealed to offer nicely cooled fizzpacks, the microwave flashed images of the day's specials, the screenwall flicked through channels she often watched, and the outdoors inspired terrace lit up with artificial sunlight.

Lili selected the cereal option on the microwave, and as the rays constructed the food and bowl, she watched the screenwall while KimLe, a particularly popular journalist seemed to be wrapping another report up.

"Leaders are in hiding as they discuss their heir crisis, somewhere away from suspected exits of the underground Rogue cities. Meanwhile, as they debate supremacy, our World is breaking up and our lifestyle is unsustainable."

KimLe's enhanced lavender eyes were peering keenly through fashion glasses. That alertness was what had gained KimLe her popularity, as most reporters obediently read the Leader approved bulletin scripts from their Brainwave vision rather than speaking directly or with personal feeling.

But KimLe had always been subtle and smart – she'd never been this outspoken.

"Latest measures have been to control the public and Soldiers with an iron fist, but Leaders still don't appear to have any real strategies for healing our World rather than dominating it." KimLe's knuckles were white as she clasped her digiscreen. "Interestingly, top historian Doctor Hiro Dotus quickly took ill after comparing Ultimate World Leader Uthoria Pendragon to dictators from the distant past. He even suggested that our wealthiest, Ultimate Leader's heir, Cam Pendragon, was *not* abducted, but instead fled Leadership." She was rushing now. "Soldier sector Administrator Sid Dides was also taken into custody after writing a report that revealed Leader approved upgrades to landscapes and Soldiers have been causing even more outbreaks of negative human and natural behaviours. It seems the World needs to be guided to health, but our Leaders' strict control is only stifling it ..."

The screen flickered for a second, pausing on KimLe's taut face, and then the camera-bot was turned away from KimLe, now showing a blonde reporter clone, who was clearly reading internally.

"We regret to announce KimLe's resignation after a stressful personal issue. We apologise that inaccurate information was broadcast. There is nothing to be anxious about, as Leaders do all in their power to maintain order for nature and humanity. Leaders all come from a long line of intelligence. Their ancestors invented our way of life, they sold it to us. They own all information. So they know what is best. Your screen will now connect to your Brainwave so that you receive the health and peace you deserve."

Lili swiped downward with a motion in the air toward the screenwall so that the connection died. Any civvies who had caught KimLe's conspiracy theories were now meant to be receiving a calming release of endorphins from Brainwave, but Lili focused on finishing her cereal instead.

She let the bowl disintegrate, the pixels returning to the microwave storage as she moved to the indoor terrace, climbing the vine covered wall and pulling herself onto the second level.

The mineral waterfall wall always made her tired muscles feel better, restoring and literally washing away pain. But she couldn't get KimLe's face, and what an early retirement could mean, out of her head.

When she laid down, Lili didn't push away the Dream-Dictator's prongs as they sought to hook into her mind. Instead she moved the setting from Soldier Drill Dreams to Numb.

Excerpts from: The Collected Tales of Mythological and Historical Heroes

This is a first edition text, published by the World's third generation of great Leaders. Congratulations – you have purchased one of the last Leader approved hard copy texts!

On the subject of religion:

In many of the eradicated religions, angelic beings featured as divine helpers and guiding lights to humanity. It was often believed that they were born at the beginning of time from the brightest lights within the hearts of the stars – 'heavenly bodies'.

In fact before internal maps were invented, the stars were referred to as literal points of guidance and direction by travellers and sailors. The stars were apparently much easier to see back then, and it is said that they could be made out in shapes such as a lion or fairy figure.

'Star signs' or 'zodiac signs' were even seen to dictate the course of a person's life.

Depending on the religion, the names or forms of angelic beings varied. Angels, seraphim ('the burning ones'), avatars, jinn, devas, bodhisattvas, daemons and spirit guides were just a few of their titles.

It makes sense that beliefs in beings like this were needed by people in a pre-World world.

| 5 |

– The Star –

I'd known she was the target as soon as I'd seen her in the café. For a second, it was like I'd recognised her. But there was nothing in her soul that I could remember, and my essence felt the normal pull, like being in a dream where you feel yourself rushing forward and are about to fall.

She'd noticed me too, which was fine. They always became familiar with me from a distance. It was better that they thought nothing of seeing my face around in the background of their lives for as long as they needed me.

I also knew that some others of my kind had felt me, and at least one was on his way for a meet up. Which was unusual, seeing as they normally shunned me.

All of my kind never could help being drawn to each other. As if they were caught in an intense gravitational pull. But I was generally ignored, and it suited me.

I was still having fun peering over my novel and trying to work out what my new client's dream could be when the chair across from me scraped back.

And Butch sat down.

A puff of hazy golden dust shimmered around him as he settled because he was never careful enough with his sand.

I sighed.

"Butch."

"Why do you insist on calling me that?" he growled.

"Brother, it suits you."

"What name do you go by in this century? Mitchell is it? Last time I saw you it was Mikaeel."

"I can't help that the names people give me are always beautiful."

"But you feel *Butch* for me?"

"More so than Gabe, angel face."

Gabe – Butch's – white blonde hair and face were hidden by an ill-fitting hood. Strange for such a proud being to hide, I thought. And hiding in a hood was more conspicuous anyway.

He really didn't have a subtle grain of sand in his essence.

"Are you ever going to get over yourself?" he glowered. "Eternity is a long time to be pissed off with no one to trust."

"Better to be pissed off than dead, brother. I could forgive and forget, but nobody else has."

He bristled, his cheeks turning to a puce colour. "You have *not* always made the correct choices." He crossed his arms and almost burst the seams of his sleeves.

"There is a difference between correct, and right," I sniffed demurely.

"Well," he began stiffly, pausing for a moment. "So it would seem."

I sucked in a breath and put my hands on the table.

"Wow." I shook my head. "Just wow. I never thought I'd get an ounce of agreement out of you. I feel like I let that happen too quickly. I wasn't ready. I didn't get to savour it."

Gabe rolled his eyes.

"Next you'll say, 'sorry I organised with the others to have you killed, Michael'." I waved an admonishing finger. "That was not your purest deed Butch ol' boy."

"Stop reminding me that you're a criminal, or I might seek your demise again," he warned heatedly, and I grinned.

"Criminals don't always break laws that are *good*," I countered. "Or have the support of the judge, like I did."

"They are still *laws*," he spat, and then visibly composed himself. "Listen. I'll get down to business." He peered around furtively. "We are in danger."

"Whhyyyy?" I sniggered. "Ya break a *law* or something?"

Gabby had always been so clean cut, intent on being the bearer of good or bad news to inspire his dreamers. So he ignored my quips and ploughed on.

"How have your enlightenments been this time round?" he asked pointedly.

I shrugged non-committedly. But I was intrigued. I had felt oddly behind in this lifetime, when the powers that be normally overloaded me with all I could need.

"You feel it too," Gabe sounded abnormally relieved to have found some kind of common ground with me.

I frowned and started to take more interest. Maybe this wasn't our usual threat sesh.

"I was given a mobile device instead of something called Brainwave," I admitted.

"I knew it," the table shook as he slapped it. "We can't be updated any more than we have been," Butch – Gabe declared zealously.

"And why might that be?" I tried not to sound convinced. "I still have the same assignment-y feelings, ready to set up another world shaping destiny."

As I said it, I watched my target leave the café. I started when I noticed a glimmering design running along the skin of her fingers, hand and apparently continuing under her sleeve. It looked like she had silvery-blue power lines beneath her flesh.

"Because in this era, to be updated would mean to be controlled. Their technology would be so invasive that we would no longer be independent beings." Gabe/Butch was agitated. His pink features crinkled in earnest like a true, oversized Cupid.

"Hmm." I wasn't going to disagree, brain chips and internal technologies were rather intense.

"I also think …" he said in a low, nervous voice. "I also think I'm being followed. Hunted."

I exhaled finally. "It's probably your assignment getting chased. Greatness attracts danger. Maybe your job is to save your assignment so that they can just *live* their dream."

We'd all had to get our hands dirty at intervals in history to help our dreamers out. I remembered how frustrated one of my more detested colleagues, Aris, had been while he'd tried to just tutor the petulant Alexander the Great.

"Don't assume to lecture me Michael, I've been doing this as long as you have."

"Almost," I granted, not mentioning old tensions over the fact that he was doing it *because* of me.

Gabe furrowed his puckering brow anxiously. "And I've only been here two days. Haven't even made proper contact to start making dreams happen for my assignment yet. What's more, I felt Evangeline arrive and extinguish within half a day. I don't think she made any dreams come true in that time. And she hasn't yet reappeared here to finish her job."

"Now that's tricky," I admitted. "But not a shame. Evangeline is not always such a good little angel."

I had a flashing memory of a fiery backdrop and her impartial face as she plunged her hand into my chest and tried to extinguish my essence for all eternity.

"You're aware I would never come to you, of all beings, for help," Gabe followed his usual policy for honesty.

"Yes, yes, scum of the Underworld, Earth, Heavens and Universe. All that."

"But if the powers can't enlighten us, and we are being chased, it seems we have arrived at a time worse than all others."

"Worse than that time in the Cold War when the world nearly ended? That was MAD. Or worse than …"

"Worse. Because we were around to make the right people's dreams come true. We also knew the world could balance itself out with cleansing natural disasters."

"Mmm," I grimaced. "Cleansing."

My eyes flicked to the screen on the café wall, still showing images of natural disasters being averted. A volcano had somehow been exploded out of existence. Saving millions. Surely that should be a miracle. But really, it was just millions of people who had been meant to move on in their journey. And now they would go on in an existence where there weren't enough of us to get around to them – while their spirits could go no further in this cycle.

"You can see the world doesn't have room for all this," Butch gestured at the screen, which was now showing plans for sky high living capsules which were designed so that those millions of people could live one on top of the other. "And," he said insistently, returning to his danger theme. "You know things will be catastrophic if we aren't around to push humanity in a positive direction. I'm not just trying to save my own essence here."

"The world would suffer without me constantly popping up," I agreed.

"If there is no future to return to, and we aren't being given the chance to fulfil dreams here," Gabe said with suspense. "There will be no more 'popping up'."

I tapped my chin. "This is a bit bad."

"Terrible!" another cloud of golden, fine sand puffed out as he slapped the table again. He seemed astounded that I couldn't comprehend the import of the situation. As well as disappointed by my uninspired adjective choices.

"No, I mean, *bad* for real. Dreams will become nothing. People will go nowhere. We'll be redundant." I felt sick as I said it.

Gabe lowered his head. "So we may not regenerate. Or at

least we may not have many chances left to fix this. We have our work cut out for us."

"You sure do. I hope Evangeline rejuvenates and the others I can feel running about in panic can lend a hand."

Gabe growled like a butch little dog. "We need you too! You are the warrior of the people."

I smirked, because I knew how much that annoyed him.

"Done me so much good in the past, fighting for the good of the people, hasn't it? Best I just make sure my assignment has a great dream before the world turns to ash. Follow the rules for once, ey?"

Gabe stood up suddenly, huffing angrily. "Well you're involved in this, willing or not. Somehow they feel what you are, and now, I'm sure they associate you with me."

"I truly *am* doomed," I groaned then. "What a way to go."

"Good luck being hunted alone, brother," Gabe snarled.

"Sweet dreams against the nightmares, brother," I farewelled him, feeling almost over all the endlessness anyway.

I was scowling as I left, moving through some stragglers in the street who were talking about a curfew. The universe must have read my mood because I felt my comforting leather jacket grace my shoulders, and I pulled the collar up and hunched into it, bunching my fists in my jeans pockets.

Soon I was stopping under the flickering purple apartment building light, just as the door slid open with a hiss and a tiny female stumbled out.

She was even shorter this time without heels.

"Miss Molly," I greeted her, and wiped the scowl from my face.

"Mitch!" She put her hands on my forearms and drew me in, pushing me to the elevator. "Don't you know that if you need to go out this time of night you do it virtually? You had me worried sick."

"Virtually?" I was stumped.

She gaped, incredulous. "Upload your consciousness," she tried to prompt my memory. "Your physical body appears where you send it … Then you aren't breaking the rules."

I stared blankly at the Boof graffiti. It had changed colour.

"Always rules. Doesn't sound much fun," I answered glumly.

"I do my cleaning job in the business sector without ever leaving this building, just virtually supervising the bots. And I've had some of my wildest nights partying in the virtual-tree," she told me. "There's no risk. No STDs, stalkers, violence …"

"No hangover?" I laughed as the doors opened for her level. I put my hand over the sensor so they wouldn't close on her.

"Those are real," she frowned and shook her head in disbelief at my ignorance. "Every virtual drink leads to a release of chemicals into your physical body, and you still taste it. Of course there's also a decline in your bank account. How do you not know this?"

I winced, fishing for an answer, but she became bashful then.

"I'm sorry. Let's not focus on all that now. Obviously you've survived your whole life without needing any of it, and it never did me any good to be part of those things. And for some reason I had the best sleep last night and woke up with a whole new attitude."

Her hair was glossy and newly washed, and I could see the freckles on her clear face as she smiled.

"You sure look like you did," I agreed. Maybe I wasn't so over this gig after all.

She shook her finger at me. "I was a bit shaken though, when I knocked on your door to thank you for last night, and realised you weren't back and it was nearly curfew."

"I could go rogue and stay out for real," I grinned, before I saw the genuinely fearful expression on her face. As if someone might have been listening and I'd said something naughty.

"But no fear. I'll be good. Do what's correct and all." I crossed my heart.

"Well … go virtual if you do really want to 'stay out', or you can do the rooftop garden for freshly cleaned air." She shuddered. Technically it was only a short time since someone she had known had thrown themselves from there, even if her mind was telling her it had been months. "And don't even joke about going Rogue, in case you're heard."

"Don't you worry about me, Miss Molly." I pretended to brush her hair from her eyes and left a faint line of golden sand across her forehead.

"Ooohhk …" she replied distantly. "I think I could sleep well again tonight, you know. Without hooking up to the system."

"With the sweetest dreams," I promised. "The balm of hurt minds."

"You too …" she started to wander to her apartment, and I let the elevator close when she made it to her door.

"The sandman rarely gets to dream for himself," I said to the Boof graffiti.

Then I curled myself up on my apartment's one couch to watch the city, getting comfortable before I had a tugging feeling at my soul. As if I was being pulled to peer at something.

Another like me – Tien – had just been born somewhere close by in the world.

"That's nice," I told the universe. "She never tried to kill me." Probably hadn't received the invite in time.

I felt Ari'el – Aris – reach out to her from wherever he was in the world too. The 'lion guardian' star was smitten by the 'fairy'.

But then I felt a very different tug. And heard something I had never heard before.

The scream of a fellow star dying.

I could feel Tien's essence burning before she had fully rejuvenated in this era. Not just the body she had been re-animating. It was her essence being wounded and torn.

My hands were uselessly over my ears and my own soul seemed to scream as I felt tears stinging in my eyes.

I heard a series of other voices calling out at once in agony too. Gabe's voice, and Ari'el the lion.

And then it was all gone.

Just some faint sobs diminishing in my mind.

I uncurled slowly in shock.

My eyes were wide and my chest rose and fell rapidly as I sat forward and put my head in my hands.

The game really had changed.

Who knew if Tien could come back from that? Or if she would ever be as strong again.

A dream that would have led to a better future would not be nurtured.

I stared out at the deserted city once more, glimmering with advertisements and catchy banners.

Could I really let dreams become nightmares?

Excerpts from: The Collected Tales of Mythological and Historical Heroes

This is a first edition text, published by the World's third generation of great Leaders. Congratulations – you have purchased one of the last Leader approved hard copy texts!

On the subject of 'guardian angels':

*One of the star-angel-beings was known as **Michael**, though this name varied throughout time. He was said to be a champion of the people, being an instrument for truth and justice wielded by the heavens.*

*In many stories Michael was a leader of other star-angels, and he confined an infamous figure of legend called **Satan** to a place called hell. In other versions of the tale the conflict was held with the 'underworld god' **Hades** (overseeing the realm of the dead), or **Death** (supposedly a grim reaper collecting the souls of those ready to pass from this World).*

*According to the old tales there was also an overwhelmingly beautiful angelic being named **Gabriel.** He visited a woman known as Mary to inform her of a non-Science related pregnancy, and he appeared to the legendary prophet Muhammad to provide him with a guiding text of some importance.*

*The legends suggest that there were many other helpful angels. There was **Ari'el**, a courageous 'lion-like' battler figure. There was **Tien**, a fairy-like, gentle creature who sought to spread harmony. There was **Evangeline**, an angel of mercy, revelation and good news. And **Raphael**, an angel of healing.*

Thankfully in the modern era we don't need to put our hopes and dreams into fantasies. We can count on great tech and great Leaders to help us live truly blessed lives.

| 6 |

- The Dreamer -

Lili felt one bead of sweat make a salty path down her spine. Her knuckles were white, her lungs burned and her biceps were tight as she held up her body weight, dangling from the final stage of an extreme aerial obstacle course.

She let out a slow breath, tracing her eyes over the vine covered wall just a yard away.

It promised relief from the strain. It signalled descent. But the others on her team were only just starting to catch up, and all training exercises had to be finished as a whole group.

"If … I'd … been able to … stomach getting more than … the required fighter designs … I would be *using* them … right now …" Lili's team mate, Curtis wheezed as he swung his way from one bar to the next, coming to a stop beside her.

"I like to turn my tech off and practice using my average human abilities. No amplifying my strength," Lili told him as a bead of sweat rolled down her brow now.

"Getting implanted … with each tech design is … proof enough that you're one strong chicka," Curtis grimaced. "You got more designs than … anyone. And I know you don't … use pain blocks. Man … I want pain blocks … right … now."

"Focus on your breathing," Lili warned. "Not long to go, the others are coming."

"My hands are … shredded," Curtis groaned, though he'd only been hanging on for a minute.

"Don't do it," Lili advised calmly, feeling totally in her element – with no thoughts about abducted Leader heirs, disappearing reporters, or a breaking World.

"Ahhh shiiiii …" *szzzzp*. Lili heard Curtis' Brainwave do a correctional zap.

It was still the main method for fixing nasty behaviours like cursing, and Curtis was a prime culprit for cursing after having grown up naturally in a real, nuclear family in the outer suburbs.

Lili smelt his hair as it sizzled, and as the zap took the last of his strength she heard the squeak of his grip sliding. With a rush of air his wiry body began to drop.

Lili automatically released her grip on the bar with one hand so that she could lunge for him. She felt her hand clap around his forearm, and before her body had time to think about it, she jerked them both back upward like an elastic band snapping into place.

Then she pushed his hand to the bar, ignoring the burn of exertion flaring in each of her own upper body muscles.

"That's … why … we … have … Lili." The bar jolted under the powerful grip of Bear as he arrived on the scene, charitably carrying Jana on his back.

Bear always called his arrangement with Jana 'weight

training', but there was not enough weight on the lithe female for him to feel. Lili reasoned that it was more like carrying the World's most lethal personal guard.

"Hey-ho! Down we go!" Junior followed the duo with gusto.

"Thank fu -"

"Don't," Lili cut Curtis off, and then led the way to the climbing ivy – swinging her legs into it until she found a vine to stand on. "You let your guard down here and you can still drop to the bottom of the course with enough distance to break both legs and be healed naturally as punishment."

"Or I could just land on my head," Curtis replied sourly, now nestling his hands into the wall of vines for grip.

"You'd have to ignore the brainwashing you've had that makes you flip so well," Bear speculated while Jana jumped nimbly from his back and began to scale down the vines on instinct.

Her eyes glittered up at the team like a cat's, but she didn't falter. "Come on."

Junior whistled through his teeth, and then swung so hard into the vines that everyone nearly dropped out of them like startled bats.

"Practically a dancer, you are," Bear grumbled, but his own big body shook the vines as he trundled downward too.

When the team at last touched down they had just enough time to neaten up before they were scheduled for a techie consultation with V. They were due for the new updates that all Soldiers were to receive, and needed to be cleared for the overhaul.

"Man, I dunno if I can stomach more programming," Curtis complained when he thumped himself down in a chair beside Lili. He looked nauseas under the white clinic lights.

"It's worth the pain," Jana leaned forward and winked at him, letting her night vision flick on for a second so that her dark eyes glinted again. "Just to get hooked up with fun new gadgets."

"I'm already perfect," Curtis complained. "I shouldn't need any more enhancements."

"Lili's the only one who's been bred to perfection," Junior corrected him, unwrapping a stick of wondergum. "Now the Leaders want us *all* evolved to be so good."

"And yet the Leaders have scheduled me to be updated further too," Lili reflected. "And my Ordinary buddy always tells me I should be Biobeautying myself some more perfect features."

"Sure," Curtis chuckled. "You'd fit into the Soldier ranks with aqua hair and surgically lengthened cat-walk legs on patrols."

Jana shook her head. "The Sciences paid a lot for those symmetrical features."

"I suppose I should be grateful for any extra spending they're willing to splash out on me," Lili concluded with a shrug. "And if I ever run out of personal power to fuel all the programs they've installed, it'll probably be too late to care anyway."

"It's not fair. Nothing gets to you Lil." Curtis bounced up to pace anxiously, his commando boots squeaking on the sterilised floors.

Three squeaks later and the nurse at the desk pursed her

red lipsticked lips at him as if she had personally polished the floors alongside the cleanerbots.

"You were built to be unaffected by this and to be the best," Curtis went on obliviously. "But I'm normal, and I'm nervous."

"Normal is fine. The theory is," Lili replied. "That I wasn't built to have a soul."

"No, no, your soul is in there," Bear interjected, rocking the whole row of chairs back as he stretched. "Leaders don't have straight-out bots for Soldiers on the World force. They harvest us from around the globe to be real protectors and enforcers with a sense of humanity, for humanity. Surely they wouldn't take that away."

"Take that away and you also take away human error," Jana stated in a low voice.

"And human thought, emotion, personality," Junior sighed. "Great."

There was a beep that signalled a techie was free to see their next appointment, and Curtis gulped.

"World Soldier designer model Lili One," the stern, red lipsticked nurse called from her desk, glancing over her fashion glasses disdainfully as if it had been Lili scuffing her floor.

"Phew," Curtis grinned as he moved for Lili to pass, and she elbowed him in the ribs before crossing the waiting bay and entering the corridor opposite.

She made her way past a series of day procedure recovery rooms, which were curtained off.

A voice growled "just get it over with" from behind one curtain, before there was a crunching noise as something was wrenched back into place.

Further down another Soldier was staring out through his curtains blankly – his Brainwave plugged in to a Dream-Dictator while pixel shaped veins grew around his temples. Now that was a sad case – when the trauma was too much to program out, and the only relief was a total wipe and reconditioning.

Lili continued on past a series of operating rooms and wards, choosing the right corridor without needing her internal maps. After so many appointments and enhancements, she knew how to make her own way, and soon found a hall with offices and plain white doors – heading for the one marked 'Grand Techie V-irgil'.

"Hi V." She entered without knocking, at once becoming immersed in a lab that was brimming with ticking, whirring gadgets.

Some were beeping, others were spinning, a few were flashing, and one vibrated itself right off the desk beside V's elbow.

"Lili, my friend, my perfectly designed model!" V sat up from where he'd been filling a dropper with a thick liquid. He pushed his amplifying goggles up onto his forehead so that he looked like a goggly bug.

Rather than a lab coat he wore his favourite grey hoodie – his title of Head of Medical and Defence Tech having been earned for his brilliance rather than his image of professionalism.

"More like your voluntary guinea pig," Lili replied, pulling herself up onto his work bench instead of the hard, silver topped treatment table.

"True," V agreed. "You definitely tolerate more than most. Especially Curtis."

She crossed her arms. "I'm pretty much the reason you made it to Grand Techie."

He wheeled his chair over. "We've done a lot together, he said. But then his forehead creased. "Perhaps we've done too much too well, with all these Soldier updates we've inspired." He tugged at the cords of his hoodie. "It's just a consultation for you today though, right?" he asked. "The warnings and check-up before the procedure?"

"You'll get to inflict the actual pain tomorrow," Lili answered. "Don't be glum, you know you enjoy it."

V almost grimaced in response, scanning her briskly for health issues as if his heart wasn't in it. "You hardly even need an update, Miss Perfection On Legs."

"Since when?" Lil raised an eyebrow. "You always want to see what else we can do."

"Since all the stuff on the news," he admitted. "Anyways, your whole body practically proves you are dedicated and committed to duty already. You're a weapon. So I don't think they should take over more of your mind too."

Lili shifted uncomfortably on the work bench. The freedom craving woman from her dreams was suddenly floating at the back of her mind.

"All Soldiers are getting it done. It's completely routine. Isn't it?"

V shrugged again, non-committedly. "So far as I've been told."

"Hey," Lili leaned forward with a frown. "What's really brought this on?"

"You know me," he sighed. "I'm just a thinker, cooped up too long without natural light every day."

"*Right.*" Lili waited for the rest, and he fidgeted listlessly with a beaker for a moment.

"But … I've been thinking, and tinkering," he went on unhappily. "You know, after all you went through to get the designs done, they should really be a symbol of independent effort and of individual strength, rather than a symbol of your ownership." V took the goggles from his forehead and began cleaning the lenses. "Anyway, as the Leaders have rolled out these new rules for Soldier updates and I thought of people like you, I had an epiphany. I created a design that makes all of your internal tech belong to you. And I made a program that gives you control of your own Brainwave with one simple scan."

He finally winced up at her, his face pinched at the treasonous statements he was throwing into casual conversation.

Lili stared at him, thinking of the World class doctors who had recently disappeared, along with the overly opinionated reporter, KimLe.

"This was not how I expected our consultation to go," she at last responded flatly. "My doctor said you should fix my head with its weird dreams too. But it almost sounds like your head is the one having trouble."

"I know …" he groaned at the gravity of what he had done. "If the new design and scan data got into the wrong hands, it could mean the wrong members of the public break away from Leader control. But it would also mean free will. Your designs and mind technology would only be hooked up to your own whims and life force, not open to Leader control or awareness. You could hijack yourself online for information or power, but… You'd be free. Like no natural or created person has experienced in our lifetime."

"Ok," Lili tried to sound light hearted. "I know you love a good experiment, and I've always been your girl. But you have to get rid of these new things. You'll be put down if Leaders, or if anyone else, finds out you've taken such Rogue actions."

V was crestfallen. "Lili, just because they made you doesn't mean they should own you."

She sighed. "Of course, selfishly, I want to be my own person, but any good Soldier knows that one destabilising force can shake an entire group." She didn't voice the niggling belief that shaking up an entirely controlled group could be a good thing.

"Well," V gave a helpless chuckle. "They're in our heads, so they probably already know of my misdeeds."

"Don't laugh, it's entirely likely that they do monitor thought patterns and tendencies. You need to be careful," Lili warned. "Give me whatever it is you've created. I have access to the Kill Zone, and can have it all wiped from the face of the World. No evidence or suspicion."

V pulled a face. "Could I store the digidata?"

"Store the plans anywhere virtual and they have it," Lili told him what he already knew.

"I could do it hard copy then, like old school …" V's gaze flicked around the room to fall on his classical painting of an emo punk. "I could put it behind …"

"Not that obvious," Lili rolled her eyes.

"Right, more hidden. Hidden treasure," he agreed. She saw him glance at the floor and roof. All useless.

She held out her hand. "And the other evidence?"

His lips turned down sulkily at the corners. "Fine." He wheeled his chair back to his desk and selected a vial and a miniscule blue chip. "You change your mind and want to experiment, you've done enough of these to know how to inject the liquid tech for a design, and how to connect yourself to a chip. The know-how for the scan is just in my head."

Lili plucked the small yet incredibly dangerous items from his hands and zipped them into a pocket of her boot. "I'm on patrol tonight. But next time I'm scheduled at the Kill Zone, these will be destroyed," she promised. "Now, any advice for tomorrow?"

"Yeah," he grinned, pulling his big green goggles back on. "Don't show up."

Excerpts from: The Collected Tales of Mythological and Historical Heroes

This is a first edition text, published by the World's third generation of great Leaders. Congratulations – you've purchased one of the last Leader approved hard copy texts!

On the subject of early individuals of note:

James Dean *was an acting icon, known for his 1950s rock-star-like looks, dream boat status, and troubled ways.*

He portrayed sensitive, rebellious misfits and audiences couldn't take their eyes off him.

He tragically died in a car accident – his star extinguished too early. But his legacy inspired many rebels, encouraged many actors to reach for fame in their turn, and made him the muse of many music and film artists for generations.

It is said that he had the face of an angel. A modern Bio-beautician's dream.

| 7 |

– The Star –

Just as I was finally beginning to meditate, a horrible screeching noise sounded all around me, and I spluttered into wakefulness, nearly needing an early reincarnation.

I saw that an enormous blade-like robotic arm had sprung out from the side of the building, and it was now squealing its way down the window as the building cleaned its own glass.

"Alright, I'm awake," I groaned at the ceiling, clutching my still bruised chest.

The biggest windscreen wiper ever continued moving slowly downward, ruining my Zen zone.

A hologram banner floating near the apartment building, which had been projecting adverts about a dating site all night, immediately changed its slogan to read: 'missing something from your life? The universe will provide.' And a male model who was disturbingly similar to Gabe posed churlishly behind the slogan.

I glowered. "Actually, giant fortune cookie, my client comes before my family issues. Compulsions are tweaking at my essence. I need to get to my dreamer. My dream girl."

The banner outside flashed the words: 'fate is real. We'll bring you together. We'll sort it out.'

"You're like a love doctor?" I asked wryly.

'Yes.'

I snorted.

The banner changed. 'Trust in a higher purpose. We're the real love doctor – successfully drawing great matches together since the dawn of time.'

"You're so subtle," I told the universe. "There are probably a hundred people jumping on that dating site right now."

The banner showed a Gabe model again, but also a pouty male who resembled another colleague of mine – Raphael, and a smouldering Evangeline look-alike.

I shuddered. Those three had really gone in hard when executing me had been high priority.

"Ick," I grimaced. "It's just missing Aris. The ring-leader."

A flickering background of love hearts appeared behind the next message: 'resolve the tension in your life'.

"Look," I groaned. "I don't want dreams to become nightmares either. But I'm too tired to face the likes of Butch again before it's properly morning."

'You're a star. Born to be brightest in the dark. Light the way for others.'

I flopped an arm over my eyes to block out the banner.

"You're not even trying to sound like a match-maker now."

Suddenly an alarm, which had not previously existed in the bare apartment, began insistently blaring, startling me bolt upright.

"Oh come on! Six in the morning?" I slapped at the alarm to silence its shrill beeping.

At once the beeping changed to a song that was teeth-grindingly chirpy: 'where would we beeee, without famileeeee? How would we sleeeeep, how would we dreeeam, without famileeee?'

"You're like a cheap Confucius," I grumbled. But I rose from the couch in resignation. "I worked with Confucius you know. And he would never stoop so low."

'Famileeeeeee…'

"Alright, I *got* it." I rubbed my eyes, defeated. "I'll grace Butch with my presence. But not because of your cosmic scale bullying. It's because I care that one of my kind has been taken down for the first time in history."

As if in support of my self-sacrificing choice, the moment I got moving I found myself instantly fitted out with a fresh white tee and jeans, James Dean style.

Begrudgingly, but stylishly, I made my way out onto the near empty streets, shrugging on a leather jacket as the first rays of the filtered morning sun peeked between the shining buildings.

Refusing to be hurried along, I strolled at a lazy pace past manicured gardens, glittering shop fronts, walls of outdoor screens and endless holograms. And yet I could not deny the hints that, in this time, the world seemed to be decaying beneath the artificial, fresh perfection all around.

If dreams were dying now too, the future did not look bright – even in a watered down, filtered sun kind of way.

Particularly troubling headlines that were flashing across

one café's screens caught my attention and I paused to listen while the news anchor happily reported that more people than ever were making use of the mind-numb settings on their Dream-Dictators. However no progress had been made on finding the Ultimate Leader, Uthoria Pendragon's missing heir Cam Pendragon.

I gazed at the rotating image of the curly, blonde haired, clean shaven young man, who had a faintly noble and yet troubled countenance. The woman beside him, presumably Uthoria, had the jowls of a bulldog. And I pondered her iron grip on the poor, unhappy heir's arm until I realised I was being watched.

"Morning," I greeted the two early risers politely. They were seated outside the café, and they appeared to have frozen. They stared at me with starry gazes, remaining paused over their organic smoothies until I tugged my collar up awkwardly and moved away from them.

I cast my eyes up to the sky pleadingly and then nodded with satisfaction as a pair of cool, dark shades graced my face.

"Much more inconspicuous," I thanked the clouds.

But a moment later a girl tripped as she watched me instead of the path in front of her.

"Aaa ..." she spluttered as I caught her elbow and helped her retain balance.

"All well my dear?" I asked courteously.

Her mouth was agape and her teeth were so white that my eyes hurt through the shades.

"Aaa ..."

"A fine choice from the alphabet." I dusted a shimmer of

gold dust from her jacket, where I'd caught at her. "I like the letter S myself. Have a nice day."

I left her to contemplate the beauties of S, and tried to keep my head down – attempting not to bump into more gaping people as the streets filled.

I wondered if I somehow seemed more attractive to mortals than normal because they were so dream starved. And I also wondered why I could feel but not find Butch while I circled a building that had his beefy presence all over it.

Then it dawned on me. Somehow people must have actually been feeling an ounce of attraction toward him too. Butch came equipped with a vibe of innate hope, promise and opportunity just as I did.

So my colleague must have tried to find some way of staying in the proximity of his target without being surrounded in crowds.

I craned my neck, and thought I could see a tiny speck at the top of the towering building, like an angel Christmas tree topper.

Then I noticed two men by a nearby news screen stand, also squinting up at the speck.

They didn't seem star struck, but rather devious. As if they were plotting to do something quite negative to the speck.

Their skins were like canvases of endless tattoo-like designs – similar to those internal powerlines I'd seen on my own dreamer. And their hands rested on nasty, big shooters that were hardly hidden in their long – therefore of course suspicious and sinister – coats.

Stepping closer as if to watch the Cam Pendragon news bulletin again, I shook my own jacket and let a puff of gold dust explode around them. The deviousness on their faces turned to dopiness, and as their eyes lost focus I made for Butch's building.

I quickly maneuvered around crowds of business people, joining a line that was churning through the building's rotating doors. Feeling the powers that be at work, I got approval from the body scanner and crossed a massive foyer before quickly squeezing my way into the elevator.

Nobody batted an eye at my less than businesslike attire, as they saw a neatly suited up, dapper gentleman.

Super slick, I removed my shades and winked at a man staring openly over his palm screen. He blushed but, along with others, continued to stare until the thirtieth floor.

Finally I felt fewer and fewer eyes on me as the elevator stopped at each level, and I was the only one to continue all the way to the distant rooftop.

When I stepped out into a concrete space decorated with patches of plastic grass, I knew at once that I'd come to the right spot.

I heard Butch's growl of annoyance and headed straight for it.

"Down Butch," I smirked. "Be good boy!" I lit up a cigarette.

"What are you doing here, deserter?" Gabe continued to growl.

"Aren't you pleased to see me again so soon Gabby?" I moved across to sit on the ledge beside him, dangling my legs over.

"*Should* I be happy to see you?" his blonde eyebrows were

so far furrowed that happiness seemed to be off the table. "Just yesterday you proved that you're still totally unreliable."

"Oh yes, if I were you I would not trust me as far as I could throw me."

"I *don't* trust you."

"There we are," I inhaled slowly. "I as you was correct."

"Why are you here then? Did you change your mind?" He wrinkled his face further. "Because so have I. I don't need an outcast's help."

"Brother, an outcast is better than nothing." I let a stream of smoke pool out from between my lips. "Especially when you really are in danger."

His cherubic complexion became rather red and devilish. "I already told you that! And now – Tien!"

"Yes," I said simply. "And now – I am here. Trying to make sense of things, despite how much *I* distrust *you* too."

"*You* distrust *me*?! You've just come to plague me." He was so scarlet that he looked like a constipated baby.

"No," I took a good long drag on the cigarette. "I'm here because *broken, psychotic, bloodthirsty* angelic family or not, Tien's death means too much. And she has not been reborn yet. If she will be." I shrugged then – smoke curling from my nostrils. "I'm also here because the universe wants me to be, and because I did find two suspicious men waiting at the bottom of the building for you."

Gabe stopped swatting angrily at my smoke wisps and gasped, paling.

"Of course," I went on. "Your stalkers are now a little star struck and dazed – momentarily."

"I knew it," Gabe whispered. "I'm next."

"Don't worry. If our café date wasn't enough, I just put myself firmly on their radar too. Whoever *they* may be." I butted my cigarette out, grinding it down until it became a small pile of fine gold dust between my fingertips. "But why stay up here, if you'd guessed that they'd found you?"

"My star power was too great to go unnoticed anywhere else. And I can't just abandon my target," Gabe rumbled, crossing toned arms over a burly chest. "Maybe I can at least make one more dream come true."

"Fair call," I agreed. "But whatta ya say we try and figure out what's going on down there. Give ourselves a chance at granting more dreams? My star power's better than yours, and I'm willing to risk it."

Then I felt a hand big enough to surround my throat do just that.

Ari'el, the lion – not a fan of mine.

"Family reunion?" he thundered.

I calmly grabbed hold of his thumb and twisted until he let go. "Don't know *why* we don't do it more than every millennium or so."

"Gabriel, how is it that you find yourself in the company of one such as this?" Ari'el – Aris, spat.

"He's been insatiably attracted to me." I shrugged helplessly. "Star power," I said again, lighting up once more just because I knew the human habit annoyed the lion even more than it annoyed Gabe.

But I was glad to see that Gabe appeared as stunned as I was. Aris had sounded so far away last night.

"I felt Michael was close, Aris, and with everything that has been happening … Michael has always shone in times of trouble. He always finds a way to the light." Gabe at once became highly deferential towards Aris. But I raised my eyebrows at his kind words.

"Michael is a criminal," Aris hissed.

"Yeah, I like him," I puffed, my eyebrows dropping right back down.

"We may need to put our differences aside …" Gabe answered hesitantly.

"Or –" Aris was probably getting ready to suggest having a second try at ripping my essence out and destroying it for good, before I cut him off.

I flicked some ash at him. "Don't worry, our intriguing new enemies, who seem to both know of our existence and how to end it, are aware of me. So I may not be around to bother you for much longer."

"Good," Aris glowered, before turning back to Gabe. "We must leave, brother, and discover what we can about this strange new time."

"Great idea," I muttered, rolling my eyes.

"How did you get here so quickly?" Gabe asked uncertainly, and I had to give him credit for the appropriateness of the question. "And have you made contact with your assignment?" Further credit was transferred.

Aris bristled a little. "Dora Cate is with me. She got me here."

"Whaaaaaat?" both Gabe and I burst out at once.

"You endangered her by making it obvious who you're attached to," I accused.

Aris crackled his knotty knuckles at me. "Dora Cate knew who I was before I had even realised who she was to me."

"Now how does that work?" I enquired. "Are the old senses slowing down?"

"Dora Cate is part of a group who have access to information about many things. And they know who's after us and why."

"She went Rogue?" Gabe asked, already up to date with some modern lingo.

"She is a *rule breaker?*" I gasped.

"She saved me from also suffering Tien's fate. Her people began investigating us, and our predicament, when Evangeline and others before her were targeted. Apparently this has been happening for a while in this era, it didn't just start with our arrival here." Aris grew even more broody then. "Dora tried to help me get to Tien to save her, and brought me here to you now."

"To me?" I gushed at the flattery.

"To Gabriel," Aris snarled.

"Hmf. So how does this travel work?" I took a long drag in.

"You hack the virtualtree and come with me," a much more appealing voice cut across Aris' as he opened his big mouth again.

Gabe started, blinking stupidly as a pair of black boots stepped up to the ledge beside me.

I squinted upward, finding a very fitted black body suit, and the closest thing to a Mediterranean pixie I'd ever seen.

"Hey spunk," she acknowledged me. Her eyes were glittering brown, surrounded in black eyeliner, and her face was framed by a sharp black bob that tapered from the neck to her chin.

"Mitch," I said, reaching up to clasp her hand in welcome.

"We came for Gabe," Aris reminded her with a softened tone.

He stepped up to take her hand from mine and to draw her down from the ledge. I wasn't sure if he was protecting her from the drop, or from me.

I swivelled around to rest one leg up on the ledge, and dragged the last inch from my cigarette before releasing it in another shower of fine gold sand.

Dora cocked her head to the side like a little bird. "Mitch is like you though."

Aris was really trying not to bristle. "Hardly like me ..."

"Is he one of your kind?" she cut across his machoism.

His glaring silence said enough.

"Right," she crossed her arms. "Worth saving then. Every dream counts. And you're meant to be facilitating mine, not holding it back."

"Who knows if I can ever be saved," I acknowledged before Aris had to. "But I am interested to learn more so we might all stand a chance."

"Are we meant to just leave with you now?" Gabe asked uncertainly.

"Collect your assignment, and then you leave with me," Dora affirmed.

"I should bring my assignment into danger?" the consternation appeared physically painful for Butch.

"You're new to this game. But, if you don't belong under

Leader control, you are in a World of danger anyway," Dora answered bluntly. "Best stick together, hey?"

"What does your target do for a living anyhow?" I asked Gabe, standing up. "I've only really glimpsed mine."

Gabe scratched his head. "He works in Human Resources …"

"What does that even mean?" I laughed.

Gabe shrugged. "It's a few floors down. I can feel him from here. So far he's peaceful and safe … without me around."

"He's peaceful and safe?" I countered. "Sounds like he could do with some spice to his life."

"A touch of zest never harmed anybody," Dora nodded, steering Gabe to the rooftop entrance.

And then I saw a black dart arc past me, from where I'd had my back to the ledge.

It sliced through the air, and its needle tip embedded in Gabe's forearm – a shadowy black acid immediately starting to inject into his skin, spreading like a bruise.

Gabe cried out, and his eyes widened as he saw something rising up behind me.

After a quick glance back to find that the two tech covered men from below were somehow air-bound, I ducked forward and swatted the dart out of Gabe's arm. I quickly squeezed at the wound like a snake bite so that the black venom-like substance that had begun to spread under the surface of his skin seeped out instead, and then I hurriedly rubbed at the skin to leave a golden covering of my sand across it.

Dora hastily scooped up the dart, and then was hoisted back by Aris, who had grabbed Gabe and Dora by their collars. He forced them behind his bulk and quickly hustled them to the elevator, thumping at the button to go down.

I retreated, again catching just a glimpse of the two suddenly again devious, not dopey, men touching down on the ledge. Almost every inch of their skins, which were covered in those technological tattoos, had lit up. And somehow those designs had given them the ability to fly up or scale the monster sized building.

"Jackpot," I heard one of them hiss to the other, before there was a miraculous *ding* and our group tumbled into the elevator.

I jabbed the elevator button again, and the doors closed behind us – right as a second dart struck the metal doors.

"Michael covered it, and it was only a surface wound," Gabe was reassuring Aris as I turned and we began moving downward. "The damaged skin should regenerate."

Even as we travelled away from our mysterious attackers I heard heavy pounding travelling down the elevator shaft while they tried to break the rooftop entrance and follow us.

"I think we should clear out," I said conversationally, pushing the button for the next floor.

The moment the doors parted again we spilled out and hurried to a stairwell.

Aris brusquely pushed past me to take the lead on the stairs. "Right, we'll get to Human Resources and collect …"

"Theus," Gabe answered breathlessly.

"He does sound in need of zest," Dora said with pity, before we burst out onto the Human Resources level, and paused immediately.

Even the office itself was boring.

A sea of desks in a drab, undecorated room.

The one standout feature was a nearby sign that read: 'Who keeps taking our resources?! We're running low!'

And while we all paused and blinked at the room, the room stared back. Fingers paused from tapping on or swiping at screens, styluses were lowered and digipads were dropped. Our fast entrance had probably been more action than they'd ever seen up here.

"Which one is he?" Aris panted, eyeing the countless office workers – all so alike in blazers, knitted vests and collared shirts.

"I can't see him," Gabe grimaced back. This world was just crawling in people.

"Who are you after?" a mousy man asked politely from his desk by the door.

"Theus …" Gabe answered awkwardly.

"Anyone seen Theus?" the man called obligingly.

"He won't be long," a lady called back. "He's making a sandwich."

"Right," Gabe answered uncertainly.

Then a lanky young man backed into the room, pushing the swinging door to the lunch room open with his behind.

He was humming, and carrying a sandwich.

"Theus!" the lady called.

Theus jumped, and his glasses went askew. Perhaps he hadn't been brave enough to zap out any sight imperfections as everyone else seemed to have done.

"You're wanted," the mousy man nodded his head helpfully at us.

"I … was just making a sandwich," Theus answered in confusion. "I forgot my pre-packeted lunch."

"Resourceful," I commented. "Humanly resourceful."

"We don't have time for this!" Dora hissed at Gabe. "You grab him. I'll start hooking up a portal."

Gabe nodded, and ploughed through the aisles, charging toward the wide eyed Theus.

Dora seized hold of the mousy man's floating desk-screen, making his holographic family pictures pixelate with the jolt. She pried open a miniscule port in the side of it, and connected it to a cord that attached to a band around her wrist.

"That's not how you go virtual," the man gasped indignantly. "That's illegal. Use your Brainwave!"

"I'm a rule breaker, baby," she said and blew a kiss at him.

"She's going to go in physically!" he spluttered to his gaping colleagues. "She's opening a portal for real!"

"She's Rogue!"

"Don't try this at home," Dora smirked in warning.

The air in front of us started to flicker as if a screen had appeared there that was the size of a door.

Gabe was pulling his sandwich clutching client along by the wrist like a child.

The door-sized shape began to crack and pixels seemed to fall out of it to leave only a frame. The picture behind the frame no longer looked out onto the other side of the office, but into a tunnel with wire covered walls.

"Wow," mousy breathed. "I've only ever seen that picture as a quick subconscious connection error."

Gabe, his client-child, and the sandwich caught up to us. Before another group burst into the room.

The dream assassins had made it into the building. Their technological skin designs were flaring so brightly that they were the very image of aliens, or robots, or both.

"Oh *come on!*" Dora cried in frustration.

The robot-alien-dream-assassins raised their weapons.

Aris readied as if to dive in front of Dora like a protective wall, and indeed he had lifted off, before she side kicked him into the portal.

She shoved both Gabe and his charge in then, before grabbing a black sphere from her belt, where I noticed an odd assortment of shapes hung.

"Oh dear," mousy commented as her thumb and pointer finger pressed the sphere and made it beep.

She hurled it at the assassins and gestured for me to step into the virtual world she had opened, just as the techgrenade went off.

I felt an odd sensation of being pulled into the flow of an electrical current as I entered the wiry tunnel with Dora following closely behind. She snapped her wristband free of the screen before quickly pulling her hand away from the closing portal entrance. And behind her I saw a vision of desks being exploded upward, digisheets and screens blowing out in different directions, and the tech designs on the assassins' skins flashing fleetingly until the portal snapped closed.

The uproar was replaced at once with the whirring sound of energy pulsing in the walls. Red light emanated around us.

"Kidnapped," Theus was whimpering where he sat on a floor of red and blue cords. "Kidnapped. By Rogues. Like that Cam guy."

"Now *that* was zest," I congratulated Dora.

"Mayhem," Gabe grimaced, clutching his arm and observing his traumatised assignment.

"Successful," Dora agreed with satisfaction.

"Lemme see," I pushed Gabe's hand away from the wound on his arm. The black acid had burned away some of his skin, but the dart had not penetrated enough for it to spread deeply. If it had been a deep hit the nasty liquid probably could have had quite an impact.

I gently rubbed some more gold dust over his forearm, as it seemed to have counteracted the black stain already, and would help the skin to regenerate.

"Thanks," Gabe grunted, but I had already turned to Theus.

I couldn't help frowning at him.

It wasn't his foppish curls, flopping over his eyes as he rocked himself anxiously.

It wasn't the pasty colour of his face, or his tightly squeezed eyes.

It was something deep inside *me* – an instinctive recognition.

"I … know you …" I said hesitantly, surprised.

And at last Theus blinked up from where he was holding his sandwich close, like a reassuring toy.

"You haven't been to this part of time before," Aris discounted the notion at once. He pushed ahead as Dora moved off down the tunnel.

Gabe took hold of Theus and led him along comfortingly.

So I took hold of my own self and marched along obediently too.

"No, somehow I know that guy," I persisted as I marched.

"Been kidnapped …" Theus continued weakly, glancing at the cable lined walls of the tunnel in shock.

"You know you can come across one life force in different bodies throughout time if it hasn't had a dream. It's probably that," Gabe brushed me off. He was trying to click his fingers in front of Theus' face at the same time as hurrying him along.

"Was just making a sandwich …" Theus shook his floppy sandwich so that some tasty filling slid out to land on the wiry floor.

"We should also get Mitch's assignment before we go back to base," Dora was telling Aris. "We need to protect whatever dream is meant to happen there."

Theus had started to breathe very loudly.

"I actually think we need to get my client out of the system and into reality …" Gabe cut in worriedly. "Or a dream could easily be lost here if Theus has a nervous breakdown."

"The universe promises to take care of delivering me to my dreamer anyway," I sighed. "It'll happen."

"Alright then, we'll sort Theus first," Dora relented be-grudgingly. "We've got things that can settle his nerves back on base."

"So what happens on this base of yours?" I asked Dora then. "Is it all an elaborate trap to force us to grant your dreams out of turn?"

"Leave if you're worried," Aris grunted.

"Sure. Some of my colleagues may want you to make their

wildest dreams come true," Dora winked, ignoring Aris. Then she stopped at a spot that looked nearly identical to the rest of the tunnel, except for some connection ports in the wall. She readied to attach her bracelet.

"Going in was easier to control," Dora warned. "We were just surfing our way into the tunnel on energy that was already rushing onward with the online system. It's such a strong current, that we've been sped through a journey that could take days otherwise. The process to get out of that current is a little rougher. I have to get the volts to push against the natural flow of data."

Theus dropped his sandwich and let Gabe put a big, protective arm around his shoulders.

Aris stood at the ready as if to catch Dora if she needed it.

Dora looked like she had never needed anything less, as though travelling in an online world was normal.

And I just braced my own self once again, waiting expectantly.

The pixels appeared once more, but less like a doorway to step through, and more like a suddenly smashed window.

At once our bodies were ripped from stability – as if we had been flying along nicely within the pressurised cabin of a commercial plane. And then, all at once, a big jagged hole had appeared in the lovely compartment.

Excerpts from: The Collected Tales of Mythological and Historical Heroes

This is a first edition text, published by the World's third generation of great Leaders. Congratulations – you've purchased one of the last Leader approved hard copy texts!

On the subject of early individuals of note:
Spartacus *was a gladiator slave, forced to fight for his life as a form of entertainment for others in the very ancient arena of Rome's Colosseum. He was inspired to lead a slave revolt and became a formidable rebel who later symbolised noble struggle. The celebration of such Rogue actions highlights how unrefined pre-unified World people were.*

| 8 |

– The Dreamer –

Lili had been oddly flat after stashing V's contraband in her microwave, and she'd hooked up to powernap mode to recharge before night patrol.

She was still momentarily groggy when she woke, until she registered that she was hearing the sound of KimLe's voice carrying to the upper level from the screenwall below.

Now entirely alert, Lili sprang out of bed to dash across the room.

"I feel much healthier today," KimLe was saying. "I believe leaving the media will be the best thing for me, so I can focus on being a good citizen. I am very lucky to have received help in time, as I hadn't even realised that I was becoming weighed down by unnecessary and inaccurate worries."

Lili dropped herself over the top room's ledge, sliding down the leafy wall to catch the last bit of the screen cast.

KimLe still looked like herself. Her light, fairy floss hair was trimmed to perfection around her face, and not a crinkle furrowed her shimmer powdered eyes. In fact, her expression was serene.

"I have received treatment that has released me from uncertainties and burdens, thanks to a free program being offered by our caring Leaders. I urge all citizens, who deserve to be peaceful, to use this treatment too."

A series of wellbeing and obedience ads started up on the screenwall, and Lili only shook herself back to the present when another segment began – once again pleading for the knightly Cam Pendragon to be returned safely. His blonde curls, strong jaw, and yet defeated stance were rotating before Lili's eyes again. But she powered the screenwall down, instead powering up the Biobeauty machine.

Breaking all of Tiff's cardinal rules, she kept the machine on its most basic three minute settings, stepping inside to be stripped, rinsed, dried, perfumed, lip glossed, pony tailed, and fully dressed for patrol.

Impeccably neat and clean on the surface, but strangely worried on the inside, Lili had to force a neutral expression when Curtis and Junior joined her, crossing the stretch of real grass towards the base armoury.

"Ready for some Ordinary supervision … and maybe some good ol' Rogue hunting?" Curtis grinned, stepping over a gardening drone.

"You make it sound so glamourous," Junior drawled, chewing on a tooth-pick as he watched lines of citizens heading home while the sun set. "I'm not even really that bothered by the Rogues."

"Well shi –" zzzzzp. "No Soldier is," Curtis winced. "Without the Rogues there'd be no sport. We'd just be babysitters of already obedient citizens and a few curfew breakers. But chasing a Rogue down when they pop up on night duty, now *that* breaks up the monotony."

"I do enjoy their company for the transport," Junior agreed. "But no matter how much of a laugh they give us on the way to lock up, we'll never see them again."

"Rogues or babysitting, either way get ready to rumble," Lili told them. She switched her Brainwave to Soldier mode and felt her left ear become heated at the same time that her left eye lit up with the connection to base.

"Right you are," Junior agreed, and both Junior and Curtis blinked, bringing a light into their own left eyes that showed they were on duty and online too.

Jana and Bear were waiting in the base armoury, having already donned their tech survival packs. They were flicking through the settings to ensure shield features and laser gun extensions were fully charged.

"I don't know why you even use all this equipment, Lil," Curtis puffed as he suited up. "You could warp gravity yourself."

Lili shrugged on a tech pack. "There are better ways to get around and be part of the team."

"And who wouldn't enjoy being part of our team?" Bear smiled widely. "Or having such high-tech toys."

He pressed his palm over the sensor in the strap crisscrossing over his chest, and at once the pack elongated to flow down his back and legs like fluid. At his knees, there was a quick bend so that he was seated. Then the rest of the material moved around to encase him in a wasp shaped airbike.

"You haven't even left the building," Jana scolded him. "Your legs will forget how to walk for themselves."

"Bet I beat you lot outside though," Bear's jovial voice sounded in each team member's internal ear piece. Then, chuckling, he was gone – the bike encasing him hardly rippling the air as it flashed out of the armoury.

Lili tapped her own chest piece, leant forward, and wrapped her hands around the fast forming handles in front of her. Bringing her face close to the protective screen as the fluid material hardened into a shell, she flashed outside too, with the others fast following her out into the deepening night.

Lili's ear piece picked up some faint half curses and a series of correctional zaps as Curtis observed that the already near empty streets were going to offer no fun. Any last minute stragglers were picking up their pace to disperse as they saw Lili's team cruising.

"Fu – zzpt – ing babysitter I am," he was grumbling.

With a slight smile, Lili led the way. Junior trailed Curtis to her right and Jana trailed Bear to her left.

But as usual the most activity came from whirring droids, the mechanical arms of the building window cleaners, and Curtis keeping up his cut off cuss filled commentary while they cruised through deserted streets.

When they'd swept their part of the inner city, Lili led the team further out to the older outskirt streets that were due to be erased. They had all expected more routine boredom – until a lone figure appeared out of nowhere in the middle of the street.

"Yeeha!" Junior called, and the team sped up, falling in behind Lili and keeping eyes everywhere in case the single chap was bait.

Hurtling towards the suspect figure, Lili launched the airbike upwards and forwards so that she lifted like a jet and soared over the person's head. Rotating mid-launch, Lili landed on his other side while the others closed in.

"Foot Soldiers," Lili ordered, and her team quickly followed suit as she let her airbike unwrap itself and retract back into a pack.

The figure was very still. He had nowhere to go.

"It looks like we've found a Rogue rabbit hole," Curtis chortled excitedly, and Junior whistled through his teeth.

"Reach for the sky," Lili commanded, stepping closer to the figure.

"Yes ma'am," the figure replied as he heard her voice and turned to face her slowly. "I just knew the universe would bring us together."

Excerpts from: The Collected Tales of Mythological and Historical Heroes

This is a first edition text, published by the World's third generation of great Leaders. Congratulations – you've purchased one of the last Leader approved hard copy texts!

On the subject of the ancient 'gods and goddesses':

In early beliefs the overseeing presence of the World – a 'God', 'Allah', 'Universe', 'Zeus', 'Ra' (there were many names used for this presence), created others to do their will. One such servant was said to have been the wise god **Prometheus***, meaning "forethought", who was tasked with creating the first people out of the great garden's earth. His brother, the more thoughtless, foolish* **Epimetheus***, was tasked with making animals.*

In the tales Epimetheus carelessly gave too many gifts to the animals, leaving Prometheus' mankind unprotected.

The stories describe how Prometheus could not leave mankind without defences, and so he stole the fire of the 'gods' to give to mankind. He was in turn punished – being chained at the top of an isolated mountain. Trapped, he was sentenced to be attacked eternally by a mighty eagle, which would descend each day to tear at his flesh and organs.

Prometheus was not freed until another figure of legend, named Heracles, Hercules or in some versions Samson, was inspired to use his incredible strength to break Prometheus' chains.

| 9 |

– The Star –

The rush of air, or of the energy currents, was deafening. My feet instantly lost purchase as I was pulled forward, flipped messily, and then sucked through the portal hole in the wire wall.

We were all bashed unceremoniously together and I had a flashing image of Aris' squeezed, puckered face being much too close to mine. I felt Theus' dropped sandwich whip past my cheek. I saw Dora's boot nearly clip my eye. And a whirlwind of our sandy dust was combining as we lost control of it for a split second.

Then we were hurled into reality, pelting into a strategically cushioned wall in a nicely padded landing room.

At once the pixelated hole sealed over, while we – all chewed up and spat out – bounced around the room like toppled bowling pins.

"I hate that," Aris growled, entirely undignified with his legs up over his head. Dora was in turn already on her feet and offering the lion her hand.

"I can't believe we were in an online dimension," Gabe wheezed in wonder.

"Here," I passed a piece of ham that had got stuck to my cheek to Theus. "I think it would wish to be given back to you."

Theus appeared on the verge of passing out, and he jumped as a door beyond the padded section of our landing room slid open.

"Hey Dora!" a young man exclaimed cheerfully, and if I hadn't noticed a complete lack of varied languages and accents in this time, I would have expected a Scottish lilt in his voice to suit his flaming hair, ruddy cheeks and robust build.

"I've alerted the boss lady and medics to your arrival," the energetic Rogue said, stepping in to shake Aris' hand good-naturedly.

"Perfect Will," Dora told him delightedly. "And I've brought us some stars."

Will reached out to pull me up with a strong grip. "Not just stars though I take it?" he eyed off the pale faced, dazed Theus.

"We got a dreamer too," Dora agreed. She came to stand before Theus and sized him up.

"We're trying to help with dreams," Will rubbed at the bright stubble on his chin. "But maybe you broke this one."

"Ye of little faith," a new, direct voice cut across their speculations. "You ran into trouble Dora?"

"Jo," Dora said respectfully. "We were pursued, with one star hit, but not grievously. Unfortunately there wasn't time to be subtle in saving Gabe's assignment. Probably going to seem like an abduction again."

"You did a great job collecting everyone at the right moment, then," Jo answered fairly. "We should have expected some trouble. We've had enough warnings, and you do always attract chaos."

Dora smiled with an impish twist of her lips. "It's true."

I reached out a hand to Jo. "Mitch," I introduced myself.

She took my hand in a warm grip and I felt my skin prickle under her knowing gaze. Her eyes seemed to belong to one with a terribly old soul.

"It is a pleasure to meet you, Michael."

Then she turned to Gabe, tucking her shortly cropped, light brown hair behind an ear. "Gabriel," she greeted him calmly. "Ari'el was keen to save you."

"Gabriel," Will, rolled the name around his tongue thoughtfully. "I hadn't expected you to be so ..."

"Butch?" I supplied politely.

Gabe didn't acknowledge me. "What exactly is going on here?" he turned to Aris, but it was Jo who answered, beckoning for us to follow her from the padded landing room.

"We are Rogue exiles from the society you saw above," she explained. "We are not subjected to any of the daily programming that citizens are subjected to by the plutocracy. As a result, we are the only ones who can guess at what is happening, and we are the only ones who are willing or able to try to stop it."

Jo led us into a board room, and Will and Dora sprawled out in swivel chairs on either side of Jo as she seated herself at the head of the expansive table.

Gabe and Aris joined them solemnly, followed by the still

dazed Theus, but I was intrigued instead by the room's floor to ceiling window.

The view showed that we were in some sort of colossal underground cavern. There was a vast, rocky wall a great distance away, but something far below was emitting an orange, fiery light that filled the board room with a very warm ambience.

I wandered closer to the thick glass, and my eyes widened as I first craned to squint upward, and then down.

We were deep below the surface world – just a distant rocky roof above. Our one room was connected to countless similar ones – all carved into what had to be the core of the Earth itself. And far below us, letting off the glowing amber cavern light, there was an expansive, thick carpet of lava.

"*Hell*," I breathed.

I'd been here before.

Excerpts from: The Collected Tales of Mythological and Historical Heroes

On the subject of the ancient 'gods and goddesses':

Like the wise Prometheus, the foolish Epimetheus was not unscathed by his errors. His carelessness had caused the plight of humanity – their weaknesses. They had no claws, no fur, no scales, no means with which to protect themselves. And so it was decreed that people would be given challenges to overcome in order for them to gain qualities like strength and intelligence for themselves.

Epimetheus' punishment was to be unable to protect his brother's people from the harshness of these challenges while they slowly suffered and learned through the ages. His punishment was also to have to watch while these challenges were unleashed, knowing that every moment of human hardship was his own fault.

*However, at first Epimetheus mistook his punishment for a gift. When a beautiful woman was sent to him by the other gods, he welcomed **Pandora** into his home, along with a box (or in some tales jar) – which they were warned had to remain sealed.*

*Unfortunately, Pandora had been created to be insatiably curious and Epimetheus was careless again. He did not guard the box, and Pandora's nature meant she could not resist opening it. In doing so, she released the terrible contents of the box, sometimes known as **'the evils'** – diseases and flaws, or 'seven deadly sins' – all designed to test mankind.*

It was believed that hope was the only positive item in the box, and that it was this that allowed people to continue to live on in the face of the plague of unleashed challenges.

If you ever feel 'plagued' by 'evils', make sure to visit your local Sciences branch for a mental perfection check and helpful chemical updates.

| 10 |

- The Star -

I remembered being cornered down there, over that pit of molten lava and fire. The air had been almost too harsh to breathe. Too heavy for lungs to process.

But every angel had come for me. Wanting me, and the trouble I caused, to stop for good. It had been at the very start of things.

"Over generations we have built our city down here, tunnelling away from civilisation," Jo was saying. "But luckily for us, we have advanced and strengthened rather than suffering in our isolation. We are more connected and aware the further we disconnect from the World above."

"Going Rogue in fact means seeking a safe haven away from total control, and breaking only the rules that are unhealthy," Aris explained in a low voice to Gabe. "It is often the most intellectual or empowered and passionate individuals who join the cause to create change."

"We have become outlaws," Dora asserted. "We refuse to be manipulated and owned, and most of us are willing to fight to stop the people above from being controlled too. I am sick of the World being ruled without care and I, for one, feel that if I don't do something, I will be responsible for the evil in this World continuing."

"We are considered rebels," Will commented. "But choice – *liberation* – is my dream. All I want is to save society from being suffocated, even if that means people fear me for disrupting their comfortable lives."

"We're not after lawlessness," Jo added gravely. "We just want free thought. And if possible, we want to save the World from its decay. The Leaders have been masking problems instead of solving them for too long."

"Sometimes the greatest good is not achieved by something that is wholly good," I remarked under my breath, still gazing down at the hellish scene below. "You must break from tradition and break from the crowd."

I felt both the eyes of Aris and Gabe burn into me then.

And I remembered their expressions as they'd held me down – the unbearable heat from below and the amber glow of the magma illuminating their features. All still so distinct.

I remembered the betrayal and resentment creasing Gabe's smooth brow. The loathing from Aris as he snarled like the lion he was. I remembered Evangeline and the hands of the others reaching for me. Angels of vengeance had come for me that day, fearing and misunderstanding me, and punishing me for seeming so rogue in the beginning myself.

"Some of us were raised World Soldier. We bring the strategy, strength and revolutionary drive to the Rogue force," Will explained.

"You bring the brawn," Dora laughed. "Some of us originated as Ordinaries, and take on functional jobs to help our society run smoothly down here. Or we train with the Soldiers until we can join them." I had a feeling that nothing about Dora had ever been ordinary even above ground. In fact I felt a bit like I'd met her once before too.

I shivered. So many things were giving me a sense of déjà vu down here.

"Some of us bring the brains, too, but they are all working hard right now to equip our society below and to find solutions to the problems of the society above," Jo went on. "Our intellectual types make our lifestyle possible, designing sustainable systems and technology that surpasses even what you would see on the surface."

"And you helped us because…?" I asked.

"You are one more thing that stands for people having minds of their own," Jo answered. "You facilitate the types of minds that could help our World, the people who might be able to address the issues it faces."

"Sometimes our own order is not so good at change," I cocked an eyebrow, and this time returned the stare of only Aris as Gabe glared down at the table.

I was certain that Gabe recognised the hell-like scene beyond the window too.

"But for humanity," I went on, "I am of course willing to complete my assignments as best as I can."

"Who were the hunters that came for us?" Gabe changed the subject.

"Leaders control them. They are so 'Soldier' now that they're more robot," Dora explained. "Soon all Soldiers will be like that, but Leaders have kept the effects of the updates quiet."

"We've faced soldiers and weapons in the past. But we've never been targets. How can soldiers of your time know of us? And how can they hurt us so permanently?" Gabe asked with a grimace.

"You've entered a time of total surveillance," Jo told him. "*Everything* is discovered. And since they discovered and started hunting your kind, they've come up with weapons to be used specifically against you."

"Your sand is gold," Will nodded at the dust that I'd spread over Gabe's wound. "But theirs comes from dead pieces of fallen stars. Black rock that has been harvested, treated, manipulated and that they use to make a liquid poison. It's like the opposite of what you guys run on."

"Exactly how much do they know, and how much do you know for that matter, about us?" I asked then. "In all of time I have only been recognised for what I might be a few times – and never was I fully understood or spoken to in this much depth about it."

"I've only told them what they've needed to know," Aris rumbled gruffly – simmering as if I had accused him of more.

"We don't know the ins and outs of your history or power, and I doubt the assassins do either," Jo agreed thoughtfully. "I've learned some things through different premodern religious recordings that have survived, detailing your actions throughout time. But I have also been very aware of you in other ways."

"In what ways?" I prompted her, curious.

Jo tapped her fingers lightly on the table. "I was raised in an Ordinary family, but taken from them to boost Soldier ranks at thirteen. Then it was discovered that I was one of a very low number of people who have a mental disorder that cannot be programmed out. I was not perfect enough to be a Soldier, and no longer belonged amongst Regulars of more mundane sectors. And ... I was hearing voices," she gave a small smile. "I managed to find a place down here, and was helped to learn of my condition. But, though I could hear what others couldn't, I was not treated as faulty. I became an asset to the Rogues, taking on a leadership role. Because the things I was hearing made me into something similar to a faulty radio, picking up on a wavelength I wasn't meant to be connected to. And I believe it is the same wavelength that each of your kind have been connected to. Some greater power that has been known by many names among scientists, astronomers, and all pre-modern religions. So I came to recognise each of you, just as you recognise each other, and I came to feel connected to the power that each of you are connected to."

"That," I said slowly in surprise. "Must have been a burden. But if you are connected as we are, then it is no accident. Human beings are in part made of the same material that my kind were made from, and a person's soul can transcend the bounds of mortality when it reaches the right level, accomplishing what it must. Normally that's what we're here for – to facilitate the right dream and put our client on the right road. But it sounds like you're on your way all by yourself."

Jo's serious face lightened with gratitude. "That is something to hope for then," she replied. "After a lifetime of being imperfect."

"Never imperfect," a musical voice disagreed as a slender, exotic looking beauty entered the room. Her hair fell in a sleek black line down her back. She seemed a little older and wiser than the other Rogues so far, but her beauty was deep and mesmerising.

"Queenie!" Will greeted her, jumping up from his chair like an excited puppy and draping an arm over her shoulders. "Here's one of those smart people we told you about, who makes Rogue Headquarters actually function. She's our Doc."

The door slid open again as another man followed Queenie in.

"Hands off the Queen," the new, rugged man ordered Will churlishly – speaking gruffly into his short beard.

He fit the definition of rough rebel as he peered around the office, but his only weapons were a glass of water in one hand and a pill that had to be a sedative in the other.

"Hey, 'm Ned." His eyes fell on Theus, and he crossed to the pale man at once, setting the tablet and water down on the table in front of him.

"Queenie thirsts for knowledge, but in her spare time she trains Ned to be less angry," Will explained.

"We're medics," Ned grumbled.

"Here to check in with our guests," Queenie added.

Dora and Aris then bombarded her and everybody's attention, telling Queenie about Gabe's arm, and whipping out the dart that Dora had retrieved.

I refocused on the view from the window, and only turned when I felt a bump at my elbow.

Theus had been slumped in his chair beside Gabe the last time I'd noticed him, but his untouched pill was still back at the table, and here he was, apparently in no way sedated.

"Hey buddy," I said carefully.

"I think I know you too," Theus swallowed nervously, referring back to the odd sense of spiritual recognition I'd had in the wire tunnel. "I've travelled through the virtualtree, am trapped underground, have been stolen by the Rogues, am now standing over molten lava … and yet the fact that I suddenly feel like I've met a stranger before seems more important than anything else."

"I *knew* it," I frowned. "But hey," I said. "It's been a tough day, let's not worry about it too much."

"What are you? Why do I feel like I know you?" Theus questioned further, clearly perplexed.

"It's nothing to worry about, I've been around for a long time," I told him. "We may have been connected somehow in the past."

"*How?*" Theus exclaimed in frustration. "Tell me how come I feel, with all my being, that I know you. A stranger!"

The others stopped to glance over at us, just as I felt Theus' hand grab for my shoulder to shake me.

At once I gasped as an unbidden image burst through my mind, as if in response to the abrupt contact. It was a memory of something I'd watched a terribly long time ago, when I had still been just an invisible spectator of life's creation.

I clutched my head and Theus' hand felt as if it had locked onto my shoulder as he watched the vision too.

I saw two nearly identical brothers working side by side.

They would come to be known as gods, for their job was to create life, just as we stars would be called angels for guiding it.

There was the smell of soil and pure, untainted air. One brother was covered in mud, his loin cloth filthy as he toiled to form two human shapes from the wet earth. He carved each face with tenderness and forethought, following divine inspiration to make the forms of a man and a woman – the earliest human beings. His name had been Prometheus, and he had become a great friend of mine.

"Those brothers –" I heard Gabe's very real and very present voice exclaim. "They look just like Theus. But they lived so long ago!"

"This is incredible," Will's voice called out, as if from far away.

"How are you all seeing this? What's happening?" I groaned.

"Your eyeballs are projecting images! It's like a hologram," Will advised in a chipper tone – sounding like all he was missing was some popcorn. "Is this not normal for you?"

In the memory Prometheus continued working on the human figures, his hands like those of a clay master.

"Do not forget to save good traits for my people," Prometheus' voice came from the memory.

"Of course not, brother!" the second god chuckled – busily designating an abundance of qualities to the first animals of the world. "Aren't the birds beautiful with the wings I've given them?" he, Epimetheus smiled happily. He carelessly threw more qualities to the different animals in his excitement.

And then the vision in my eyes shifted to show Prometheus – his people finished but his head in his clay covered hands. Epimetheus held his brother, his own cheeks tear streaked with remorse. He had forgotten the people.

When that image faded, the sweet, floral scent of a blooming garden almost made me weak at the knees as I remembered what came next.

I watched as, to keep the first humans safe, the world's first haven, a bountiful garden was made – springing to life almost instantaneously. Green, healthy, coloured vibrantly by fruits and flowers.

"This place is divine!" Queenie breathed.

And yet we watched the first human woman leave the first man, running away from the garden unprotected.

"Is this the story of … Adam and Eve?" I heard Jo ask in a wondering voice. "I didn't know that Eve left first."

"Eve wasn't the first woman," Aris' voice growled. "This is where Michael made himself visible to the true first woman, breaking all of the rules to change the course of history instead of watching it unfold."

I blindly turned my head towards him. "I couldn't allow people to be stuck in, or to suffer beyond the garden," I retorted. "It was in their nature to make mistakes, while the consequences never fit the crime. And I was the star who had been created to protect people. To be their champion. Even if that meant I broke my own maker's rules."

"So you'd been *made* to break the rules!" Dora exclaimed. "It was in your nature to help them, and in their … our nature to need it."

My mind burned again and refocused on the image of Prometheus, standing beside me and holding a flaming torch out to a group of figures huddled in the darkness. Together, we had stolen the fire of the gods, and together we gave it to the mortals and taught them of its ways.

"People were not *meant* to be aided in their trials," Aris rumbled in quiet fury.

It was not good for him to remember every reason for hating me – what was the universe doing?

My skull seared with the next memory, which was with Epimetheus, this time.

"Please help me!" he had cried. "Prometheus has been punished by the other angels! He is high in the Caucasus Mountains where I cannot reach him!"

I had swept my way up the mountain to find Prometheus' lithe body straining against shackles that bound him to a massive boulder. But worse was the swooping of wings, the crunching of pebbles, the tearing of my friend's flesh as an eagle so mighty that it almost blocked out the sky ripped through his skin and muscle.

I'd tried to shelter him, but the eagle had been unstoppable – punishing him for changing the world.

The sound of his screams, long past, rocked us all now. And there was the sound of my own sobs from that awful time too.

I heard Gabe's intake of breath as the memory showed the sun going down, the retreat of the eagle, the smears of blood and gore, and me sitting down beside Prometheus. I was taking a manacled, torn hand in my own.

"It is the same every day," Prometheus had cried and bled against my shoulder. "But *you* know. *You* know what it is to be punished for doing what is right."

In the memory I spread my sand all about, bringing sweet dreams and forgetfulness to Prometheus, and promising to return with help.

"You … broke the rules *again*," I heard Aris' now more sickly voice cut in from reality once more. "That was a trial that had to be undergone by Prometheus in that life cycle. It made him into a figure of sacrifice and legend."

But I was grimly happy to watch the memory as it revealed my role in leading another of the first ever dreamers in the world, Hercules, to free Prometheus – making Hercules' own dreams of proving his great strength come true.

"So many of us had wanted to do something to end Prometheus' trial," I snarled at Aris. "But, yes, I broke the rules and interfered. I only regret that I wasn't there in time to help Epimetheus too."

My head felt like it was splitting, and I heard Theus groan at the same time as I did when the vision melted again into a new one, showing the second brother once more.

"We need to help them," I heard Dora's voice, and then I felt her try to free Theus' grip from where it was still clawed around my shoulder.

This time the pain became overwhelming as my memory was churned out of me, to be channelled toward two people.

The image played on to show Epimetheus again screaming at me for help.

"It's all my fault!" he wailed.

A terrible vortex was opening up in his home before my very eyes. A tornado of furious, rushing power cracked and then pulled down the stone of the walls. The apocalyptic sound was deafening as the swirling storm grew, ready to consume us, and *everything*.

Fighting my way forward I found Pandora – Dora – in the centre of it all. She had been cursed to open the box and now the world would become consumed in a storm of evils.

I felt plague gnaw at my bones, and suffering inflict my soul. I felt heartache and sorrow and heard cries of misfortune. And Pandora, devastated at what she had unleashed, could not close the box as each horror escaped to whirl around her.

I had reached her only as the last evil had been unleashed. But I had stopped her from closing the box.

"You *didn't*," I heard Aris grunt hoarsely. "That box had been meant to be opened. It contained the tests that all humanity was, and is, meant to face – as our maker deigned necessary for souls to be able to grow in each cycle."

But, without hesitation, the memory of myself reached forward to place something else in the bottom of the box. Something that I had been endowed with, that was part of my own being upon creation.

"You broke the rules in so many ways," Aris' voice was cracking as we all watched me place a ray of hope in the bottom of the box.

Then I had asked Pandora to open it again, so that hope was released into the world and so that humanity might survive the horror that it was to be tested by.

I had never seen Pandora or the two brothers again. Each of them had performed their roles, but their dreams and their unhappy souls had not been satisfied, and they had continued on in a cycle of lifetimes, searching and waiting …

"I really *did* know you," I wheezed as I felt my eyes clear, right as Dora and Theus began to sink to the ground.

I caught both of them mid-collapse, one in each arm. But I felt unstable myself, incredulous that I had known them a million lifetimes ago.

"Medic?" I asked huskily, squinting up at the almost comically frozen room.

Queenie and Ned rushed forward, with Will and Jo quickly following to help. But Gabe and Aris were stunned, watching me.

I gripped the back of the closest chair for strength. "The eyes really must be the windows to the soul," I said sourly.

"You did so much –" Gabe began.

"More rules broken. More things I don't regret, brother," I scowled and straightened before an attack could start.

They'd all tried to kill me for just one of the first infringements I'd ever committed, and here I'd gone displaying a few more.

They both took steps towards me, but I pushed my way between them and crossed to the door, hurrying down the winding corridor, suddenly chafing to leave.

Just as I'd taken one too many speedy turns, I ran into an older gentleman, with long white hair plaited down his spine. He gave me a calm, appraising expression.

"Star born?" he asked respectfully.

"Yes, my friend, and I need your help."

"You're lost?"

"For most of my life," I agreed. "But can you point me to the fastest way to the surface? I don't care about travelling great distances through wiry tunnels, just about getting to the outside."

"It will be curfew out there now," the man warned.

"It's fine," I said quickly. "I have lived this long taking care of myself, and it's the safest I've ever been."

The man inclined his head. "If you're willing to risk it, you can scan yourself here," he answered, leading me to a similar kind of scanner that had been used for identification and entry into buildings on the surface. "If you choose to be scanned you will be sent from here to the closest scanner on the surface. It's Rogue technology."

"So, it'll be like I am being faxed?" I asked, and he peered at me quizzically.

"Never mind, I'll take that option," I went on hurriedly.

He made the selection for me, and I was aware of the laser light running down my body while I stood in the hall.

I heard Butch and Aris' voices begin to follow me down the corridor. Then there was a moment of darkness and disembodiment. Before I felt a new scanner run its rays back up my body.

I could feel sensation returning to my feet, ankles, calves, all the way back to the top of my head.

I blinked, suddenly finding myself in the middle of a dark, empty street under the sky.

I had been scanned out of existence underground, and then back into existence above it.

"Thank my lucky stars," I smiled to myself.

Before all hell broke loose.

Excerpts from: The Collected Tales of Mythological and Historical Heroes

This is a first edition text, published by the World's third generation of great Leaders. Congratulations – you've purchased one of the last Leader approved hard copy texts!

On the subject of early thinkers:

Aristotle *was a famous Greek philosopher and scientist. His teachings made him a treasured star – inspiring others to learn and to grow for generations.*

He taught Alexander the Great – an early conqueror of the ancient World, but he despaired when his pupil made harsh choices that went against moral rules.

He believed that a person must create happiness for themselves in this and the 'next life' by following a correct, virtuous path and by undergoing a journey of growth to be their best self or form.

| 11 |

– The Dreamer –

Lili raised her eyebrows as she registered his face.

It was the magnetic rock star from the café.

"Know this guy, Lil?" Bear asked, holding his laser up. But even Bear sounded a tad taken aback by how attractive this stranger was.

"We've made eye contact," Lili shrugged. "Be wary, team. Where there's one rabbit, there's many."

"Look, this rabbit feels he's got off on the wrong hop," the rock star lifted his hands innocently. "There are no Rogues here."

"Step away from the entrance and we'll find out," Jana's voice was velvet as she stared through the sights on her own laser.

"Entrance? Oh no. No entrance," rock star promised. "I lost my contact lens. That's all. It's around here somewhere – but never mind. I'll be on my way."

"Contact lens?" a new, disembodied voice echoed from within the Soldier circle, making the rock star quickly move aside.

Not a moment later the feet and ankles of another male began scanning into existence within the perimeter – the rest of his body following, right to the tips of some very red hair.

"Contact lenses are so ancient," the newcomer chuckled with easy cheer. "But good effort to cover for us."

Despite the Rogue's rosy nature, the laser baton held ready in his grip made it clear that he meant business.

"Hey there Will," rock star greeted the red haired Rogue resignedly, taking another step back as two more pairs of feet appeared.

"I brought Ned and some others," Will grinned. And he was quickly flanked by a surly, bearded Rogue. Along with a tall male of such a noble countenance that he seemed like an old-time knight. That particular Rogue was vaguely familiar with his wild blonde curls and strong jaw.

"Where have I seen that guy before?" Curtis mused in Lili's ear piece.

"Branch out," Lili told her team, squinting to search for the miniscule tech that the Rogues must have planted in the gravel. "We've got a whole rabbit warren."

"Now, ma'am, can't we just collect our friend and call it a good evening?" Will asked good-naturedly.

"You made it a good evening the moment you scanned top side," Curtis beamed just as cheerfully. "Right into our circle. You've made this easy."

"Nothing's ever easy," Lili warned, stepping forward to seize her rock star as the Soldiers widened their circle.

"She's smart," yet another voice joined in. "And she's correct." The voice was accompanied now by its owner as a young, serious woman with short brown hair scanned in, accompanied on either side by two massive, impressive men. They had a strange charismatic appeal to them, almost like Lili's rock star had.

"Jo," Lili's rock star grimaced. "You brought Butch and Aris?"

"They thought it was important they help us to find you," Jo answered calmly. "Though finding you hasn't been too tricky."

"Detain. Use stun settings," Lili ordered, feeling the excitement of her team.

"Seven to five," Junior sniffed. "Let's round 'em up!"

But as both opposing groups became abruptly animated; some moving to defensive stances and others moving to attack, a foreign noise – a wave of rumbling vibrations began to grow in the distance.

"What is that?" the noble, knightly blonde Rogue asked before he caught Junior's fist to the face.

"Focus on the job at hand!" the red haired one, Will, yelled, before Bear threw Jana at him, and she swivelled around the Rogue's body like a hula hoop – bringing him down quickly.

Bear gleefully charged at the two big rock star-type males, Aris and Butch, and knocked them over like bowling pins.

The sound continued, an alien background noise, but the two groups kept moving and Lili turned to regard her own rock star. She had the oddest sensation of being drawn to him ... very strongly.

Junior ducked a stun blast from Jo, the short haired female, tackled Ned, the cranky bearded Rogue, and at the same time collided with the familiar, knightly Rogue – his blonde curls bouncing everywhere.

Curtis rushed in to help, pure joy written across his face.

Lili encountered zero resistance from her rock star as she tugged him closer, but she followed his gaze upward as his eyes worriedly searched the sky.

Then she frowned as she sighted a dark, fast moving cloud. A cloud which was emitting the intensifying sounds.

"Alert!" Lili yelled at the top of her lungs, startling all participants of the scuffle. "Eyes skyward!"

Everyone stopped mid roll, kick, duck or hula as the sound was suddenly accompanied by a flood of light.

"What the fu …" a little zap came from Curtis as he paused, holding the gruff bearded Rogue by the collar.

"Assassins!" Jo growled.

And, blurring to a stop in the air, soaring over the Rogue and Soldier groups, were four new opponents.

Lili felt her heart shudder – for these people were covered in designs beyond even her own. They would no longer be able to think in an even remotely human manner.

"Ahhh, are they Soldier?" Junior asked. His curly blonde, knightly opponent was just as transfixed beside him.

Jana scanned the newcomers from where she crouched with her knees pinning Will's wrists. "Maybe they once were."

"Well they aren't Rogue," Jo stated flatly.

The four 'assassins' seemed to have found what they were scanning for as they raised brutal shooters, and aimed them at the three members of the rock star family, including Lili's prisoner.

Lili immediately let her own designs light up, dragging the rock star back.

"You are interfering with our watch and with our prisoners. You approach unlawfully. Stand down and identify!" she ordered the figures above.

Instead, they loosed fire.

"From arrest to protect!" she yelled at her team.

So as the first shots soared toward their enemies-turned-victims, Lili's team flew into their new course of action.

Lili growled as her enhanced sight fell on a shot that was slicing towards her rock star.

With accelerated speed, she twirled him away and the shot ricocheted off the gravel, spattering some form of dark liquid.

But behind her Junior let out a sharp cry.

Junior had jumped in front of the rock star called Butch and the familiar knightly Rogue, but now a poison dart was piercing Junior's shoulder.

Junior sank to his knees and the knightly Rogue quickly caught at the Soldier, yanking the dart out of Junior's skin and throwing the still spurting injection out of harm's way.

A burning smell filled the air and smoke sizzled from Junior's clothes – until Butch reached a hand over Junior's shoulder, pressing the wound so that Junior surprisingly groaned in relief. When Butch lifted his hand he left a gold hand print on the Soldier's vest.

But before Junior's first cry had even finished ringing out, Lili had already bent her knees and lifted off in fury.

She had shot through the air, her pulsing designs flaring so brightly that she'd struck like a slash of lightning.

Lili grabbed hold of an enemy's boot and yanked it downward so that he was ripped out of his hover cycle and crashed down to the road, leaving cracks in its surface.

Still soaring upward, Lili booted the next attacker so hard that he projectile vomited onto the 'assassin' next to him.

Below, Bear dodged the back splash and hoisted the other rock star – Aris – behind himself before tucking the Rogue named Jo under his arm like a doll. He backed them toward an abandoned shop wall, which was somewhat sheltered by its dilapidated front veranda.

Curtis pushed Ned; sending him back-pedalling towards the veranda and out of harm's way too.

Not far from there Jana was somersaulting over the red head of her captive-turned-citizen-to-protect-and-serve. She pulled him up over her body by his wrists, and then catapulted him away to land in shock against the shop wall.

Above them, Lili clobbered the vomit man with a glowing fist and heard his jaw crunch. Then she threw him at his soiled comrade so that they arced away from her in a rush – smashing into a distant warehouse.

"Lil, listen, there are more coming," Jana's voice cautioned in Lili's ear piece. She and the others had now collected most of the Rogues under the shelter of the veranda. Bear was just running out again for Junior, Butch and the knight.

"I hear them," Lili responded, registering the dull electrical humming that seemed to accompany the flight of these new beings. "Sounds like a whole flock."

Without pause she hurtled into the other two assassins so fast that the three of them all spun around each other like a giant pin wheel – whirling crazily until Lili turned off her anti-gravity designs.

Weighing the two attackers down in a free fall, Lili snapped the neck of one brute on the way down, and then levered herself around the body of her final opponent to surf his struggling form down to earth.

She put her heavy boot on his head so that he hit the gravel face down.

"I have visual!" Jana warned more urgently. "They're distant but coming in fast and hot."

Lili stepped quickly off her last opponent's head, eyes on the many shadows becoming visible in the skies as the humming grew unbearably louder. "They're within range," she yelled to everyone. "Get to cover!"

Bear was now picking first Junior and then the surprised knight up, easily tossing one and then the other to where Jana and Curtis waited to catch the two men – as though they were all in a tumbling act of talented circus acrobats.

But even as Bear began to drag Butch backward too, there was the crack of a weapon firing again – and a dart was spearing down towards Butch's chest.

The one called Aris cried out from the shelter.

And Lili's rock star, who was still standing where she'd pirouetted him to just a minute before, now leapt forward – catching the dart square in his own chest.

"Mitch?!" Butch grabbed at Lili's rock star as he slumped.

Almost immediately burns began to spread across Mitch's exposed flesh, growing outward from the likely fatal wound as the poison spread.

Butch yanked the deeply embedded dart out, and Mitch

shuddered as Butch tried to smooth gold across the damage, but the burns continued to grow.

For no explicable reason, Lili was outraged.

"Lil!" Jana yelled this time. "There are too many!"

Lili's designs burned with aggression as brutish 'assassins' started to rain down from the sky – landing heavily on the road.

She flew through the air so fast that she got past the guard of the nearest two. She picked one assassin up and threw him into a parked hovcar.

She hauled the other up over her head. Then brought him down with a crack over her knee.

Even as she threw him away from herself, three new enemies turned toward her and she blurred forward to tear them apart.

But more assassins touched down near the shop, launching at Lili's team and previous prisoners.

Bear went hurtling one way, Jana was sent rolling the other. Curtis was trying to shield Junior while the Rogues circled the two Soldiers protectively.

Lili was there before she'd had time to register speeding forward.

She caught one assassin's hand before it smashed into the knight Rogue's face.

With a death kick she propelled the assassin backward like a repulsed magnet.

"They're breaking our exits!" she heard the Rogue named Will cry, and she saw groups of the enemy gathering to stomp on different parts of the gravel. The simple might of their legs was crumbling the road, along with whatever minute Rogue scanners were hidden there.

"You're the only one strong enough to hold them off and fly to safety," Jo yelled at Lili. "Trust me to get your team out of here."

For a fleeting moment Lili sucked in a breath. Then she nodded to the tough female Rogue.

"Retreat!" Jo at once yelled over the chaos, stooping to help Curtis lift Junior. "Lead the way!" she ordered Ned, who was hustling Jana and Bear up to follow him.

Ned didn't pause, but ran for where the tech covered assassins were destroying the gravel with sheer brute force.

Lili steeled herself, angling her shoulder and blurring across the distance to crash into the assassins – flinging them away from the invisible Rogue rabbit hole.

"Go!!!" Lili roared as her team looked to her.

She felt the impact of fists and boots from all directions, but was satisfied to see her team get moving, as well as Butch and his big fellow rock star carrying the slumped over Mitch between them.

"The scanner's too damaged!" Will groaned when he reached the rubble, trying desperately to press at a cracked part of the road.

"We'll have to scan manually," Jo answered grimly.

Lili growled in frustration as her lit up vision flickered a little.

"I'll stay behind," Ned rumbled, and stooped to hold the invisible button down.

At once the gathered crowd of Lili's Soldiers and Jo's Rogues began to flicker and fade with the beginnings of a mass scanning. But before he could disappear, Mitch detached himself from the other rock stars, and stumbled across to Ned. He flopped down gratefully, pushed Ned into the disintegrating group and quickly placed his hand over the same, unassuming part of the road.

"Got it," he rasped, holding the cracked gravel until the increasingly mirage-like assembly had vanished to safety.

Then Lili at last burst her way free, done with being a distraction.

She threw herself backwards, sending three opponents flying as she sped to where Mitch laid, and she quickly looped his arm over her shoulders as he passed out.

She unhooked a tech grenade from her belt, pressed it to life and tossed it into the pack of assassins as she kicked off.

The destructive sonic blast popped her ears and there was a wave of terrible heat at her back, but the crashing gale force winds helped to speed her and Mitch away even more quickly.

She blurred them over the city, and toward base rather than the Rogue Kill Zone, so that she could hide her dying rock star.

Breaking countless Soldier protocols, she smuggled him into her apartment, which already contained V's contraband and her own brooding doubts.

Excerpts from: The Collected Tales of Mythological and Historical Heroes

This is a first edition text, published by the World's third generation of great Leaders. Congratulations – you've purchased one of the last Leader approved hard copy texts!

On the subject of influential early historical figures:

** In this section people, lands and cities that are believed to have existed prior to the unification of World are mentioned.*

William Wallace *was a leader of a Scottish rebellion, rallying previously separate tribes in an attempt to overthrow English control. The English had stripped the Scots of their liberty and rights, and until his capture William Wallace successfully drove his English suppressors back, battle by battle.*

It is fortunate that there are no longer different races of human beings. Because we are one nation, no such division exists today. And no such need for blatant, messy disobedience.

| 12 |

– The Star –

I could feel myself slowly dying.

But I wasn't there yet.

It was rare that I had been made to suffer a long, drawn out end, and even Tien's death had sounded quick enough. But then again, none of my kind had suffered a real, everlasting end such as those assassins had just guaranteed me. The poor universe was probably trying to get its magnanimous mind around it.

"Ouch," I rasped as I felt myself being propped up to sit against a wall.

Then a heavenly light pattering of water was turned on overhead, and I leaned my head back against the wall so that the drops touched my face like kisses.

"The waterfall wall has healing properties," a voice told me. "Hopefully it can flush out some of the poison still on your skin, and soothe the burning."

I sensed my assignment as she sat down opposite me in the shower. I felt her strong hands take hold of my shoulders, and pull me forward so my head rested now against her own shoulder. She didn't seem to care about the wet.

She pushed my jacket back, and pulled my T-shirt over my head. Then she let me rest back against the cool wall again.

My burning skin felt as if a miracle poultice had been poured over it rather than lukewarm water.

She sponged at the wound with a towel wrapped around her hand, and pain came flooding back. Without mercy, she tried to scrape away any black poison that still clung to the edges of the burnt out crater in my chest. Amazingly, it had hit right where I'd been shot in the sixties just a day or two before.

That death had been much more sudden. Much more peaceful.

"Sorry ..." I felt my numb lips mumble through the wet. "Normally you wouldn't be the one helping *me* on my path."

I felt her fingers on my wrist and then at my neck. "Normally?"

"Normally you could let me die and you would actually feel better about it," I knew I was rambling. "This is too drawn out for either of us to enjoy. And I haven't been able to help you enough for this death to be meaningful. It's totally uninspiring," I sighed.

"I don't know how many deaths you've had, but they sound better than I've been led to expect," she answered bluntly.

Too honest to deny death was inevitable. Probably as shocked as I was that it hadn't happened already.

"There," she said. "I've got as much of the poison out as I can."

My eyes were shut but it still felt like the world was swirling around me. "Oh. Good."

Then I heard her sharp intake of breath.

My own blood must have finally had the chance to begin to flow.

I peeled open an eyelid.

Little rivers of red were darting down my chest and stomach, mingling with the water.

But she was examining the blood on her towel.

"Now what kind of underground, messed up narcotic have you been taking to get like that?" she asked in fascination.

"Magic," I grinned at her lopsidedly.

"Never heard of it," she cocked an eyebrow. "And I've never seen blood that shimmers gold."

"Lili ..." I tested the name out that the others had used for her.

"The first model," she agreed. "And you, Mitch, really are something else." She stood to turn the water off.

"Quite the star," I confided in her.

"You're soaked. I should get you down to the Biobeauty machine ..." she mused.

"Why?" I winced. "I am beautiful enough."

"Well," she informed me, "I don't usually dry and strip down strange men." She stooped to sling my arm over her shoulders.

But even *I* hadn't expected the inhuman cry that tore from my throat as she shifted me upwards.

I felt the heat in my chest become ashes and char.

"I'll dry myself…" I panted, trying to fight a wave of nausea.

She walked and half dragged me over to an expansive bed, lowering me carefully.

"Just need a towel," I added.

She appraised me thoughtfully. "I've never needed to own more than a hand towel before. And you wrecked that one."

"Got a paper towel?" I managed. "Or dish towel even."

"Who washes dishes these days?" she snorted. She disappeared for a minute, and returned with a fluffy dressing gown. She had somehow returned in a dry state, with fresh clothes and immaculate hair, but the dressing gown was for me.

"To die with dignity," I said wistfully.

"To live a little in luxury," she pointed out.

She helped me into the robe, and closed it around me before pulling my saturated trousers off.

"I rarely even need to undress *myself*," she was saying wonderingly.

"There's something to be said for it…"

"The Biobeauty just does such a good job."

"Stirling performance on you at any rate," I agreed.

She opened the top of the gown again and paused.

We both blinked at the gold dust clinging to the inside of the garment.

It was falling off me like the dust from a moth's wings now.

She placed gauze over my chest and then put pressure on

it. Strangely, I felt the gauze start to take to me like a second skin. It clung on, a new layer to cover and fill the cratered wound.

"I think we have some things to discuss," she told me.

She was leaning back on the pillows beside me now, watching me.

"Time might run out before we're done," I said a little weakly. "But I'll find you again if I get my next life," I promised. "I have unfinished business with you, and the universe has OCD. It would sort it out."

"Is that so?" she pondered my half lucid words. "Are you always so philosophical?"

"Oh, always a mix between realist and dreamer," I sighed.

I could feel my chest more powerfully than any part of my body, but I wasn't sure if that just meant my extremities were going numb.

"What unfinished business do you presume to have with me, seeing as you only just learned my name?" she enquired.

Very cautiously, I tilted my head and focused my eyes on her.

"Tell me," I began with a shallow breath. "What would your wish be, if I could grant you one to fulfil your dreams?"

She was taken aback for a second. But she obviously wanted to accommodate the dying man.

"I would wish," she said thoughtfully. "To save people from the oblivion and obliviousness that we are all sinking into. To give everyone free choice. And I really wish it wasn't treasonous to say such things."

I furrowed my brow. "I'm not sure I have the revolutionary energy to inspire change on that level," I replied sadly. "That's a good one though."

I sucked in my breath, awash in pain for a moment, before I could go on.

"I think that's why my kind are being killed off really," I speculated drowsily. "Wishes on stars and dreams being inspired don't fit into this modern world. Everyone has to follow, not stand out ..."

"Have others been killed off?" she asked, obviously concerned about the strange new police force she had encountered.

"Yes. But they were nowhere near as lovely as me," I informed her. "I would be careful," I added. "I do believe you've become entangled with a dangerous force. You might be in trouble."

"The Leaders have never needed their own police, not with the World Soldier forces," she frowned. "But those things ... they have been constructed from Soldier technology."

"So they were Soldiers once, like you."

"Probably very similar to me actually. They would have been raised Soldier. But they must have recently received updates that changed them. Too many designs to live with and still be independent though."

"You were raised Soldier, Lili?" I asked.

"Not just raised. I was a Soldier construct," she answered easily. "An experiment that probably led to the creation of our new assassin friends. What were you before you went Rogue? I can't pin down what role you would have played in the community. And you aren't built Soldier."

I pouted weakly at that. "Hmmf. This is a great body, thanks."

She laughed dryly. "No, literally built. I've seen a fair bit of you tonight, and you have no designs that they give to Ordinaries being made into Soldiers. And no markings that are given to ones like me, who are constructed in labs. We're given internal technology straight away from our infant design."

"So … you weren't born to a family?"

"I was made in the test tubes, and I grew for a time in a lab. Then like all Soldiers, I was sent all over the globe to live for long periods, serving the entire World."

She appeared to realise something then, something that she would never have to consider for herself.

"Do you have family that I should connect with?" she asked.

"Oh," I grimaced. "They would all be aware of what's happened."

"Do you see them often?"

This time I scowled. "Sporadically."

"Family sometimes seems more trouble than it's worth," Lili granted.

"It never ends well," I assured her darkly.

One day and night in their company for the first time since they had last tried to kill me, and look where it had got me.

"I am the greatest disappointment to my siblings," I went on.

"Then, the big guy that you saved, and the other even bigger one …"

"All greatly disappointed," I promised.

"Even after you sacrificed yourself?"

"Too little, too late," I rolled my eyes. "I have not always done the right thing, in their opinion."

"Got caught in the wrong crowds?" she asked sympathetically.

"Only depending on the way you look at it," I coughed. "Not all rules that are made stay relevant or right. And not all rule makers disagree with the rule breakers at times. But that's hard for sticklers to see. They are unswervingly good, and I can be bad."

She pondered me wryly. "So your family doesn't like you too much, and you believe that is somewhat justified. You and your family are being hunted, and now your life hangs in the balance."

"I don't sound like the stuff dreams are made of, do I?" I smiled a little at her sum up.

"At least you belong to the Rogues," she offered. "Better to belong somewhere, hey?"

I shook my head. "I only met them today. They just wanted to enlist me to work for them instead of dying. It didn't work out."

"You only met them today? What have you been doing with yourself then? And why the dying and hunting part at all?" she was confused now. Everyone in the modern era had to belong somewhere.

"Actually, I have been doing an awful lot. Every day of my existence has been about doing what needed to be done. But I haven't been here in this part of my existence long enough to complete my task, of helping you. And I really am sorry for that."

She didn't seem sceptical, just interested. She probably thought I was hallucinating.

A gold haze *was* starting to frame my vision, creeping in, and I had rarely explained myself to an assignment before.

"Your task of helping me," she repeated slowly. "Give me an example of how you help."

A warm smile touched my lips as I remembered the countless dreams I had facilitated. I didn't always die in order to inspire someone, sometimes I lived long enough to push them to achieve it and see the results. Then just passed quietly away to my next job.

I remembered one special time. I had been allowed to guide a boy as he grew up. It was one of the longest stages of living amongst people that I had been granted. It had been at a turning point in human history; the late 1400s in Renaissance Florence.

"Once I helped a talented young boy, who had in fact been named after me. He was a misfit, but a brilliant misfit. He created such enchanting statues and works of art."

For a moment I remembered the tinkling sound of tools inside a quiet workshop. The bustle of the streets and markets outside as people passed and carts were drawn along the cobble stones. I remembered watching steady, precise hands working to carve a face, which was emerging from the stone as if it were alive. I remembered my client saying that he could see the statue in the stone, waiting to be freed, and I would encourage him on, lighting his way.

"You are like a teacher?" her voice was uncertain.

The gold light across my vision was shimmering over everything else in her room.

"No." I shook my head.

"Are you some kind of magician?" she joked.

I let my eyes close. I really was very tired.

"I just make dreams come true. In sleep, in life, in hours, days or years with the person I have been chosen to help."

"I don't understand," she admitted, sounding frustrated.

"Well, you know how you were … constructed … by science to be Soldier? I was constructed a long time ago too. I don't have designs that give me power. But I do have power."

I felt her sweep my hair away from where it clung to my damp forehead. I felt her pause as she must have noticed the tiny glittering particles that I had perspired.

She didn't push me to explain that, but I could sense she was thinking hard.

"Are you in pain?" she asked after a while. And I was surprised. I couldn't feel anything much anymore. It was close.

"No. All I can see is gold. The sands of time. My hourglass is nearly up."

"You don't see your life Snaps?" she was curious.

"Like my life passing before my very eyes?"

"No … images from the Brainwave chip you've had since *birth* …?"

"I don't have Brainwave." I could feel her staring at me in shock. As if I'd finally stumped her. "Explain what the Snaps are?" I asked.

She drew a deep breath to compose herself, readying to humour me.

"There is a chip that captures key moments, or Snaps of your life. It can transmit moments from your own memory or share other people's stored files of you. You can access them and share them at any time in life, but generally they automatically come on when …"

"Mine would be too long to watch," I told her.

"How long?"

"Well, technically for here and now, I am only two days old," I amended.

"What if you don't count here and now?"

"Longer than human life has existed."

"The boy you helped …"

"I met him in 1475. His mother wished me to be his guardian. His guardian angel. It was part of her dream, so I got to stay to see the world break free from the last grips of the Dark Ages. I got to guide her son as he inspired the world to see divinity in art and humanism. He had quite the cantankerous nature, but he understood me completely."

"He was named after you? Mitch."

"My true name is Michael. But I have been known by others. Michele, Mick, Mitch are the ordinary ones."

"His name was …"

"Michelangelo. It means -"

"Michael Angel," she breathed. "He was known as the Il Divino, the Divine One, for his visions of beauty seemed touched by something *sacred*. I read about him. I have a real book about the ancient world."

"So, do you believe me?" I tested. It didn't really matter. But it would have been nice, if this was the last time, to finally be totally trusted and known. To be believed in.

"I don't know," she admitted. "But right now, you don't seem to be dying like anyone else I've ever seen."

"I normally resemble a mortal as I die," I frowned.

"At the moment," she hesitated to explain. "You're faintly glowing."

"Ah. Not normal." I wondered why I looked different. My mask was slipping.

"What other names have you been known by?"

I drew in a breath. "By family – traitor. By my creator – archangel. By history – 'like God'. By children – The Sandman," I smiled faintly. "I like that one, it's cute."

"Sandman?" her voice was shaky. "That story about –"

"The man who brings sweet dreams to children? Yes. That's nice isn't it? Better than traitor." I raised my hand and opened it for her to see. I knew my gold dust would be clinging to my fingertips. I definitely wasn't bothering to keep it in anymore. "I deserve both names though. I am not wholly good."

I felt her take my hand in hers in a more tender gesture.

"So what is happening right now, if you are meant to be immortal?" she asked.

"I have died so many times," I reassured her. "It's just normally quicker than this. And less final."

"Can you explain to me?"

"I have died in the place of my assignments, I have died saving my assignments, I have died in accidents near my assignments for them to save, and I have died fighting for my assignments – for their goals to be met. Every death is my sacrifice so they are inspired or moved to live and achieve as only they can. Then I come back in another place or time, ready to start again. My death for their dream to live."

"Don't you get to live your dreams too?"

"We *are* dreams. Each new life is a new beginning of opportunities. Maybe it would be possible that we could sacrifice so much that we could be given the chance to live a dream of our own. But this was meant to be your turn."

"I don't know how you could make my dream come true," she remarked thoughtfully. "The old cliché dream of World peace and empowerment for the people. If it hasn't happened yet, why would it happen now?"

"It has happened bit by bit since the dawn of time," I disagreed. "The world can't be improved without taking steps to learn how to be better, and neither can people. But there are those who have fought to limit corruption, injustice, persecution. There are those who have tried to eliminate flaws that hold the world back. And those who have inspired something better or revealed something beautiful in humanity."

"Michelangelo?" she tried.

"Hammurabi and his first laws. Rome's establishment of architectural order. The discovery of gravity and penicillin. Aristotle's theories. Aris; one of my kin had a hand in that. The first time Ari'el was open minded enough to let new ideas into the world, and it changed him so much he is known more now as Aris."

"My turn would have been a tricky one at any rate," she reasoned.

"Every dream, whether it involves finding cures for illness, making grand discoveries, or even just having the confidence to go for a job interview or put pen to paper; each one is special. And if I was sent to you to facilitate yours, it is possible. Maybe, unlike normal dreams, all I had to do was wake you up."

"What if a dream does not come true?"

"Your soul keeps living on in further cycles, waiting," I grimaced. "If I die too soon, I can normally come back to help. Not everyone has had their turn yet either, and there are always new souls beginning the cycle."

"And this time?"

"I have never died in this way. Nobody has ever tried to kill my kind for what they are specifically. I don't know if I will ever come back."

"So someone is trying to end dreams, which are what build the future. Who would want to damage the dreams of individuals, and put an end to the most glorious parts of being human? The human ability to progress, to hope, to be inspired, and to achieve?"

I shivered involuntarily. "This era felt suffocating as soon as I woke up in it. I could feel that individual thought was being constrained. Because, while we specifically follow the deepest dreams and nurture them, normally dreams of all kinds are ricocheting off every surface like fireworks, even changing in shape and form within seconds. There was none of that." I shivered again. "This world is so controlled that it cannot stomach dreams that will bring change. So we are not wanted by those who would benefit most from the status quo."

I felt her sink back beside me.

"Leaders," she uttered. "Leaders are willingly killing off World changing dreams."

I opened my eyes and tried to look at her again. But my vision was completely overcome by curtains of gold now.

"I will try my very best to find my way back to you. But I have seen you in action. And I have seen the Rogues who think and fight freely. I believe people can still make their own dreams come true."

I felt her breath on my cheek as she lowered herself down to lie with her face beside mine.

"I don't know what will happen now," she admitted.

It was the first time I had heard a trace of vulnerability in her voice.

"All I have ever had to worry about was being Soldier. But I don't want to become what those things were tonight."

"Your whole team needs to be careful," I warned.

And then the apartment shuddered with an explosion of noise as a door was blown in, followed by yelling and running feet.

I felt her tense and leap up from beside me.

"STAND DOWN SOLDIER!" a superior voice barked and I heard the sound of blows as she was circled and restrained.

Then I felt rough hands seize my arms and haul me up.

"What is he wearing?" a rumbly voice asked.

The pain sensors in my body came flaring back to life, and I roared in agony; buckling until they dragged me forward.

I heard her yelling.

Then nothing until I came to and realised I was being transported.

Excerpts from: The Collected Tales of Mythological and Historical Heroes

On the subject of influential early historical figures:

* In this section peoples that are believed to have existed prior to the unification of World are mentioned.

Michelangelo was seen as a miracle from the moment he was born – his supposedly barren mother having prayed for a child to the angel Michael. Michelangelo's mother is said to have named the future artist 'Michael angel' following the wonder of her son's birth.

Though Michelangelo was tragically orphaned quite young, and was noted to have been an isolated, hot tempered, eccentric person – it was as if the stars really were smiling on him. For he was taken in by impressive mentors who allowed his talent to shine, and he was also widely adored rather than spurned for his oddity and his genius in a time when these things were little understood.

Michelangelo developed in skill and fame in a period of history that was known as the Renaissance – an era following the Dark Ages that focused on realism and beauty rather than suffering and fear in art. Michelangelo excelled in his painting and sculpting, presenting such sublime beauty on the ceiling of the Sistine Chapel and in his Statue of David that he was often referred to as "the divine one".

If some higher power truly was guiding Michelangelo, it can be described as a cheeky one.

He is said to have been inspired to paint his enemies into his great artworks so that they could be immortalised as fools, with features like donkey ears and snakes biting off their genitals.

You can now do virtual gallery tours with Michelangelo's censored works – with the actual uncensored masterpieces long crumbled to dust to make way for our un-religious World.

| 13 |

– The Star –

I blindly felt the motion, but no sound of tyres on a road and no loud motor.

I remembered I must have been in some modern floating vehicle, and that I couldn't see for good reason, and was in pretty big trouble.

I felt my head and upper body being cradled.

"Are you harmed?" I asked Lili.

"No."

"Are you restrained?"

"No."

"You could light up and tear your way out of this?"

"Yes."

"But you won't?"

"I am Soldier. I am theirs. And I need to see what is happening," she answered simply.

"Do they know what I am?"

"*I* hardly know what you are, but they traced you for a reason."

"Good, those assassins like a fast execution," I felt surprisingly satisfied. Even if it meant no return, I had been around for so long anyway, just surviving and watching and guiding. I was tired. And at least Lili was starting to want to find things out for herself, and would perhaps make some life changing decisions of her own.

"It actually sounds like an execution *won't* be happening," Lili replied in a low voice.

"I beg your pardon?"

"How do you feel now?" she answered with a question.

I pondered it, and realised something with consternation. "Slightly less dead than before."

"They have been back here twice with pulse shots to keep you suspended in life; fooling your body. I had thought pulse shots were banned after some test interrogations on the mostly dead were deemed too cruel."

"How …" I didn't even want to comprehend what it would be like chatting to a corpse whose soul had 'mostly' fled.

"Soon it will start to wear off and death will creep back in to take effect. But they will also creep back in and give you another shot."

"Why?" I spluttered.

"Apparently you are the first of your kind to survive such a direct shot for so long. They feel you may be special in some way. Worth examining. They want a closer look at you."

"No," I said firmly.

She was silent, knowing what I meant.

"Lili?" I asked.

I was starting to wince and my breath was coming fast.

I stifled a moan as the vehicle rose and fell over some kind of air rift.

"Lili, I am not something they should know any more about …"

I gritted my teeth as I heard movement from beyond our holding cell. Coming from the front of the vehicle.

"Please Lili?" I reached for her and missed, but she took hold of my hand.

I drew her hand down to my chest.

"Please?"

I felt her body swell and then release with a drawn out breath.

It sounded like someone was pulling at a door that must have been dividing us from the enemy in front.

Then I felt a sizzling spread of energy under my hand as Lil's fist must have lit up.

"I wish you sweet dreams, Mitch," she whispered.

Before a pulse of sound.

And nothing.

Excerpts from: The Collected Tales of Mythological and Historical Heroes

This is a first edition text, published by the World's third generation of great Leaders. Congratulations – you've purchased one of the last Leader approved hard copy texts!

On the subject of places, events, conflicts and movements:

** Note, in this section, lands that are believed to have existed prior to the unification of World are mentioned.*

The 1918 **Spanish flu** *was named thus because the Spanish were more honest than other countries about how great a crisis the flu was. In order to avoid mass panic or an image of weakness many countries did not admit how significantly they were suffering. In reality the influenza hit the World so harshly following World War One, that some cities ran out of coffins and the flu was compared to the Black Death – which had wiped out one third of the World's population in earlier history.*

Other health crises rocked the World in 2020 when the Covid-19 virus caused people to stockpile necessities like an old manual hygiene product called toilet paper. In the 2030s the World's overproduction of waste and unclean energy also caught up, causing terrifying mutations and also the need for mass huntings of these unsightly abominations.

It is hard to imagine such hardship in our own time, where even a case of the 'common cold' can be programmed right out of us, and where larger issues or defects can be avoided pre-conception by DNA scans.

It is also nice to know that Leaders would never allow mass panic, as terrible news will always be softened for us.

| 14 |

– The Dreamer –

"Bad news. No need for more shots," a voice growled. "He's unsalvageable."

Two tech filled eyes glared nastily at Lili before the robot-like Soldier slammed the hatch between the holding cell and the front of the hovcar closed.

Just moments before that Lili had placed her hand over the hole in Mitch's chest, blasting a deep volt of energy into his body. Then his skin had radiated with gold light, and he'd tensed upwards in her arms before relaxing limply back against her.

Whatever secrets Mitch had needed to keep would be kept, and now Lili found herself alone, contemplating her choice to be disloyal despite all of the conditioning she'd ever undergone, and despite the fact that her entire identity was that of a dutiful Soldier.

She was straight backed and ready when the hovcar cruised to a stop, and when its back doors were wrenched open by two brutes who hardly knew their new strength.

Lili remained impassive as the assassin Soldiers pulled her

roughly from the vehicle, where she saw that they had taken her all the way to The Centre, where Administrators and Leaders conducted their business of pulling all the strings.

She allowed them to restrain her with laser cuffs, and to lead her to the nearest building while their vice-like fingers dug deeply into her arms.

They keyed in a code at the entrance, selecting a room to be scanned to. And even during the scanning process, as Lili was reassembled into a windowless, entirely concrete interrogation room, she felt their grip biting into her skin.

"Ah, good, you're here."

Lili was greeted by two Administrators in immaculate suits – Leader pen pushers.

"Have a seat," the men gestured, taking seats of their own behind a steel table.

The chair Lili was forced into was lined with wires and prongs that could animate and extend – able to hook into a prisoner's Brainwave at any moment.

Lili stiffened defiantly, but they didn't hook in right away – one of the suits instead perusing through a brightly glowing hologram of Lili's details, which floated above the steel table.

The Administrator swiped past an unflattering profile picture, flicked through a file detailing Lili's accomplishments and services, and scanned through reports on experimental procedures and updates she'd gone through from the moment of her creation.

"Let's get some more personal background information on World Soldier design model Lili One," the second of the suits requested, and his colleague brought up a new file that Lili had never seen.

Tiff's model-like identification picture popped up with that file, along with report entries Tiff had apparently submitted over the years that were titled 'reflections on my buddy'.

For a moment, Lili was simply stumped that Tiff really had always completed her homework assignments. But then the first suit stopped skimming the entries when he found a highlighted quote.

"'Lili is of course different to me,'" the first suit read out Tiff's quote. "'But she's also different to most Soldiers. She goes blank on the surface, but it's because she's a real thinker.' What a nice thing for your buddy to say," the suit commented.

He smoothed his moustache thoughtfully and flicked to another of Tiff's highlighted reflections. "'Lili is so strong. She can probably singlehandedly save the World if the Leaders can't.'"

Lili kept her face neutral.

"There's a note here too," the other suit commented. "From your mental perfection checks. The doctor says you're a real dreamer. You've been glitching – dreaming about freedom and rebellion." His eyebrows raised. "Now that's troubling."

Lili remembered the woman in the cave. Craving freedom for everyone, as she had been granted herself.

"So not quite Soldier, and not at all Regular …" the moustached suit mused. "Are you perhaps somewhere in between? Somewhere that goes Rogue from what is allowed?"

"Your patrol went a little differently than usual tonight," the other suit stated then. "Where is the rest of your team?"

Lili shrugged. "They escaped with their lives."

The hologram changed to show footage of Lili tearing apart design covered 'Soldiers' as her team disappeared with the Rogues.

She cocked her head to the side. "Taken prisoner then."

The two onlooking assassin 'Soldiers' beside Lili's chair crossed their arms as her hologram self busily ripped up their buddies before charging at whichever one the footage had been salvaged from. There was a close up of Lili's snarling face and then the vision distorted.

The non-moustached Administrator smoothed his wiry hair. His hair implants had been cheaply done for someone in such fine attire.

"Why were you attacking fellow Soldiers, Lili One?" he asked sternly.

Lili cocked an eyebrow. "I've never seen fellow Soldiers like that. And they attacked my prisoners. They were inhibiting my work."

Moustached suit frowned. "Your automatic reaction should be to stand down for superior officers, Lili One."

She snickered. "They weren't too superior. I broke most of them pretty easily."

Her guards shifted on either side of her.

"Don't you care about what happens to you for impertinence, Lili One?" moustache asked.

She settled back into her chair. "I am Soldier. I answer to Soldier Leader Con, and I serve for the World."

Hair plugs in turn leaned forward in his chair. "It has been determined that all Soldiers will be updated to follow as these fellows do. Your Business Leaders outrank your Soldier Leader. And your World needs control."

Lili glared over the table at them both. "Then, no. I no longer care what happens to me for my impertinence."

The suit with the hair plugs leaned back again. "Your team and yourself attended a pre-update check today, didn't you?"

Lili's mind flashed to V, telling her not to go back for the real thing tomorrow.

A churning feeling clotted in her stomach as she realised the assassin 'Soldiers', stripped of all individuality, really had been just like her. Even the two oafs at her sides.

She had been one update away from joining them without realising. And she now hated that she had dispatched so many of her earlier opponents.

"In the next few days all of the Soldiers in this area are due to be updated," he continued. "And though, as model one, you were instrumental in getting us this far – we now have to decide if you've become a faulty experiment or if you can be salvaged."

"Can be made into a walking Leader program, you mean?" Lili asked.

"In the line of duty," hair plugs nodded.

"In the line of dictatorship," she corrected.

"You are being quite disagreeable," moustache warned.

"Not quite Soldier, not at all Regular," she agreed gruffly. "I don't think I can be salvaged for reprogramming. I am a completely corrupted piece of hardware. The best thing is to take me to the Kill Zone."

"Perhaps you could still be helpful, though," hair plugs

said. "We haven't been able to reach your team, after they were 'taken prisoner' in such Rogue territory."

Moustached suit rapped his fingers on the steel table. "But they might answer if contact came from you."

"You're right," Lili agreed – suddenly feeling very helpful. "Allow me to make contact?"

They brightened then, and nodded smugly. "Make sure we can hear what you hear."

Lili's left eye lit up as she obediently switched on her SoldierBrainwave connection.

Hoping that Junior was being patched up, which would mean that Jana and Bear would be on protective mode, she decided that her best option was Curtis.

She sent out the signal.

The suits were abundantly satisfied as Curtis connected with Lili immediately, his vision now being cast as a hologram in front of her for them to view.

Curtis quickly found something reflective to look into so that Lili could see his expressions, however she had nothing reflective and he was left to see Lili's line of sight, rather than her face.

"Shi –zzap- t Lil, where are you? We're down the burrow," he said hurriedly before he registered what he was seeing and what Lili was looking at.

Then he paused. "Ahhh …"

"Soldier, your orders are for yourself and your team to return for updates or to be considered Rogue," moustached suit enunciated clearly.

"Lil, you ok?" Curtis ignored moustache.

Administrator hair plugs interjected then. "Soldier, we are

giving your orders now, on behalf of the Leaders. We demand your immediate action and respect."

Lili tried not to roll her eyes so that the vision wouldn't roll. Nobody should have to demand respect.

"Right," Curtis seemed to be realising that things had changed pretty massively from what he had known of the World just hours before.

"Good," moustache looked gratified.

"Lili, what are your orders?" Curtis said then.

The outraged suits couldn't quite muster anything good enough to be proper growls. But there were sounds alluding to outrage.

Lili quickly shifted her head and glanced to either side of herself at the two assassins.

"These are Soldiers now. The newest update," she said. "Stay rabbit."

Curtis' reflection registered worry and understanding before Lili cut off the connection, and felt herself being slammed down to the concrete floor by the two 'Soldiers'.

A design covered forearm was pinning her throat, a boot was grinding into her wrist, two fists were pinning her shoulders, and her legs were squashed by her glowering colleagues.

Lili let her designs light up – wanting the Kill Zone instead of the update. But then there was a hiss as the door opened.

And in stepped V.

The three struggling Soldiers and two suits all froze as V entered, his vintage sneakers squeaking on the polished concrete floor.

He pushed his green goggles up to sit on top of his head,

glancing at Lili for a second, but showing no outward sign of recognition or care.

"Grand Techie V-irgil," moustache coughed.

"The body turned to sand before it could be properly studied," he informed the suits.

"To sand?" hair plugs asked stupidly.

"First I thought decomposition must've sped up and I was looking at bone dust," V continued. "But it was all shimmery. So I took a sample, and it turned out to be nearly one hundred percent stardust."

"Stardust?" plugs was still being insipid.

"Yep," V confirmed. "Materials of the heavens older than time itself."

"How is that possible?" moustache chipped in this time.

Lili gurgled in annoyance.

"I don't know yet," V shrugged. "What's been decided about Lili One? I have spent an awful lot of time on her you know. And an awful lot of Leader currency."

Moustache crossed his arms. "She is Rogue. Rogues are destroyed."

V whistled. "That's billions wasted right there. Lili was the experiment that made all of your current upgrade plans possible." He walked around Lili, eyeing her.

"She actually has higher grade technology than any of your Soldiers could survive without their chip," he added. "It would be a shame to put her down when you've got your top techie here. I'm happy to reprogram her with a wipe, a new chip, and by taking her mind offline like you've done with these final versions."

Hair plugs stroked his face as if he were the one with the moustache.

V ploughed on. "She could just be one more brand new Soldier; no fuss and no waste of currency."

Lili felt her temples throbbing – she was purpling in the face.

"But if she's stronger than the other newbies," plugs began to speculate.

"Oh she would surely be an asset under your control," V nodded.

"An asset to control," plugs considered, nodding.

"We could send her to fetch her team," moustache decided. "Yes."

"I'll shut her down and your newbies can transfer her to the lab," V was being very agreeable.

His face stayed blank as he withdrew a small vaccine gun from his coat. "Lights out," he told Lili as he pressed it into her neck.

She held his eyes with her own until her eyelids slowly shut of their own accord.

Excerpts from: The Collected Tales of Mythological and Historical Heroes

This is a first edition text, published by the World's third generation of great Leaders. Congratulations – you've purchased one of the last Leader approved hard copy texts!

On the subject of early individuals of note:

Virgil *was a famed poet of ancient Rome, with his most recognised poetry being about the creation of a civilised, positive life and World. His works often spoke of a more moral, simple, beautiful life. Like ours.*

However, he also wrote of the importance of an individual overcoming crises, or even taking Rogue actions to create such a life.

He stated that 'fortune sides with him who dares', though modern readers would know that it is most important to follow, not to overcome or challenge.

Virgil died before completing his final epic work, the Aeneid, about refugees from the ancient, destroyed city of Troy. Themes of an individual following their fate and founding a new way of life – the establishment of Rome, were explored.

It is a great relief that our Leaders oversee and ensure that the arts left behind by our society are always consistent and favourable.

It is also important to keep in mind that fate and dreams are unneeded fantasies in a World where your next step forward can be earned and inserted with an easily accessible, relatively painless update.

| 15 |

- The Dreamer -

The sound of a beeping machine.

Of someone moving nearby.

The feel of ten needles being driven into each arm, and a tugging sensation behind my ear.

The discomfort of energy flowing from a Brainwave prong, into my cranium.

Then the machine's beeps withdrawing, and the needles being lifted out from my punctured skin.

"Come on Lili …" a coaxing voice.

The pull of the prong being detached.

My eyes flew open.

"YES!"

I whipped up into a sitting position so fast that it felt I had left my brain back where I'd been laying.

"IT WORKED!"

I stared at V wildly.

He had just wheeled out of my way, ecstatic.

I gasped at the searing pain, like a pick axe chipping into my skull.

"Give it a second," V told me. He sounded like a proud father, but looked like a frog in his goggles.

I spluttered as I tried to speak and nothing came out.

"You're rebooting," he explained. "Here," he helped me swivel my legs over the side of the work bench.

My eyes tried to focus past the dizziness as he tapped at my legs for reflexes and then shone a light in my face to check my pupils.

The torch beam budded and exploded across my vision with more pain but the other lights in his office were dimmed to infrared.

Machines spun sickeningly around me and I felt heavily intoxicated.

My eyes struggled to take in the room as things shifted around me, coming into focus and then seeming to rotate away.

"It'll improve," he took my face in his hands and forced me to focus on him. The room faded to spin behind him. "You've gone through worse than this. Just not anything similar to this. Concentrate on getting yourself back online."

I took steadying breaths, filling my lungs. I flexed my stiff, clammy fingers. I straightened my aching spine and let my legs click.

"Try to say something," he encouraged excitedly.

I noticed my mind was starting to catch up and objects around the room were beginning to stay in their designated places.

My throat hardly felt like my own, and I wondered how long I'd been out.

"Jerk." I managed.

"She's back!" he crowed.

"What … happened?"

V grinned his toothy grin at me and pushed his goggles back, rubbing at his stubble.

"Lights," he demanded, and the normal lights turned on.

I winced, and raised a shaking hand to rub my eyes.

"You've been offline and technically brain dead for three days," he told me enthusiastically.

I frowned at him in disgust.

"Don't worry, I froze all bodily functions too," he smirked. "It will take a little bit for your body to catch up to what I've been up to."

I swiped his nearby mug and took a swig of the real style alcohol I knew would be in there. "What exactly have you been up to? Why am I still me?"

"Ahh. Well, you're actually more you now than you've ever been …" he hinted. "I had to shut the old Lili down to take some pretty drastic measures, and to take you from their reach. I couldn't wake you up until I'd worked it out, or they would know I hadn't reprogrammed you."

"But I'm online again?" I questioned in confusion.

"Yes, but not on *their* line. You're operating on your own now. On your own line."

I stared at him. Staggered.

Nobody in memory had existed separately to the rest of society. Even Rogues had just had to damage and alter their connections so that they couldn't be found, but they were still connected to each other and society, like online pirates hacking into the power and hiding to avoid being recognised by it.

Only Mitch claimed to have been different, I thought. And I felt a pang at the thought of the man I'd hardly known.

"You did those new tricks on me? The ones I told you never to try?"

"Yep," he admitted to the magnitude of it. "Your designs and mind technology are now only hooked up to *your* whims and life force, not open to Leader control or awareness. You're free – the narrator of your own story. Nobody can even check your database unless they physically hook into you. Today, with your new chip, is your new birthday."

"This is going to baffle any scanners," I grimaced, feeling my ears pop and suddenly hearing everything more crisply – as if cotton wool had been muffling the World before.

"We could do something about that," he promised. "You know, I had to sneak into your place," V fished for compliments.

"Very spybot of you," I commended.

"I tore the place apart," he went on, and I remembered where I'd stashed the things I'd meant to destroy – the contraband that had now just saved my life.

"How did you –?"

"I gave up and went searching for food in despair," he grinned. "Who stores contraband in a microwave? My emo painting would have been much more fitting."

"V … What does all this mean?" I asked. "I was built to be Soldier."

"You can be anything you want now. No role in society

has been dictated for you," he shrugged. Just as miffed by the possibilities as I was.

I couldn't comprehend the freedom I had now, and also the outcast that this made me. I needed direction. Purpose. Rules.

"And you probably have about a day before they realise you aren't the delightful new toy I promised to give them," V informed me. "A day to get used to your own mind and strength."

"So my designs, they're all running on my own energy, and I'm completely without any other connection or source?"

"Yep. I was worried that would mean you would burn out. But I actually think your own strength being amplified could be more powerful than eking it from the same bandwidth as every other person and machine in our World. We'll see."

I let out a big breath. The pain had faded to a distant memory.

Apart from being sore where he had worked on me, I felt uncommonly strong and alert. I felt a type of new, vibrant energy and hope that I'd never felt before. Because for once it was all my own.

My mind flickered again to the dream woman in the cave. And then to the wish that I'd told Mitch I would have wanted granted. That I would want to free people. Maybe, just maybe it had to be me first. Then others?

"What will you do now?" I asked, very aware of the danger V had put himself in.

"I'll say I broke you and had you destroyed ..." he didn't sound convinced.

"Nope. It won't work." I shook my head. "You know that

even if they can't read my mind or hack my body, they can register my face every time I'm scanned. Even if I change dramatically, the systems will pick up on the slightest trace. They'll know I'm alive, and that you did it."

He shrugged. "This is what I do, all my life – my stuff – is here."

"You know, I've just recently experienced what it is to lose all of that," I replied dryly.

"I'm the Grand Techie," V pouted. "The World would be lost without me."

"Well, I think *I* am going to need to find my team," I answered. "They'll still be off the grid."

"Rogue?" he asked.

"Yes. And Grand Techie or not, you'll be coming with me." I could not let my lifelong friend and creator be liquidated for me. "You and I can work out how to liberate others too, seeing as it was our research that has caused so much harm."

He thought about it. "Rooooguue," he tested the word. "Has a certain charm."

"Then you'll come?"

"I'll come with you," he clapped his hands with a touch of excitement. "It'll take time to work out how to help others who aren't as strong as you are. But I bet I could add to Rogue knowledge."

"Good," I nodded. "I don't need much time to say goodbye to my life up here."

"Give me half a day," he begged. "I've been looking into

the star-boy. Or what was left of him. I want to get all my research together."

My interest was piqued, and I leaned my elbows on my knees, craning to see the data on his screens. "You've been very busy. What did you find out?"

"Well," V held up a diagram that made no sense at all. "Every human is made mostly of water. But about forty percent of our atoms are made up of material that can be traced back to stars." The diagram still made no sense and had no apparent relevance.

He tapped it to draw my attention.

"Right. I didn't know that," I admitted. "I'd just figured we were all mostly technology and fizzpacks."

V cackled. "When supernovae exploded billions of years ago, their sand fell like fairy dust across the galaxy and became part of the chemical makeup of every molecule and living thing in our World and universe. In turn, as we absorbed, we also reflect. Our anatomies are so complex that each person is like a universe themselves. Connected to all the other universes around them by common matter."

"I feel enriched," I grimaced at the level of natural connection he was hinting every organism had, without even mentioning technological connections.

"You look pained," he told me bluntly. "Anyway, your boy was ninety eight percent pure star and two percent person. Almost as if he had just been wearing a human suit."

"Woah..."

"I know! Have I made progress in the last few days or what?!"

"Or what," I replied. But he could tell I was impressed.

"Who knows what it means, though," he shrugged. "Except that he was much older than most things in existence. No wonder he has the Leaders freaked."

"Well you have half a day to get yourself organised and then we can work it out with the Rogues. They must know more – they were protecting other star men from the new Soldiers themselves."

"Half a day," V promised in a tizz, wheeling his chair across the room. "You keep your head down in the meantime," he ordered over his shoulder.

I slid off the bench and found that I was much steadier on my feet than expected. I felt great.

"I'll be ready for lunch when you come back for me!" he warned again as I pinched one of his hooded jumpers.

"Of course," I answered as his door opened for me, pulling the hoodie on. "I owe you big time my friend."

The clinic was still dark with the early hours of morning, so it was easy to ghost down the quiet hall.

The curtained emergency rooms were now silent, no judgmental receptionist sat at the desk out front, and I opted for the little-used fire escape stairs instead of the lift to avoid being scanned for as long as possible.

The heavy stair-well door was surprisingly not heavy at all, and I winced as I nearly ripped it off its hinges. Closing it more carefully, I began to quickly make my way downward, but started with surprise when I paused at a landing and read a sign that suggested I'd somehow descended four flights of stairs.

"No way," I frowned, moving down the stairs again.

"Yes way," I breathed. Because suddenly I was on the ground floor.

I exited the stairs cautiously, deciding I was going to have to get used to my new self – and that the next way to test my skills would be to cross the lobby undetected.

There were not many people moving about yet, but when I saw someone approaching the scanner to enter the hospital, I dashed across the lobby, darted around the last cleaner bots, and practically flew through the door past the person that had just been scanned through.

Then I sped my way easily out into the wee hours of the morning, only stopping when I reached a deserted alley over-shadowed by two buildings.

Ducking in for cover, I immediately tried to focus on using my brand new internal hardware to make a connection, thankfully knowing my team's ID numbers by heart.

I tried Bear.

Probably asleep.

Tried Jana.

Too smart to answer a surface call.

Tried Junior.

Most likely still on meds.

"Heyyy pardner. Whaaat timeizitt??" Curtis' bleary half-awake voice nearly shattered my eardrums. He always sounded like a legendary cowboy at rodeo.

"Early," I whispered.

There was a pause as Curtis realised he was talking to his Brainwave, not to someone else in the room.

"Lili? Is zat you?"

"Better than your average wakeup call," I affirmed. I

peered at a nearby window so he could see me in the reflection, and he scrambled up off the bunk he must have been sprawled over, tripping his way toward a small, dark bathroom. He appeared quite dishevelled in the mirror.

"Where have you been?!" he exploded. "I … I'm not getting any trace of you or your details Lil …" he said then in confusion. "It's like I'm getting pranked by an unknown number. But every number – every person is registered … And nobody on the surface should be able to use the government connection to call me now the Rogues have got me hidden."

"I can," I shrugged in the window reflection.

"Lili …" he breathed in uncertainty. "What's happened? The last message we got from you …"

"Still stands," I affirmed. "It's Rogue or robot. Soldiers are all to be updated into those hybrid machines we fought the other night."

"That is unacceptable," I heard a softer, feminine voice come from behind Curtis' head. He looked up so I could see Jana, who had probably come to wake him.

"We were one of the next teams to be fitted with the final updates," I affirmed.

"After we have been nothing but dutiful anyway," Jana hissed.

"How did you get away?" Curtis asked, knowing that I would rather termination than brainwashing.

"V convinced them that updating me would be more cost effective. Then he used some new tricks to hack me out of the system instead," I explained in a low voice, hugging V's hoodie around myself gratefully. "He freed me from government control."

There was silence and there were raised eyebrows for a few moments as Curtis and Jana took in the fact that they were looking at the first free human in generations.

"Do you think V could come up with a way to make this work for all of us … Rogues? And maybe even Soldiers who used to be like us?" Curtis was starting to get excited.

I grinned. "He's packing up all of his research now. Which is why I'm reaching out. We need a pick up."

Jana cracked her knuckles. "I'll let the others know. It will be easier for us to come to you and V in the ward than for you to get to a gateway."

"I look forward to seeing how the Rogues have always jacked into the system to do that," I cocked an eyebrow.

Jana nodded, and then disappeared from view.

"Lili, be careful. Having no registered identity also makes it tough for you to survive out there," Curtis warned. "You can't even transfer digits to buy food."

"It's tricky, but V thinks he can do something about it. I need to get V out as soon as possible," I said. "He's the only one who knows how to do what he did, he has all that re-search gathered up, and he risked his neck for me." I moved from foot to foot. "I need all this to happen quickly."

"We'll be ready when you are, just prank me," Curtis as-sured me, delivering a flippant salute before I pulled V's hood up and let our connection drop.

I rolled my shoulders, leaving the alley and making my way to base.

I held my head up confidently as I crossed the familiar lawns and into my building, slipping in amongst a group of Soldiers as they filed into the elevator.

I kept my eyes forward and exited calmly at my level, but when the elevator doors closed I hurried to the end of the foyer, opened the window at the end, and pulled myself out to sit on the sill.

I couldn't scan myself into my own room.

So I lit my designs with my own power, intending to gently levitate up to the window of my apartment.

Instead I shot like a bullet from the sill, flying so high up that I hit my head on the building's window wiper, where the arm rested at the top floor.

A foul word slipped from my lips before I could stop it and I rubbed my head.

Then I realised I had not been zapped for swearing. And that I had just found flight, without any effort to launch, to be ridiculously easy.

I grinned, and swore again. Just to be sure. And not one iota of corrective electricity pulsed through my nerves.

Elated, I let myself drop back down a few floors to my level, and then easily caught myself.

Shaking my head in wonder I reached out and traced my glowing fingers across the glass in a circle. When I was done I gently, gently, lowered the precise glass cutting down into the room to rest on the carpet, and no alarms went off.

I was relieved that the apartment hadn't been stripped yet and things weren't on high alert, but, for the first time my kitchen and living room did not register who I was. They did not welcome me home with whirs of life and greeting beeps. The screenwall didn't flick to my favourite channels, the microwave didn't offer any specials, and the lights over my terrace didn't even flick on.

It was like I was already gone and had never really been there.

My bedroom up top was still chaotic, with the bed covered in a fine gold dust. But I avoided thinking on that, grabbing a bag and dropping back down to the Biobeauty to fix the damage of three days lying prone in a lab.

I emerged fresh in a flexible body suit, and then set the microwave to whip up a couple of greasy souvlakis for V.

I stashed them in the bag, along with some more clothes, boots, fizzpacks and the one personal, prized item I owned. The lone book on my shelf by the screenwall. 'The Collected Tales of Mythological and Historical Heroes.'

I wrapped it carefully in V's hoodie, cushioning it nicely in the bag. And then I was good to go.

I subtly made my way off base again, and tried to appear unconcerned and casual on the streets as I passed civvies and the usual adverts. I only half listened to another report on the search for the curly blonde, tragically noble looking Cam Pendragon, whose Leader mother, the biggest Business slayer in the World, was stopping at no expense to find him and keep power in the family.

I nearly missed it when four new images and a new bulletin appeared on the advert walls. Four familiar faces. Labelled: 'Soldiers Gone Rogue.'

Bear, Jana, Curtis and Junior.

I stopped short on the street. "Please let that be it ..." I whispered.

Then the photos were replaced by another. Labelled: 'Escaped Traitor – Highly Dangerous.'

My face looked back at me.

"V ..."

I dropped all pretence of subtlety – breaking into an unnaturally fast sprint that carried me across busy streets, through bustling crowds and back to the hospital.

I pranked Curtis at the same time that I squeezed in amongst a bunch of visiting Soldier families as they were scanned through the doors, all leaving a trail of metadata behind them like good citizens.

I ploughed straight to the stairwell while every other normal person rode the lifts, and I burst from the fire escape and back into the waiting room.

The snobby nurse was at her station, her bright red lips forming an 'o' of surprise as I skidded across her floor, barged though the emergency rooms, and barely managed to stop as I got to V's lab.

Or where it had been.

There was the smell of burning, but it was faint beneath the odour of cleaning chemicals.

Some kind of techgrenade had been set off in there. And all of the objects within that space had been blasted away.

There were no beeping machines.

No goth paintings.

No goggles and no wheelie chair.

Not even the 'Grand Techie V-irgil' name plate over the door.

Instead, there were piles of dust. White, bare walls, and clean shelves.

As I watched, frozen, a team of cleaner bots rolled in to take care of the dust. In seconds, it was as if the room had always been empty.

"Are you here for your updates?" one of the nurses from the recovery ward asked in passing.

"Where's V? I'm due to see him," I swallowed hard.

"He took a sick day," she lied.

"He never takes a sick day," I grunted. "Where's all his stuff?"

"Tell her the truth. Soldiers don't react to much anymore," another nurse down the hall commented without interest from behind her desk, not glancing up from her screen. "Nobody in this ward even cared that a techgrenade went off."

I realised she was right. There was a distinct lack of uproar from the curtained recovery area. Instead, Soldiers were lying obediently, blankly, in their beds.

"This one hasn't had the update yet," the first nurse replied.

The other nurse, eyes fixed on the screen, shrugged one shoulder. "Well today's the day – nearly everyone else is done. Doesn't matter who does it for her."

"Where. Is. V?" I bit each word out.

"Well Soldier," the nurse nearest me replied. "He was a traitor. He had to be put down. It's your job to understand something like that. Doctor R can see you though."

I hadn't even realised I was capable of the sudden swell of electrical power that burst from my fists as I bunched them just then.

The nurse screamed and dodged the unexpected blast, and it was as if an alarm had been set off.

Every unmoving Soldier who had been keeping to their respective curtained rooms, suddenly sat bolt upright.

Simultaneously, they swung their legs over the beds and stood.

Simultaneously, they began to advance.

They seemed able to ignore plasters on their legs or stitches being popped. Some hobbled forward with bad backs. Bandaged hands reached out to me.

But a spontaneous hole opened in the air beside me, and a girl with a black bob, Jana, Bear and Curtis took in the hellish hospital scene with shocked faces.

"The walking dead …" I heard Curtis gasp in horror.

"V?" Jana cut to the chase, her eyes taking in his empty room.

I shook my head.

"Just you then!" the girl with the bob yelled as the portal sparked and sent rifts of air around the room. She grabbed my wrist, and pulled me in.

Excerpts from: The Collected Tales of Mythological and Historical Heroes

On the subject of modern perils:

Before the first Leaders rose gloriously to centralise every element of life, technology was developing at an alarming rate and the law could not keep up with the ever evolving nature of a more advanced World.

The first Brainwave chips were being implanted globally – with most families opting to have updateable children from birth. The great convenience of this was that the child had immediate access to sleep pattern and toileting controls, could upload skills by age group, and would grow up to their full potential. Nobody wanted to give their child less of a chance to succeed.

However, the fear of missing out led many families who could not afford the original brand of Brainwave to shop for less secure alternatives. The market was not yet controlled or kept under the strictest of surveillance, so these cheaper copies were often in fact virus infected fakes.

Hospitals were flooded with glitching, unstable or at times literally sparking children. But worse, hackers could take advantage of these faulty children.

A particular hacker group, known only as The Mutineers, led the great metadata and internal tech hack of the fortieth century – with mass data leaks and mind control of youth.

In the course of one night, The Mutineers drained billions of bank accounts across the globe.

Thankfully this inspired the first Leaders to take control of the law and technology globally.

It is now both a right and a requirement for every World child to be fitted with a government issued Brainwave chip, so that no child falls behind, and no harmful alternatives are needed. It is illegal, and unimaginable to live separately to Leader-issue Brainwave control.

| 16 |

– The Star –

The lines across my palms.
The fine hairs on my arms.
The tiny corners of my lips.
The bends in my elbows.
The creases behind my ears.
Were burning.
Parts of me I had never spared much thought for.
And every single other part of me.
Scorching.
I remembered my vision turning to darkness. Then nothing. Then worse than nothing.
This.
Awareness of every inch of my essence sparking back to life.
Never had rebirth felt more like the end.
Never had I wished more for it to be.
The pain of it.
I remembered feeling ready for the end. And accepting it.

Accepting that I should die for our secrets and so that maybe a few more dreams could happen.

I remembered a brief flash of a different emotion before my awareness had died completely though. A quick thought that I would have fought for them. For the people to have better lives. I was Michael. I had always been the people's champion, even when it was against the rules.

Maybe that thought. That certain thought of who I was and what I would stand for. That thought of what I would sacrifice. That fighting thought, had brought this upon me.

This surging,

ripping,

curling,

fierce,

burning.

I did not feel entirely present. But with great certainty, I knew I was existing more ferociously than ever before.

I could not feel another body; a human that my essence had found to weld itself to.

Instead I felt as if I was forming my own physical anchor in this world.

It hurt.

It was consuming.

Waves of boiling heat.

My blood felt as if it was swirling in a frenzy. Bubbles surging to the surface of my veins.

Cruel, divinely burning, dancing, licking flames. Like tiny demons prancing viciously, pinching and lashing wickedly, twirling savagely, across the surface of my skin.

Wavering, marching, spreading lines of flickering sparks; budding, stabbing as they travelled under my skin. Trails of destruction.

My tongue; a desert that had faced the detonation of a thousand bombs.

My throat; a collapsing tunnel of ashes.

Heat like cracking whips across my rib bones.

Magma where my marrow should be.

Crackling, sizzling pores.

Molecules melting and reshaping. Dripping like globules of melted plastic.

Charred lungs.

Frying fingernails.

"Oh my Lord…"

My burning skull resonated with the sound of a familiar voice. My hearing was profound. But my vision was just golden light.

I hated that voice.

"Evangeline, it's him," I heard Aris whisper coarsely.

"What's happening to him?" Gabe actually sounded concerned.

"He's … being reborn …" Aris sounded uncertain for once.

My teeth were gritted and bared. It felt like they were glowing, like red hot iron in a forge.

My fingers curled in claws.

"How is that possible?" Evangeline hissed. "Tien hasn't even reappeared yet and it's only been a matter of days for him. It took me weeks, and I certainly wasn't reborn like that!"

There was the sound of running feet.

"What in the hell?!" a Rogue voice summed up exactly what kind of burning I was suffering.

I felt my back arch as a lightning bolt of flame surged down my spine.

"He's on fire! Put him out!" Another Rogue.

"We can't," Aris answered.

More like won't, I thought. Oh Lord above, *please* put it out.

"His skin," one Rogue's voice sounded mortified. "It's glowing. Radiating."

My neck lolled of its own accord, dragging my skull against dirt.

"EMBERS JUST CAME OFF HIS CHEST!"

"What is going on here?" it sounded like the leader, Jo, had arrived. Then she must have seen me. "Is … that Mitch?! He's smoking!"

Not in a good way.

I opened my eyes towards where I thought her voice was coming from, and my jaw unclenched to try to speak.

There were gasps.

"There's fire inside him!"

Then they cried out as I did.

I felt a massive explosion of heat from within my core as my heart sped up. I couldn't inhale as a stream of golden fire burst out from within me, raking its way free in a golden surge that erupted from my eyes and mouth.

I heard feet stumbling, and people landing in the dust.

A force of burning air, like a bushfire tornado, had just hit them. Had sent them flying. And it had come from me.

"Help him!" I thought it must have been Dora Cate. Her voice was raised and was getting close again.

Aris would have stopped her. I was a danger. As always.

"Don't touch him," Aris had to raise his voice over the roaring of the flames inside and around me. All over me. Eating me up. Bringing me to life. Obliterating the ground I laid on.

The rushing sound wasn't just in my ears then.

"Touch him? I can hardly see him!"

"I think that it will soon be contained within him," Evangeline explained, loudly. She sounded shocked, as if she had reached some realisation about what she was seeing.

"What is it?" Jo demanded.

"He …" Aris cleared his throat. "He is burning with heavenly fire."

I felt my eyes widen, and my heels dig into the dirt with agony, and knew they were ducking down as more heat suddenly radiated outward from my body.

Heavenly fire.

The heart of all stars – my angelic essence. Really taking on its own form?

"We have to move him! Get him below!" I felt someone try to sling a jacket over me, to cover my nakedness. Then I heard them cry out as the jacket burst into flames with a rush of hot air.

"There's no way he won't be picked up by sensors, even out here in a wasteland," another Rogue voice agreed. "We hardly needed other stars to find him."

It was as if my ears popped then, and simultaneously, my mind became fireworks.

I could feel *everything* suddenly.

Everyone.

The Rogue with the beard, Ned, had lost his jacket.

Dora Cate.

Jo.

Evangeline.

Butch.

Aris.

But beyond them.

I could feel tiny pin pricks of life.

Everywhere.

Above me.

In the stars.

All around me.

The people in the cities.

Echoes of voices from far away. My kin. Thousands of them. All struggling to make sense of this new world. Many being hunted. Many turning their attention to here.

To me.

They could feel me.

No longer with spite.

With wonder.

"You want to take him underground?" Evangeline asked. "He's a bomb waiting to go off. He could bring down your entire operation."

"He is your kin. Are you telling me you don't want to take him to safety?" Jo asked coolly.

"I would not leave him here to be used by the enemy for

their test results," Evangeline sounded stony. "But I would not bring something so destructive into my haven."

"It seems Mitch is like a weapon," Jo said then. "Which really, is exactly what we need."

I felt Dora move closer to me, despite Aris grunting. She held her hand close to my skin for a second before it got too hot.

"How can we take him down?" she asked as I convulsed.

There was silence for a moment. Before Gabe spoke up.

"We were born of the same star fire originally. It is part of us too, even if we haven't had it woken in us again yet. I think I can take him."

Finally: "I will help," Aris said gruffly.

"Fine," Evangeline gave in sourly. "Let's take the danger into our midst."

"We'd be stupid *not* to take 'the champion of humanity' with us," Dora retorted in a prickly voice, and then I heard her storm off before Aris sighed and bent beside me.

"The heat is calming," Gabe said. "The fire is moving deeper inside him."

I realised the pain was less intensely catastrophic. As if the lava inside me was slowing to ooze and gnaw at every extremity more slowly. But I must have passed out when my family managed to lift me, because I was next aware of a bench beneath me.

Possibly an operating table.

By the sound of things industrial fans had been brought in to surround me, and they whirred on high speed.

But sweat poured in torrents down my chest, my forehead, my neck. Saturated hair was clinging to my face. There was the smell of ash and smoke.

I could tell that my body had slightly melted what should have been the flat steel table, as I felt as if I was lying in a body shaped mould. I had sunken into my own stencil shape.

I was aware of a beautiful voice humming in the background. I could register the owner of the voice, and remembered her ... Queenie.

I caught the smell of sweet perfume. "Come back to us Mitch," I heard Dora Cate whisper. "Theus and I need you. We think you have answers for us. Please? And, you know," she sounded deeply surprised. "I think I like him. The Human Resources guy."

A while later there were more voices. Less friendly.

"I can feel it," Evangeline was saying. "He's more than what we are now. He's not just a dream worker. He's ascended to ... to ... I don't even know what."

"He exists in his own right," Gabe was agreeing thoughtfully. "Like, he can act independently, on his own power now. Probably for the same cause, part of the same grand plan, but as himself."

"Why though?" Aris asked in frustration. "What allowed him to change so dramatically? To come back in this way?"

"Why *him?*" Evangeline actually seemed pained by the idea. She had been put down unnaturally, just as I had been.

"Mitch said to me, just the other day, the most intriguing thing." I heard Jo enter the room at precisely the right moment. She had another presence with her – someone I wanted to reach out for.

Someone *I* liked.

"Mitch explained that I may have my condition for a reason. It may help me progress toward the level of understanding and fulfilment that all souls spend each lifetime searching for, before their dream is complete and they can ascend."

I could imagine Evangeline gaping in a terribly un-angelic way. She would hate how easily I'd bandied around angelic insights.

If I hadn't been catatonic, I would have laughed.

"Perhaps other stars, such as yourself, have just not progressed to Mitch's level yet," Jo finished.

Icing on the cake, and cherry on top.

"Now, if you'll come with me, I've brought Mitch's dreamer with me and I think Lili should get to spend some time with him herself."

"Of course," Gabe answered respectfully. But I could sense that Evangeline was simmering so much she could have burst into flames herself as they followed Jo from the room.

"I think your friend Evangeline finds Jo's tough love refreshing," I heard Lili say, her lips close to my ear.

I fought to move toward her, just an inch.

"It's best not to touch," I heard Ned rumble from what must have been further into the ward. "He's still supernova inside."

"It's fine. My designs should chill him out," Lili replied, before I felt her hand settle over my sternum and a soothing cool sensation spreading from her touch.

It was the most relief I'd felt since rebirth, and the tension seemed to leave my muscles as the cold settled over them. I almost felt my shoulders slump down to relax.

"No wonder you didn't feel the need for me to contact your loved ones last time you were dying," Lili spoke to me again, and I could have sworn that I felt my mouth tug in a faint smile.

Excerpts from: The Collected Tales of Mythological and Historical Heroes

This is a first edition text, published by the World's third generation of great Leaders. Congratulations – you've purchased one of the last Leader approved hard copy texts!

On the subject of structures:

** Note, in this section, places that are believed to have existed prior to the unification of World are mentioned.*

Some of the most important structures to be removed in the first Leader era were those that symbolised a previously divided World. Leaders oversaw the destruction of old national icons like a seemingly pointless Eiffel Tower, now useless palaces, the no longer necessary 'wonders' (like the Great Wall of China), and religious sites (like Mecca and the Vatican).

Sixty thousand year old 'Dreaming Stories' painted in caves by the first people of Australia had already been demolished during the mining boom, the Rosetta Stone (which helped early historians to decode ancient Egyptian hieroglyphs) had been defaced beyond repair, the Taj Mahal had been turned into a refugee centre, and many other problematic locations had faded with the tests of time.

Conveniently, many other sites and structures, such as the Sistine Chapel and Stonehenge had also already been destroyed in World War Five.

However, Leaders had to cleanse the World of a number of other religious structures, statues and art – putting down any early Rogue protesters who refused to see this as progress on the way to moving forward.

Aside from religious or national sites, outmoded structures also had to be wiped. Transport in particular needed re-vamping, and systems like the famous London Tube and New York Central Station – famed for a ceiling painted to reflect the heavens, had to go. These were from a time where railways helped people travel large distances (before mass carrier hov-vehicles were created).

| 17 |

– The Dreamer –

"Hey."

His voice rasped as he forced the one word out.

"You … cooled me down," he husked. "I started dreaming of all the nice places I'd ever visited."

I sat up from where I had been flicking through a real magazine. Queenie had thought they were quaint, and had added them to her ward for looks more than entertainment.

"Hey," I answered. "Ready to grant all my wishes?"

He groaned and laughed in a puff of smoke at the same time.

"Where are all my other admirers?" he asked then.

Apart from some dark circles under his eyes, he looked great. More than great.

God-like.

His temperature had gradually dropped enough to stop breaking thermometer scans, and Queenie, Ned and I had turned off all the fans. We'd moved him to a proper bed, and had found an imprint of his body melted into the bench he'd been on. I had done my best to reshape it for Queenie.

"Actually they're all undergoing a bunch of tests and some research," I answered.

"My kin?" he was surprised.

"No, you asked about your *admirers*," I teased. "I was tested as well. The Rogues have become very interested in how you apparently know Theus, and maybe Dora too. They're looking into the genealogy of anyone interested, trying to see if it's possible that we have all lived before."

"Course it is," he grimaced, sitting himself up gingerly.

"That's what the other super stars said."

He appeared ill just thinking of them. "Did they explain that everyone keeps reincarnating until their soul's purpose has been fulfilled? They move on when their dream is inspired and carried out."

"Check and check. You'd already told me those things too."

He pushed his hair back from his eyes. They were flecked with gold. As if tiny flames still burned inside him. "You say you were tested?"

"They're trying to see who we may have been in the past. In this life, I'm a test tube baby. But I was interested to see if anything about me would be explained by other lives I might have had."

He was observing me with his magnetic gaze, searching me quizzically. "You're different from when I last saw you."

I nodded, putting my hands in the pockets of V's hoodie as I thought of him. I sure felt different.

"So are you."

"What happened after we last talked?" he asked.

"After I killed you," I summed up our last time together more accurately. "I was confronted by some life altering changes. I realised exactly how strict surface surveillance is. I found out that all Soldiers are to be like those assassins we fought – they've probably finished updating the World forces by now. And I found out that it was best we joined the very Rogues we used to hunt for our day job."

He whistled through his teeth. "That is some serious learning. But I don't think revelations are what have changed you. How did you get away?"

I sighed. "I was created by a great techy. He was one of the leading creators of the internal designs used for enhancing human strength. He gave me each of the designs I have, and was a close friend of mine. However when he learned that his designs and experiments with me were not going to simply help to enhance people anymore, but would be used to totally control them, he tried to warn me and came up with a kind of cure. When he found out I'd been taken, he came for me. He disconnected me, cutting off all control Leaders could have over me, and made me into the first free woman of our age."

Mitch reached out and opened his hand. I wasn't normally the hand holding type. But, surprising myself, I automatically placed my hand in his, feeling the heightened warmth of his skin.

"What happened then?" he asked softly.

I blinked. And took a breath.

"I convinced him to go Rogue. But by the time I'd contacted my team and packed some things, he had been put down. Somehow they'd worked out what he had done for me."

"So your genealogy isn't the only thing the Rogues are testing you for?" he squeezed my hand, sending a peculiar thrill up my wrist and forearm.

"No," I answered. "I could be the key to finding technology to free everyone from Leader control. They need to work out what V did to me."

"V?"

"His real name was V-irgil. But he hated that."

Mitch raised his eyebrows. "An impressive namesake. If we are talking re-incarnation and dreams being fulfilled, Virgil would have had a grand one. He was a poet who would often describe the beauty of simplicity. He believed individuals deserved a civilised world and a simple life. So maybe," Mitch continued, "Virgil fulfilled his dream when he set you on this path. You could lead the way back to a more pastoral life, free of artificial control."

I regarded him thoughtfully, a feeling of uncharacteristic warmth budding in my stomach. "I appreciate you saying it."

I felt his grip tighten around mine again for a second, and his face became stony before the automatic doors beeped open.

The one called Gabriel walked in.

"Brother, I felt you were awake."

"Butch," Mitch nodded back, his tone flat.

'Butch' scowled. "Well, what's new?"

It sounded like a casual question, but seemed to mean more. It wasn't exactly a caring, friendly check in.

Mitch shrugged. "Me."

Butch – Gabe – sighed in exasperation. "In what way?"

"No blink updates."

"No … blink updates?" Gabe echoed, astounded.

"Didn't need 'em."

"Didn't …" Gabe's eyes were wide.

"Could just sense it all myself," Mitch sniffed.

"Your power source? Its changed hasn't it?"

Mitch showed no signs of being the warm, compassionate fellow I had just been dealing with. Petulance was written all over his face.

"As I'm sure is imprinted in your memory, it's the first time I haven't been reborn fully clothed and provided for. But don't you worry yourself, I can still access what I need, it's just that I can do it for myself now."

Gabe's mouth hung open a little.

"My sand is surging in me like it wants me to use my own power. But it's nice to still be connected to home." Mitch flexed the fingers of his free hand, and a cigarette appeared in them.

"See? All me." He was a little smug as Gabe guffawed, but he put the unlit cigarette down respectfully, his eyes flickering to where Queenie was moving about the ward.

"Could hear an awful lot of things, too," he said then. He gazed down at my hand in his. "When I was burning to life."

Gabe frowned.

"It's great to hear Evangeline is back, and just as opinionated about me as before," Mitch went on, seeming deeply interested in tracing the lines of my palm now.

"You *are* a felon among our kind," Gabe rumbled. "You are still seen that way by many."

"I remember vividly how others have viewed me. I remember how *you* viewed me. What about now, brother?"

Gabe looked carefully at Mitch. "I do not know how I see you. Still a rule breaker. But somehow, more progressive than the rest of us."

Mitch was impassive now. "I *am* a felon. But I appreciate you helping to bring me here. I know it would have burned you."

There was a pause. Gabriel shifted uncomfortably.

"Well," Gabe said at last. "Criminal or not, both mine and Aris' charges seem to think you can help them to learn of their dreams."

"Now admitting *that* would have burnt you even more," Mitch smiled faintly. "Who is Evangeline's dreamer? I could probably help out there too. Really make her want to destroy my essence again."

Gabe crossed his bulky arms, refusing to be antagonised. "I guess that wouldn't be so easy now. With you being stronger than us."

"I'm just more of an oddity again," Mitch shrugged. Then he seemed to have had enough of talking to Gabe.

"Well, nature calls," he stated flippantly, squeezing my hand before releasing it, and swinging himself up and out of bed.

I put a steadying hand on his elbow as he faltered for a moment. Then he straightened, and walked confidently to the bathroom – somehow even looking good in fitted hospital shorts.

Gabe grimaced, giving up and leaving. But I scooped up a

loose shirt and pants from a trolley, and made my way into the bathroom block.

Mitch's bare back greeted me. He had saturated his hair and face at a basin, letting the droplets run down his neck.

"Still need to cool down?" I asked, seating myself on the bench.

"I had thought this was the male area," Mitch answered wryly. "But, yes, I am cooling down for a different reason. Eternity was not long enough between family reunions it seems." He straightened, and turned to lean against the bench beside me.

"I wouldn't know," I replied pleasantly, and he elbowed my knee apologetically.

"I think you have a very loyal family," he said. "Your team know you and respect you. That's what family should be."

I leaned closer to him now, peering at the smooth skin across his chest. "Not a single bruise," I remarked, changing the subject and touching where I had detonated the kill shot just days before.

"Not a blister of poison or burn mark or hole," he agreed. Again, he put his hand over mine for a moment, so my fingers were pressed to his chest and I could feel his heartbeat. "I did not get to properly thank you for your kindness, by the way."

"Here is a further kindness," I said, and then waved the clothes under his nose. "You can shower, get dressed and emerge from the infirmary as a new being. The Rogues have a spare room for you."

"Do those clothes really count as a kindness?" he wrinkled his nose at the grey comfort-wear in distaste.

"They're the best you've got for now," I said with a grin at his fussiness.

"Yes. Well," he muttered. "I'll see what I can do for my own self later. That cigarette was a bit of an effort, but I had to piss Butch off."

"I understand," I leaned back against the wall as he disappeared into a shower booth.

"This isn't quite like that waterfall thing you had back at your place," he sounded distasteful again.

"Nope."

"Have you got one of those in your new home?"

"Yep."

"Do I?"

"Maybe."

"How do I work this one?" he sounded uncertain.

"Just get in!" I encouraged.

"Woah!" I heard him jump as the shower jets sensed his presence. "It just shot me with soap!"

"Mhmmm."

I was amused by his fascination as he commentated on how the shower was going.

"Did you know this thing is screening me for what water pressure, temperature, soap sensitivity and scent I require?" he chuckled then. "Apparently I've burned off anything that might have needed exfoliation. No loofa for me."

"It's not quite as good as a Biobeauty machine," I replied as I heard the jets switch off, but I felt my breath catch a moment later as he emerged looking like a completely Biobeautied glamour model, even in comfort-wear.

He had somehow become even more noticeably beautiful

since rebirth, and while Queenie managed to retain her composure when Mitch approached to thank her, the infallible Ned was a little ruffled as Mitch shook the medic's hand.

Mitch's magnetism became especially noticeable as we stepped out of the ward, and he was clearly uncomfortable at the impact he was having as he followed me down a busy hallway where many random Rogues simply stopped to watch him pass.

But he cheered up when I accidentally brushed by one staring Rogue – and nearly sent her toppling with the force of the slight contact.

"It's nice to know I'm not the only one adjusting to a new sense of strength and independence," Mitch said, following me carefully as I threaded my way onward to the quarters my team had been given.

There had been a spare room in our section, and another near the other stars, but Jo had tactically decided it was best for Mitch to stick with my team.

"We're both discovering our new selves," he went on pleasantly.

"Sure," I agreed. "We have an identity crisis in common."

"Lili!" Curtis burst out of his room as he heard my voice. "It's not a crisis – it's a dream come true!" he declared cheerfully. Then Curtis' eyes fell on Mitch. "*Wow*, man, you look better," he said.

I leaned in Curtis' doorway, peering into the bunker-like share room to find the nearly healed Junior sprawled out on his bottom bunk.

"Mitch is definitely doing better than you, poor Junior," I

sympathised as Junior grinned up at me. "You found yourself shot one day and then stuck sharing with this wild card the next."

"Even sharing with Curtis hasn't ruined the high all that gold sand gave me when Gabe saved me from the dart," Junior said, stretching luxuriously. "And Jana and Bear are just next door if Curtis' antics get too much."

I ducked back around Curtis, and re-joined my bemused star. "It turns out you and I are the only ones going through an identity crisis," I mused to Mitch, pulling him over to his own door then. "My team doesn't seem at all worried by their dramatic shift in lifestyle."

"*Your* lifestyle hasn't changed!" Curtis chortled after us. "Your room has a rope ladder to the second level."

"That's why we didn't want it," I heard Junior chirp in before Curtis grinned and closed their door.

"Your room's quite large like mine, but don't worry – no ropes," I told Mitch. "Go in and rest. I'll be just across the hall."

"Thanks Lili," he told me as I retreated. "I'm sure I'll re-emerge all rested and ready for your wishes."

Excerpts from: The Collected Tales of Mythological and Historical Heroes

This is a first edition text, published by the World's third generation of great Leaders. Congratulations — you've purchased one of the last Leader approved hard copy texts!

On the subject of places, events, conflicts and movements:

** Note, in this section, lands that are believed to have existed prior to the unification of World are mentioned.*

*Before being conquered by Rome, ancient Britain had already faced difficulties from a people living on the fringes of northern Scotland. These people, known as **the Picts** or 'painted people', were made up of different warring clans.*

Accounts describe the Picts as being highly mysterious and even fairy-like. Certainly they were a strong people, having already defied Viking attacks, but it was only the continued threat of the Roman conquerors in Britain that forced the Picts to unify under one ruler, the King of the Picts.

As we know in our own time, strong Leadership and imposed unity are the only path to a successful life.

| 18 |

– The Star –

"So …" I said slowly, circling the large room, listlessly tracing my hand over the polished concrete walls. "Does this mean I'm your universal favourite?"

There was no miraculously appearing hologram banner or alarm clock playing cheesy tunes. I did not feel alone, but I was not answered.

"If there's no response in ten seconds I'm going to assume I've been promoted to employee of the millennium."

Nothing.

"What does it mean if I am now a completely existing being?" I wondered out loud. "Will I still pass in and out of the ages, stopping only for brief visits? Will I come back if I lose my life? And which world am I part of now? I'm entirely heavenly star, but in an earthly body. That's not normal."

Still nothing. But I paused and held my fingertips where they were on the wall, finding that I had circled the entire room. And that I had left a ring of gold dust everywhere that I'd traced.

"I miss the stars in the wide open skies," I said to the studiously silent universe. "I wonder if I could bring some cosmos into the underworld."

I waited a moment, observing the golden ring I'd made around the room.

"If you don't speak up, I'm going to take it that you think this is a good idea."

Not one sign was delivered.

I smiled and started to run then, drawing thicker, crazier circles around the room. I wondered how well I could spread my sand, now that it burned within me and wanted to pour from my soul – so I threw a handful at the roof, and it burst like tiny stars, glittering against the concrete. I raced to the middle of the room, closed my eyes and started to spin in a circle, getting faster and imagining the galaxy above me. I let the sand pour outward, rushing around me crazily like a storm.

I was panting when I at last spun to a stop and opened my eyes, ready to admire my first piece of the underground universe.

"WOAH!"

The roof was inches from my nose.

I promptly dropped about two metres, and cast my arms out in desperation, waiting for impact.

Instead, my body managed to automatically catch itself mid-air.

"If I'm really levitating," I panted, eyes popping. "I'm going to presume that I *am* the favourite."

I blinked downward.

And confirmed.

Yes. I was definitely airborne.

"Thank you. My status has at last been recognised," I gasped, but my mind was reeling as I straightened myself in the air.

In the scripture of cultures long past, they'd said we had wings in our true form. And in the beginning we *had* been blessed with flight. All of us had been able to be as I was now – the sand swooping outwards from my body, holding me up like wings.

I had never felt the strange lump in my throat out of happiness for *myself* before.

I … had really progressed.

I let out a whoop of joy and sped around the room in a golden rush before coming to land with a bounce on the couch below. I put my arms behind my head and gazed at the masterpiece of glittering lights above.

"Remember Central Station's heavenly ceiling? I think it looks like that," I confided to the air. "There's more sand than that time you assigned me to the desert," I went on with a grin.

Then I frowned. "The layers of robes, the desert winds, the beating sun. They were merchants," I reminisced fuzzily. "Whose dream had that one been? I can hardly remember his name. But I remember he was a good man. Deeply lined cheeks and forehead, and hazel eyes. He gripped my hand when the time had come. He stayed with me. And he was inspired to research and trade in herbs of healing after that. The Middle East was going to really start advancing in medicine, and little by little he would spread what he knew." I yawned. "A Middle Eastern skin tone suited me."

I felt myself slipping into meditation at last, seeing visions of different dreams that I'd helped to come true.

I remembered one where I'd been swimming through clear island waters with a spear in hand. The taste of salt, and cool drips had traced down my face and there had been giggles of joy and some splashing.

"You're doing it!" the island language had sung from my lips. *"You're good at this!"*

I had been teaching a small girl to fish – her dream had been to be able to help feed her mother and sisters. The waves had made us bob up and down, and I had reached out to pass her my spear. Her black hair had clung to her face, but it had not been able to cover the widest smile rounding her cheeks as I'd shown her how to live.

I remembered dragging a bedraggled Pict warrior into the woods, back from a fight with a battalion of Roman soldiers. Blue body paint had been seeping outward from his skin to cloud the puddles like blood, and thunder had clashed as loudly as weapons and war cries. Mud had made it hard to see and the grit had been all I could taste.

"You're needed. You must wake!"

My rescued Pict warrior had opened his eyes in time to warn me, before a Roman sword had burst through my stomach. He had been inspired to rise and fight on then. To lead the Picts, become the first King of the Picts, and seek alliance with the Scots.

I remembered so many faces, languages, environments,

wonders, horrors, eras. Biting ice and sabre-tooth tigers. Mammoths that could be hunted and frozen, used for meat for months. Jostling boat voyages to new promise lands. Temple sacrifices. Jungle fevers and Spanish flus. Masquerades. Chains of slavery being broken. Voices echoing through theatre stalls and from elaborate stages. Scenes of political intrigue. Heroic last stands.

I remembered the start of democracy. Spartan fervour against Persian conquerors. Inventions like the printing press. Type writers. Carnivals. The birth of cinemas. World Wars. Hot wars and Cold wars. Peace and more wars.

I remembered working my way through disillusionment, tragedy. Cures. Epic journeys. First loves. Literature and art. Expressionism. Enchantment. And sacrifice.

"Hey mate, stay back there with your camera. It's not safe."

I remembered dense jungles and orange gases in Vietnam. Repetitive bullets firing one after another. The sound of helicopter blades and whirring explosives. Land mines tearing up fields – and tearing up the body I had been in. I remembered the cry of the photographer. The smell of bloodied soil and smoke, and that it had been only halfway through that rotten war, but that my death had been caught gloriously on camera. It had moved the photographer to fight in the only way he knew how – capturing moments of the war, showing the world the true horror of the conflict as booming explosions and toxic poisons had consumed village after village ...

I blinked as a booming sound that was not an explosion from the memory startled me back to the present.

More like a banging sound actually.

I let go of a pent up breath.

"Coming!"

I winced at the tracksuit I was still wearing, and gazed up to the powers that be in exasperation. But maybe I could do this myself.

I glanced back down.

"Slick!" I grinned.

My tee was back, and the jacket and jeans too. All on my own steam – or sand.

"Snazzy," said Curtis appreciatively as I opened the door.

"Hey, that sure wasn't in my uniform pack," said the one who had to be Junior, who was also waiting for me outside.

"Your admiration feels much better than when I was just a 'rabbit' you were ready to hunt," I beamed.

Junior rubbed at his buzz cut awkwardly, but Curtis laughed boisterously and clapped me on the back. "Lucky for you, bunnies are off the hunting list."

Then his eyes were caught by the room beyond me.

"WOW! What happened in here?!" Curtis slid the door open wider and Junior whistled.

"I did," I said sheepishly, suddenly wondering how the Rogues would like the new decorative scheme.

"You did that?! CRAZY!" Curtis rushed past me to get a better view. "WOW!" he said again, craning his neck upward. "Junior you gotta come here and feel this!"

Junior stepped around me apologetically. "I'll just get him." But as soon as he stepped into the room, he stopped in wonder.

"What?" I asked curiously.

"This place feels like the stuff that hopes and dreams should be made of!" Curtis called back excitedly.

"Ha," I said. "Not bad." I scratched my head then. "So, did you two come just to talk fashion and décor?"

"Ahh, no." Junior pushed Curtis back to where I was waiting at the door. "We're meant to be taking you to a meeting. A screen cast actually."

"Right…"

"See, you and Lili, and the other stars, are the only ones not linked up to the Rogue systems, or any systems. So you didn't get the alert."

"Right…"

"Unless you turned on your screenwall first thing this morning, you wouldn't have seen that a mass screen cast is going to be aired today."

"Okay," I gestured them onward. "Lead the way then."

"We're as green at being Rogue as you are, but we've been given access to internal maps that guide us through this entire complex," Curtis informed me enthusiastically, taking the lead. "You need a toilet? You ask me. A cafeteria? I got you covered. A –"

"I think he gets it," Junior cut in. "You're a perfect tour guide."

"I would be lost without you," I reassured Curtis as we passed more people and took an elevator to a higher level.

"Well," Curtis said, walking confidently through any Rogues who stopped to stare at me. "It wouldn't do to miss a screen cast when you're one of the stars!"

"I am?" I asked weakly. It didn't sound like he was referring to my genetic classification.

"We all just have to stand there in the picture I think," Junior assured me, before Curtis burst through some doors and led me back into the meeting room with the view of the core of the Earth.

"Guys, you should see what Mitch did with his room!" Curtis exclaimed at once, and the original Rogues I had met, as well as Lili and the rest of her team, Theus … and my estranged family, all peered up from where they'd been selecting their seats.

"He's made it look like outer space!" Curtis went on excitedly.

"Vandalism," I heard Aris mutter, with an expression that said he hardly expected anything less.

"Art!" Curtis corrected him. "It's bursting with good vibes."

"I'm pretty sure it will dust right off," I winced at Jo.

"Nonsense!" she smiled. "We need some splashes of hope around the place."

Aris and Evangeline appeared mildly disappointed that I hadn't been told off, though they didn't say anything further and I remembered Lili's observation that Evangeline seemed less hostile in Jo's presence.

"There's a spare spot over here," Lili rescued me, and I made my way to sit at the long table beside her.

I noticed that there was a floating sphere, like a mini moon hovering near the window.

"Okay team, I'm going to inform the Rogues about how our new members have brought us a touch of that hope I was just referring to," Jo explained. "It's exactly the kind of news we all needed. Twenty thousand uncertain Rogues are less effective than twenty thousand rebellious ones. We can talk more amongst ourselves after, but just face the screen-cam confidently for now."

Twenty thousand people was a lot. But not against an entire brainwashed world, I realised. Especially when many Rogues were like refugees rather than true rebels anyway.

Jo took her seat, and a light flashed in the moon camera to start the filming.

"Good morning," Jo greeted, and then got straight to business. "We know from recent surface reports that the Leaders have gone one step further in their control by removing all human emotion from Soldiers. They are tightening their grip on people by hiding information, eradicating free thought and killing off all who have opinions. This way they stay in power, the World is ordered and people are up to date, even if it is to the cost of human choice – and to the detriment of the planet. The wrong decisions are being made, putting all of life in jeopardy."

I tried not to appear glum at all that as the moon started to rotate to scan the faces of everyone at the table. It paused for a short span of time on the stoic, noble face of the knightly looking Rogue from the night of my supposed rescue. Those blonde curls and that strong jaw were so familiar – but the confident, assured young man was new to me. No soul recognition there.

"However," Jo continued. "While our Rogue goals are not to end the surface way of life and impose our own rule, we do want to protect the freedom to express our human nature, and we do want to protect the natural World itself."

The moon panned over me and I felt how normal people must feel when being hit with the Happy Birthday song.

"We have recently made gains that can help us," Jo said then. "One surface doctor sacrificed his life to reprogram Lili One –" the camera panned to Lili, who seemed undaunted. "And Lili is now the first free woman of the modern era. She is willing to do what it takes to find the way to make true freedom possible for all of us."

The camera panned back over my face and then over to Gabe, Aris and Evangeline next. They all appeared mighty angelic right then.

"You will have also heard rumours that we've been joined by entities who are dedicated to being humanity's muses. These rumours are true, and these beings are here to work with us to ensure humanity has a future, and can continue to dream and hope. These beings are made of star matter, and they have access to a non-technological power that allows them to inspire change and progress in the World." Jo smiled. "Thank you."

The moon's light switched off.

"Well said!" the red haired Rogue, Will, declared – and he dropped the official act at once, sipping at a fizzy drink he'd been hiding under the table.

Dora Cate leaned back in her wheelie chair. "Hope my makeup's alright. It's eeealry Jo." She was still one sharp human being, and Theus was watching her with his mouth slightly agape.

"You are the most beautiful woman to have ever lived," he told her and she smiled at him, wheeling her chair a little closer.

"So test results are back," Queenie announced then. "We had a huge response of people interested in getting analysed and traced, and our Sciences did identify a pattern in the data when they searched back across online records for as far back as they could."

"Was there any pattern with us?" Dora asked excitedly, gripping Theus' hand.

"There were patterns of varying length with nearly everyone tested," Queenie answered patiently. "When we came across matches – with people popping up as having identical records across different generations, we no longer assumed it could mean an ancestor had been found, but that we may have come upon an earlier self of the test subject. When looked at like that, it seems that nearly everyone who was tested would have been in this World for a lot longer than this one lifetime. Only some people could have been classified as brand new, with no other closely enough matching records existing before this lifetime. But," Queenie warned. "We can't trace too far back. Only into the early thousands, when the Sciences started to really take off."

Dora slumped back in her chair. "I am certain the ancient girl Mitch saw in his vision was me."

"It's possible," Queenie agreed. "If we do accept that the test subjects who kept 'popping up' throughout time have lived multiple lives."

"They are dreamers that have not had their purpose fulfilled," Aris affirmed. "They are reborn until that happens. But there won't be many people like that who have had their dreams unmet for as many ages as what Mitch saw. Maybe a handful of generations might have to be lived before someone is able to find fulfilment and progress onward – either by learning and realising their dreams themselves, being helped by the universe or by being facilitated by us. It wouldn't take eons worth of time though; the universe wouldn't allow it."

"You sure?" I asked.

Aris was immediately offended that I would challenge him – his eyes bulging.

"I'm almost certain Theus is connected to one of the very *first* beings I ever came in contact with," I explained. "One of the very first rebels. And I feel that I have come across Dora a few times too."

"I'm just the H.R guy," Theus interjected weakly.

"Human Resources …" Gabe pondered thoughtfully, rubbing his broad chin.

"Think about it," I persisted. "Could that be the universe's number one biggest hint? Who is the world's ultimate human resource provider?"

Aris crossed his arms. "You're saying he could be Prometheus? Or the brother, Epimetheus – the proverbial fool?"

Theus gaped in horror. "Which one would I be?"

"He'll have to work with Gabe to see which way his dreams are inclined. But of course, as humanity needs a new beginning, the tragedies of unfulfilled dreamers from the past must first be solved," I said. "The ones who had the biggest dreams or biggest problems, now need to be addressed before the world can start a new age. They had to be left until now, so it could all come full circle."

"The universe has OCD, it was always going to sort it out,"

Lili quoted me back to myself, her eyebrow raised. "How is it possible that I have existed before, when I was created artificially this time around?"

"It's the essence of someone that continues to exist," Evangeline sniffed, her face stony as always.

"So we need to work out who we all are – really. Like our original selves?" Will was still sipping calmly at his drink. "Then make our dreams come true like in the ancient stories. Happily ever after and such?"

"Well," I cleared my throat. "If I feel I have bumped into two of you before, maybe I can help out there. And perhaps my colleagues can also work out if they recognise any of you. Then it would come down to research for any further information."

"The three of us would have had a flash of realisation, like you did, if we recognised anyone," Evangeline snapped, crossing her arms haughtily.

"Forgot to mention," I grinned, "but when I first woke up to your discussion of whether you should leave me to die or not, my mind was able to reach out and feel all of our kin currently in existence. I think a lot of them are on their way, seeking my comfort as we speak. So we're not just counting on *your* help. Thankfully."

"You…" Aris' elbow slipped off the table in his shock.

Gabe was impressed despite himself.

I blew on my knuckles. "Perhaps, if we have all been brought together with this group of people for a reason, some other angelic cousin of ours will have a 'flash of realisation' when they get here too."

Jo stood and began to pace. "Can the mass arrival be stopped? If they all accumulate in the one area, there is an even higher risk that they will be picked off."

"Our kind have been sending distress signals from all over the globe," Aris admitted. "They are going to be hunted no matter where they are."

"There are underground Rogue stations all over the World too though," Jo said thoughtfully. "We are the head-quarters, but your kind could seek refuge at their closest base. We could send out the images of our team; the people you think are here for a reason, and they could have their 'realisation' or recognition from afar. Then we have dreamers and their projects protected, and increase our force size and hope levels astronomically."

Everyone turned their eyes on me.

"Can you find a way to spread the word?" Aris rumbled; surly.

I shrugged. "Somehow I wound up flying around my room last night. Not sure how, but things just seem to happen for me right now, and I've got to learn as I go."

Evangeline recoiled as if I'd slapped her. "You … were granted that ability again?"

"Apparently," I was pleased to inform her.

It was dawning on her that I was fulfilling my destiny faster than any of our kin. The one who had always been wrong – somehow being the most right at last.

"So you aren't completely sure how to repeat the mass contact again?" Will questioned. "Maybe you can send out a widespread group message if the four of you all try together.

You could do it in that nice vibes room you made for your-self."

Suddenly the four of us stars had something in common.

We all looked like we wanted to be sick.

"It's agreed then," Jo smiled in relief. "Lili will help us to work out what her Doctor, V, did for her. The stars will contact their people. We'll contact ours. Then our forces are organised. Next step, try to initiate some dreams and see where that gets us."

"I don't think I can be part of our family bonding," Evangeline tried to get out of it. "I need to make contact with my project. I don't even know who it is yet."

"Perfect," Jo smiled wider. "We could not allow you to go to the surface alone. So when you are done reaching out as a family, you can become a team and work with my Rogues."

I honestly felt the need to lie down.

Excerpts from: The Collected Tales of Mythological and Historical Heroes

This is a first edition text, published by the World's third generation of great Leaders. Congratulations – you've purchased one of the last Leader approved hard copy texts!

On the subject of places, events, conflicts and movements:

** Note, in this section, lands that are believed to have existed prior to the unification of World are mentioned.*

Before modern land clearances wiped out jungles and forests for living space, Vietnam was covered in dense jungle. It was near impossible to spot one's opponents, or horrible traps and waiting ambushes.

The **Vietnam War** *was the first truly media covered war, and photography (an early version of Brainwave snaps) and television (basic screenwalls) showed such devastating images of the impact on Soldiers and Vietnamese people that mass Flower Power and Love Not War campaigns grew.*

Now our Leaders' imposed peace has made sure that war is a distant memory. Censorship means we see only lovely news. And mental health perfection checks mean that trauma can be easily wiped from our minds.

| 19 |

- The Dreamer -

Curtis rapped on Mitch's door with easy confidence and, momentarily, Mitch's miffed face appeared as he opened it.

"More of you?" the rock star exclaimed.

"Yo!" Curtis beamed, and made his way past Mitch, into the high roofed, golden sand covered room.

"What's going on here?" Mitch was flummoxed as I leaned in the doorway for a moment and peered in.

Jana, Bear and Junior had already found perches around the perimeter of Mitch's room. Dora Cate and Theus were laying on the floor staring up at the roof in awe. They were holding hands. Curtis was making his way over to the kitchen where Ned, Will and the familiar blonde knight Rogue were.

"Just what I'd hoped!" Curtis was overjoyed as Will worked Mitch's microwave into churning out bowls of fluorescent Meteorbites. "Snacks and a show!" Curtis plunged in to grab a handful, and his fingers were immediately stained orange.

There were a number of other unfamiliar, spectating Rogues who lounged around the apartment. They had laid claim to the sofa, which had been pushed out of the centre of the room, and were also taking up any other spare space available around the walls.

"Well, you *are* the star," I told Mitch. "So you must also be the entertainment."

"They want to watch me try not to puke at close contact with my family?" Mitch still had the pallor of one who was faintly ill as he thought about what was ahead.

"They want to see what you can really do, and what it could mean for them," I answered.

"Well, quick," he ushered me in. "None of the relos have turned up yet, so maybe they've backed out."

I eased past him, and immediately felt the uplifting vibes emanating from the room. The gold sand paintings had created quite the party atmosphere amongst the others, making everyone as light hearted as if this was a party scene in the virtualtree.

"Or perhaps if we turn off all the lights and pretend nobody's home they won't knock," he said hopefully then, closing the door and waving a hand so that all of the lights abruptly switched off. Except the room didn't become dark – and I smiled at the incredible golden glow.

"YEEEHAAA!" one of the Rogues yelled appreciatively.

"This is fu – zpt – n awesome!" Curtis bellowed, throwing his stained hands in the air and spilling Meteorbites in a shower. It was as if he had consumed too much contraband.

"Your sand is intoxicating your guests," I told Mitch observationally.

"At least others can enjoy themselves," he replied glumly, before there came a heavy thump on the door.

"Liliii," he moaned, his face pinched and terribly pained.

"You go take your place in the middle space," I ordered. "Make yourself ambivalent. I'll let the rest of the live show in."

With hunched shoulders, hands shoved in pockets and a dark expression, Mitch begrudgingly scuffed at the floor and turned to get himself ready.

Hyper aware of my strength now, I lightly re-opened the manual door, just as Gabe was about to thump on it again.

Aris had his bulky arms crossed. But he lowered them when I raised an eyebrow at his hostile posture.

"Well, is he *ready?*" Evangeline spoke with daggers in her voice.

Her hair streamed out in thick, fiery orange waves and her eyes were hawk-like. Her lips were sharply curved and the distaste on them right then was quite clear.

I was the one who took on the coolly hostile stance now, feeling the thrills and bubbles of power sending light into my eyes and arms as I leisurely pushed up the sleeves of V's hoodie and leaned against the doorway to block it.

She pursed her lips.

"I'm sure he's ready," I said slowly, looking her over. "But I can see why he's reluctant."

She huffed angrily and Gabe shuffled a little, until my eyes were back on him.

He cleared his throat. "May we come in?"

"Lovely manners," I smiled a wide smile. "Yes. Do come in."

I could feel the affronted disdain glowering out of Evangeline as I let her and the others pass, closing the door more sharply than I'd opened it. But I could have sworn that I saw the hint of a grin being smothered on Mitch's face as he tried with a saintly effort to appear apathetic and meditative.

"Lil! Here!" Curtis called from the seat he had claimed on the kitchen bench, waving exaggeratedly.

I crossed to take a seat by his legs, leaning my back against the bench and stretching my own legs out on the floor.

Mitch was keeping up an impassive expression as Gabe and Aris sat cross-legged on either side of him and Evangeline sat across from him. The three stars gazed at the gold, glowing marks – impressed despite themselves.

"I think we need to …" Mitch grimaced. "Join sand. But we'll do it carefully, with others in the room."

Evangeline flicked her hair and rolled her shoulders. "Of course."

Gabe seemed willing and Aris seemed begrudging.

"I'll need to work out something special for my sand, to get it to do what we need. So … you first," Mitch invited Aris overly politely.

Bristling, Aris drew himself up proudly. He opened his palms to face upwards on his knees.

A sparkling mist of fine golden sand rose from around his hands and shimmered around his form like a faint hovering cloud.

Gabe and Evangeline followed suit, so that it seemed a gleaming, translucent curtain hung around each of them.

Then Mitch released his sand.

A whirlwind of gold turreted upward and outward from

him, sweeping their sand into his. They gasped and rocked where they sat, but they all maintained concentration.

The room was erupting with bursting light and rushes of twirling air that whipped my hair about and dragged me to the side. But more incredible still, was the sudden explosion of sound – a multitude of voices that seemed to speak from the whirlwind. Some soft and distant, some exclaiming in surprise, some crying out with joy, many loud with relief. It sounded as if hundreds of spirits were circling the room.

Mitch began speaking then in a normal, level voice, and immediately I felt every disembodied presence strain to listen to him.

He explained the updates of all Soldiers, and warned them that stars were not the only ones in danger, that their dreamers, and the touches that they were meant to put on the World's future were at stake.

Panicked, infuriated or disgruntled exclamations faded as Mitch's voice went on, instructing them to find their dreamers and to go with the Rogues that would be coming for them. I could feel the emotions ebbing from the swirling mass of lights that represented the presence of each 'star', and they seemed to be feeling gratitude, or begrudging respect, as Mitch offered them some kind of salvation from the chaos they had found themselves in.

He repeated their orders, and then his swirling vortex of sand calmed, falling behind him to form a faint shape – of massive, arching wings.

He opened his eyes, and the physical gesture was like the flicking of a switch. All the voices dropped out and lost connection.

"Well, that's done," Mitch shrugged as if he'd finally made a bothersome call he'd been putting off. "You three are excused," he added gladly.

But none of the other three stars had moved. In fact, Evangeline was staring fixedly at Mitch, and reached out to him like a rapt, repentant criminal who had seen the error of her ways.

"Uh … what are you doing?" Mitch frowned and leaned back as she reached towards him. His face was a disconcerted mask as she put her hand on his.

"Mitch –" she began. But he flinched as, the moment she made contact with him, the faint sand that had been starting to ebb away suddenly burst back to life like a wild tornado.

This time I was dragged a short distance sideways to knock into Curtis' legs. He and a couple of other spectators had hurriedly gripped the bench as an anchor against the sudden torrent of air that plucked at and rushed about us.

Mitch's teeth were gritted and his eyes blazed with golden fire as the storm of sand raged around the four of them. And in the whirlwind were flickering images, heat and sound.

"I haven't learned to control everything yet," I heard Mitch moan with an effort. "Let me go!"

Evangeline didn't, or possibly couldn't reply.

As if playing on a screen, I could see the image of Mitch from another time being projected across the sand. He was hurtling through the air, rugged in heavy skins and furs as clothing. He didn't appear younger, but somehow seemed newer. And desperate.

His sand whirled around him in the image, moving like

wings and carrying him across the sky as empty, hilly lands blurred below.

Curtis had stiffened against me and I heard a few other spectators gasp as the image of Mitch glanced back over his shoulder – showing that the sky behind him was filled with a horde of other stars. They were tiny in the distance, but they were moving fast.

Their sand, their wings, blocked out the horizon and it was as if they had much greater power in this memory than they had now in present time.

The image of Mitch arced upwards suddenly, and my stomach jolted as if I was with him in the torrents of wind, racing up a mountain so high I couldn't see the peak.

Even though we were sitting safely in the Rogue compound, it got harder to breathe, and strangely hotter instead of colder.

Then he soared up over the top and plummeted down *into* the mountain, so that it became clear that it was no mountain at all.

It was not real, not happening right now, but the intensity of the heat of the volcano was suffocating, and the red lava threw a throbbing, glowing orange light all around the epic, cavernous walls.

The image of Mitch landed heavily on a ledge that was jutting out just above the lava, where the heat was so scorching that I found myself rasping in real time, and the skin on my face felt like it might crack, wither and blow away.

Mitch's image peered over the side of the ledge, his face illuminated brightly, and below him, the lava started *moving*.

A glowing face-like shape emerged from the thick magma. Sharp, ash covered features glared out of the heat. Glops of dripping lava rolled away to clear a space where a mouth should be, and a slow, hoarse voice spoke to Mitch.

My skin prickled despite the searing heat.

"You've ruined us," the voice of the lava face accused darkly, with every syllable rolling and melting in the air.

"I have saved you, and given you new purpose," Mitch replied grimly. "I was ordered to destroy you totally."

"You have cast us out of life above. Imprisonment *is* destruction," the voice glowered. I felt sick as I watched a radiating hand and arm start to snake out of the lava, struggling to reach up to Mitch before sinking back down.

"Why live in a world that sees you as an enemy?" Mitch husked, sadness on his face. "You are the passing of time, you are the root of suffering, you are sin and death. They do not understand you, or that you can be precious."

"You describe yourself as much as you describe us. And … you broke the rules for us. You should join us."

"I wasn't ordered to kill your team for being rule breakers or because you are disliked," Mitch rubbed a shaking hand across his brow. "I was ordered to end it because you did your job too well. Your team of Evils brought too much darkness into a world that needs light. There is no balance. You bring misery and then death, all too swiftly."

"I *am* Death. Pandora opened the box to let my Evils free," the voice hissed. "She was given the box by the maker. The maker made us, because those humans are so faulty, and need to learn through misery, mistakes and rebelliousness before they must come to me. What does it matter how swiftly they come?"

The furnace-like sensation, which was ebbing from the scene playing out on the screens of sand, was now accompanied by the sound of many furious voices approaching in the distance. Evangeline and her followers were close to reaching the volcano, yet the image of Mitch ignored the sound and spoke earnestly.

"The maker has seen that there are more lessons than just miserable ones, and when you work so swiftly the devastation is too great. So I have been given the assignment to confine you and to destroy your Evils."

"But instead you're locking us all down here? Trapped, but safe from the others that I hear coming. Why would you do it?" the voice hissed.

"I think it would be wrong to destroy you for doing what you were created to do, when perhaps, in moderation, you could be a very important part of the cycle." The image of Mitch was determined. "Though it is hard for the light to understand, I believe the world needs the Evils. You can guide humanity as it confronts your challenges – tests that can make or break a person. You can play one of the most important parts in a soul's journey of growth and learning. As death is something that they must face, it – you – should be something that inspires them to first live. Sickness, turmoil, strife, jealousy, hatred, famine and passion will exist, and you will understand them best. You will contribute most to humanity's understanding and growth in the face of adversity. But so will I and so will my kin. I believe that both the dark and the light are needed."

"What do you propose I do differently, great Michael?" the voice was slow and calculating now.

The image of Mitch spoke more quickly as the first of his kin became visible at the faraway lip of the volcano. "Change the time that should be given to each human, each spirit. Allow them to live, to grow, to learn – through your dark lessons and our good ones – before you take them to this final place and let them rest. Allow them to be *ready* before their spirit really leaves to come to you."

"What if I simply decide to stop, choosing to wallow in this prison, inactive for the rest of days?" the face of magma asked. "People will sicken, age, whither. And be stuck."

"I have given you a city under the world. You are king now. Peaceful Death can rule all of eternity after dreams rule all of life, you cannot allow your kingdom to be empty."

"I already hold so many souls in my embrace," the face declared. It started to sink away.

"Young, and untested!" Mitch replied. "They are not wise. They are children!" The face halted, regarding Mitch with glowing eyes. "But my kin and I can work closely with you – we'll need your help for our essences to be able to move through time in the guise of mortals. And we will work to ensure that the spirits who come to you will be finished with their cycles of living, and that they will be ready when they have faced every test. Yet without you, people will never have the need to rise to an occasion. Will never need wild energy. Or to question the rules. You must seduce them to do more than just ... be. They need that."

"So you mean to create a new way of being for yourself,

and for your kin, when you could stay as you are – just in-visible observers, comfortable on the sidelines," the magma rolled each word slowly as if time was not of the essence.

"What a terrible show to spend eternity watching," Mitch laughed sorrowfully.

"Then you wish to work with Death to nurture life." The voice was speculative. "In a way *you* would be trapped too, committing life after life of your own to making the dreams of others come true. All for satisfied souls to rest easily ever after."

"Yes," Mitch agreed. "But sacrifice after sacrifice will be well worth the pain. And I might learn some things myself."

"You are wise," the voice – Satan's voice, or Hades' or Death's voice, replied. "You shape this world more than the maker does."

Mitch shook his head. "I represent the maker, who created me to be as I am."

"Ahhh, but *they* do not understand that."

My attention was drawn again to the furious approach of the other angelic stars. I could see their storms of sand start-ing to grow in the image of the sky above the volcano as they regrouped, with Mitch trapped below.

"They do not," Mitch admitted. "I hardly do myself. It is lonely to be this way."

"They should be the ones to do some learning," the voice hissed.

The angry cloud of Mitch's kin was growing by the sec-ond.

"You may not survive their wrath. And if you do, you *will*

be alone," the voice warned. "Join us. Join with my titans, the Evils, and be safe where you have entrapped and enlightened us. I see now that you have saved us, and I can return this kindness to you."

Mitch shook his head. "No. You have your job, and I have mine. Are we in agreeance?"

"We are," the voice was just a whisper as the face sank backward, disappearing into the lava. "Good fortune to you, Michael."

"And dark fortune to you," Mitch answered, before turning to face the rushing cloud of angels as they began pouring in through the mouth of the volcano, and racing toward him in a shape like an arrow, aimed right at his heart.

His image was one of solitary strength and unhappiness as he watched the enraged angels of vengeance descending – Evangeline at their forefront.

In moments thousands, maybe hundreds of thousands, of angelic stars had landed around the walls of the volcano, watching from different rock perches and yelling in fury.

At least fifty slammed down onto the ledge, making it shudder and rumble as they surrounded Mitch and engulfed him, forcing him to his knees.

Two burly males held him down. Ari'el the lion, who was so furious that he seemed darker in nature than Satan had. And Gabriel, his face a mask of hurt and betrayal.

Across from them the image of Evangeline was snarling; ferocious as the masses of angels urged her on and she stood over Mitch.

"You have sealed the Evils away, out of reach, when you were tasked with their destruction," she accused sharply.

"Yes," Mitch answered.

"You have intervened to offer protection to the first woman, and to those who followed," Evangeline raged. "Completely altering the evolutionary pattern for humanity hereafter."

"Yes."

"You have made more than one choice that has impacted the course of this world. You have broken the rules too gravely for things to ever go back to how the maker originally intended."

"Yes," now Mitch appeared gratified. "I was made by the maker to be this way."

Evangeline was seething. "You were made by the maker to do a job and to follow instructions. But you have broken the rules."

"I would break them all again," Mitch affirmed honestly, his voice void of defiance or malice. "I believe this *is* my job."

"Then ours will be to stop you," Aris growled resentfully, pulling Mitch back savagely in an uncompromising grip.

Gabe looked afraid.

Evangeline's face became impartial, reaching a decision, and somehow the blankness in her expression was more horrifying than the emotion had been.

She placed her hand on Mitch's chest, and they regarded each other for a moment, before she pushed her hand sharply forward – and somehow thrust her fingers *into* his chest.

The mortified cry that tore from Mitch's lips ripped around the volcano, as well as around the actual room we all huddled in.

The image of Mitch stiffened against Gabe and Aris' hold. At once the crowds became silent and some lifted from where they watched in stunned reverie. But it was not his pain that had cut off the surging chanting of the massed angels.

Instead their focus was drawn by the appearance of a growing disc of solid light, brighter than the unfiltered sun, with rays that swelled to such intensity that Evangeline and all of her followers in the belly of the volcano were blinded.

The light increased until Evangeline and the hordes of angels were knocked back and pressed against the rock, as if buffeted there by a terrible wind storm. And even though I, an outsider, watched the scene as just a memory, my head and eyes felt like they would burst with the immense power of this strange, ethereal being – or perhaps beings?

As I blinked and gasped, overwhelmed by the mere image of the presence's aura, I saw the rays reach out and touch each angel, piercing their chests as Evangeline had done to Mitch.

The sand that had held them up like wings dropped away in a rush, dissipating as it landed on the lava until they were left with only the sand within them. They groaned and shuddered in fear as they were reduced, before they were lifted in groups out of the volcano and flung like dolls through the air. They hurtled away to land all around the globe and to begin a new job that would help them to understand the ever evolving nature of life and the world.

Mitch was lifted too, to be given work to do until he better understood himself and his role in the world.

Then the image of the light was gone, the sand that had been crashing around the room – playing the scene, had dropped, and I was left blinking and panting for air.

Excerpts from: The Collected Tales of Mythological and Historical Heroes

On the subject of the 'first people':

*In some of the outmoded religions there were tales of the 'first people'. These included accounts of the first man, **Adam**, being created out of the earth, and in some accounts the first woman, **Lilith**, was also created out of the earth alongside him to live in a garden known as Eden.*

However in these tales Lilith refused to be subordinate to Adam and rebelliously left their paradise. Because of her disobedient, free-willed nature she was portrayed throughout early history as a demoness spawning legions of demons. In some cases she was even told to have become a consort of Satan/Hades/Death. This portrayal of Lilith by early societies in fact reflects on the status of females and how their submission was expected, while their empowerment was judged harshly. Lilith was literally cast as the mother of all evil for her efforts to be independent.

*Adam in turn was said to have been united with his next partner – **Eve.** She was portrayed as more submissive, but also more foolish than Lilith, again highlighting perceptions of women in early times. Because Eve encouraged Adam to break the rules of their Eden they had to learn to live beyond the garden as punishment – toiling to survive.*

In other accounts the first primitive human beings evolved gradually and were originally much better equipped to survive – with tough bodies and protective hair covering their skins while they slowly developed skills and tools.

It is almost heartbreaking for modern humanity to imagine a World in which people were defined by gender, and had to toil to survive without the help of Biobeauties or pixel food. Though rebelliousness or rule breaking is of course still an unforgiveable idea, worthy of intense punishment.

| 20 |

- The Star -

I slumped, exhausted, and released from the vision at last.

Evangeline's hand was shaking and digging into mine like a vice.

Her eyes were wide, her cheeks were covered with glittering, gold tinged tears, and I was faintly stunned to see such emotion on what was usually such a spiteful face.

"Michael," she said weakly.

She'd never used a soft tone toward me even at the very beginning, before I'd done anything to irk her. It was too odd.

The sand had calmed, but traces of it were still circling us and I could see the people around my room clinging to the couch or counter or huddled on the floor in astonishment, trying to recover.

Even the indestructible Lily was dizzily blinking her vision back to normal.

I took hold of Evangeline's hand and tried to pry her fingers away from where they pinched my skin.

"You're locked on there," I said, slapping at them, grimacing at this disturbingly clingy new Evangeline. "Let go, we've got to be careful of the humans."

I frowned up at Aris for help, but felt a pang of fear to see him regarding me with stunned features too. Had the world gone mad?

Gabe reached across, as if he were in a daze, and went to put his hand on my shoulder.

"No, dim wit!" I tried to shrug him away. "Have you lost your senses?"

This was obviously not the time for his eternally late apologies. Something whacky was happening. I was even more magnetic than usual.

"Buuutch!" I cried out as he kept on going anyway, making contact with me so that at once the sand roared up and engulfed us all again.

We had been in a garden. *The* garden. The first green, life filled space in an otherwise open and undecorated land. The stars had not long been born, and we had still revelled in existing. We'd watched and we'd explored, but we'd done as we were told, and we had not intervened as other life was created for the first time.

We had seen animals and the two first people being brought to life, being given paradise, and being given rules of their own. We had played in the garden around them, like children. But they hadn't been able to see us.

Then we had seen the first woman rebelling against a submissive life in the garden, and we had watched, devastated as she'd fled from paradise.

The other stars had been distraught because they'd seen Lilith as a demonic problem for her betrayal of the plan.

But *I* had been shaken, because for the first time, I'd realised that there was a problem with the plan itself.

Gabriel and I had been the only ones brave enough to trail Lilith as she'd fled the garden into the wilderness. But Gabriel had only followed reluctantly, to try to stop me.

"We can't let her go out there unprotected. Epimetheus did not save her any gifts and she has nothing to help her survive," my young self had protested, flying easily at that time.

"She is faulty. She rebelled. The powers will make a new one," Gabriel had answered, trying to keep up.

"That's not fair, she is what she was made to be," I'd said. Watching as she'd stumbled across rough grounds.

"Exactly," Gabriel had pleaded. "So let her be as she is."

"She'll die," I'd argued, and as time had passed I'd watched Lilith's skin burn while her hands and feet bled.

"She broke the rules," Gabe had chased me, frustrated.

"She was created to," I'd cried out, urging him to understand.

Her face had been contorted as burning day had become freezing night and her soft skin was unprotected. Then as time had passed again she had become aimless and blank, wandering across the dust and becoming ever more lost.

"She is afraid and alone, and too vulnerable to go on," I'd told Gabriel in dismay. "If I do nothing she'll either die or turn mad."

"Don't, Michael!" Gabe had begged, but I'd ignored him, and had landed in front of her, breaking the rules and making my shining sand create a semi-solid form to be sure she could see me.

"It's alright," I'd told her gently, but she could no longer understand. "I'll help you to stay free. You'll survive, if I just use a little sand."

"Please!" Gabe had cried.

But I'd reached my hand out to Lilith, taking her mortal hand in mine. And as my sand had begun to swirl it had felt like making her wish come true was the most purposeful and right thing I could ever have done.

She had relaxed and she'd smiled as her hair had grown longer and her body had become covered in it to keep the sun's bite and night's chill away. As she had evolved her brow had widened and her bones had toughened. I'd hardened her body and numbed her mind to pain, and I'd known she could be free and have her own life.

"It will take thousands of years for her to ever evolve back to what she was intended to be," Gabe had spluttered.

I had been glad anyway – because she would be alright. But Gabriel hadn't spoken to me on the way back to the garden. The others had regarded me with distrust and scorn. And then when the next woman and the original man's time had come, I'd worked with Prometheus and I'd again helped to make them evolve into something stronger.

The garden had ended, the others had dispersed, but I had not been abandoned by my maker.

For, while I had broken the rules, I had been made to do so by the same power that had written them.

I'd walked the world unaccompanied from then on. Separate. An outcast. Leaving rule after rule broken behind me.

And yet I had known that I was *right* to do so.

I shuddered and blinked, finding my way back to the present. Butch was pale, and Aris and Evangeline were wide-eyed.

They exhausted me. I could not stand to be near them, or what they were doing to me any longer. Not until I was back in control of myself.

I broke their hold on me and stood before anyone could touch me again or get our sand entangled.

"I've done my job," I said civilly. "I need some space, please." Because space was something I'd become used to and was something I could deal with.

My family stared up at me, gaping.

I frowned and forced every last grain of my sand to disappear immediately so that the spell was truly broken.

"Out, please," I repeated, and I heard one person manage to break their reverie and get up, a little wobbly on her feet.

"Come on," Lili nudged Curtis and the others around her. "Up. We all need to sleep that one off."

The people around the room stirred as she went to each person, as if dispersing the drunken final members of a party at first light. They stumbled from the room and she came back to me in the middle.

"Michael," it was Aris this time, clearing his throat. I jumped back before he could think to touch.

"You heard him. Talk later." Lili somehow managed to single-handedly hoist Gabe and Aris up by their shirts and then yanked Evangeline to her feet. She hustled them to the door before they had recovered their wits.

"Not you, Lili," I said as she was about to leave too.

She turned as I called her back, with a question on her face.

I reached out and let a giant arm of sand jump out from me to drag the couch back to where I stood. I sat on it and patted beside me. "I need you here. You are my purpose in this life, and I need to be reminded of it. Of what I believe in and know."

She didn't say anything, but came across to sit on the couch.

"Pretend we know each other and that you care about me," I said, putting a cushion in her lap and laying down.

"I think we do, and I think I do," she said as I closed my eyes.

I started to sink into my meditation as she quietly uttered the words: "it's alright. I'll help you to stay free. You'll survive."

Excerpts from: The Collected Tales of Mythological and Historical Heroes

This is a first edition text, published by the World's third generation of great Leaders. Congratulations – you've purchased one of the last Leader approved hard copy texts!

On the subject of influential early historical or mythological figures:

** In this section people, lands and cities that are believed to have existed prior to the unification of World are mentioned.*

Lilith was of such a wild, dark nature that it is believed she became a consort of Satan/Hades/Death and enjoyed her time in the realm called Hell. People became even more afraid of Lilith as the stories made her into a queen of all evils, and many normal women were persecuted if it was believed that they had been corrupted by Lilith and the Devil's influence – practicing witchcraft.

The fear of such women was so great that a time of witch hunting wiped out thousands of women throughout the part of World that had been Europe in particular. Many villages were left near empty of people during this hysteria, and were instead filled more with the stakes where the 'witches' were burned.

Lilith's story can also be related to one of a goddess in Greek mythology, **Persephone***. This story tells of a woman being brought down to the Underworld to be with Hades. Some versions of the story tell of Persephone having little choice and being unhappy in the Underworld, though other versions tell of how Persephone found the realm of the dead to be a refuge and a peaceful escape from above.*

| **21** |

– The Dreamer –

I blinked up at the high ceiling, swirling with galaxies of gold, and heard Mitch moving around in the kitchen. My internal clock settings told me I had slept peacefully, even without Brainwave intervention, and also with no dreams about women who looked like me – or who really might have been me, throughout the ages.

"Where in all of the Lords' names am I meant to find a pan? A dish? A scrap of FOOD?"

Mitch's voice was less bright than usual as the noises of searching in the kitchen grew louder.

I sat up from where I'd been sprawled out on the couch.

"Did you try nuking a pack of something?" I asked, leaning my chin on the back of the sofa and watching Mitch.

"Well, I have nothing to put in the microwave to nuke," Mitch gestured at the empty counter in puzzlement. "And I was going to be thoughtful and make you a proper breakfast in bed by hand."

An unusual ball of warm tingles burst in my stomach. No

such thing had ever stirred within my carefully programmed, cast iron constitution before.

"I've never had somebody hand make my breakfast," I confessed with interest. "Or bring it to my bed."

"Never had breakfast in bed made for you?" he guffawed.

I pulled myself up to sit on the arm of the couch. "I'm not sure that I've ever had a hand made meal in my life. Or if many other people would have either."

He was genuinely disturbed. "That's just so sad."

I shrugged. "We go digital shopping, virtually selecting our groceries in packets or from restaurant menus. The packets have pixels of flavour, scent, additive nutrients and a shape that the microwave organises into a whole. Chefs have to be masters of Sciences and programming these days. But there's basically no food wastage."

Mitch screwed his face up. "Eck. Well this morning you shall dine in the old style."

"But," I cocked an eyebrow at that empty bench. "How will you manage to be traditional with no solid ingredients?"

He opened his arms out and I noticed that an apron had suddenly appeared over his clothes. Then he clapped his hands together, rubbing them, and a carton of eggs and loaf of bread appeared on the counter – looking exactly as shown in historical pictures of ancient purchased goods.

"Pretend I went out and physically bought them for you. Aside from cheating with the groceries the rest will be authentic."

"A stove?" I inquired inquisitively.

Hot plates appeared in the benchtop.

"The rest will be authentic."

"Utensils? Plates? They normally pixelate in and out of existence too. No cleaning."

Silverware and crockery rattled at once as he opened what had previously been a fizz packs drawer in the counter.

"From now – totally authentic."

My face felt oddly warm and soft as I smiled.

"What should I do?" I asked.

"Well you've spoilt the surprise by waking up, and that's not a bed. So I guess you can go shower or something and act surprised when you come out."

"Roger that," I agreed, rising from the couch. "I haven't got anything to change into though, and there's no Biobeauty in here to save me." I was still wearing V's now rumpled hoodie.

"It'll all be there," he promised knowingly as he expertly tapped an egg against the bench without exploding the fragile little shell covered ball.

I shook my head in fascination, using the holds in the wall to climb up to the nook-like room above the kitchen.

"You haven't even used the bed!" I called down.

"Who designs a place where you have to climb to get to where you sleep?!" he cried back indignantly. "Does nobody think of the disabled or elderly?"

I grinned as I stripped off and saw a neatly folded pile of gear and combat boots waiting for me on the bed – my wish being his command.

"You can *fly*," I reminded him. "And you're in the part of base where the army Rogues live."

"That's not the point," he argued, but I was too serene under the flowing water of the shower wall to bother telling him that being elderly or disabled hardly limited anyone. Tech upgrades could do wonders, for bodies and dwellings.

When I slid my way back down, feeling fresh and ready, he in turn looked like he had fallen through plaster and been covered in white powder. He also appeared to be having the time of his life.

"What happened to you?" I questioned, cocking my head as I took in the powdery mess covering every inch of the kitchen.

Mitch glanced up with a wide smile, joyfully stirring a mixture of some sort.

"I told you it would be authentic. I burnt the eggs. But then I had a great idea."

I tried not to sound apprehensive. "What idea?"

"We can make pancakes together! Come on," he gestured me over with his head. "I've already started on the mix!"

I cautiously approached the bench. "I've never cooked before."

Mitch put the mixing bowl down and was suddenly holding a pan. "Well, it's alright. I've never cooked just for the sake of it with someone else." He handed me the pan. "Now I'll do the blobs and you do the heating bit. Turns out I burn things."

As soon as my traitorous hand automatically reached for the pan, he used it to yank me closer, and then he spun me to be standing over the hot plates. In a moment he had spooned a blob of creamy mix onto the pan.

Before my eyes it spread and expanded into a nice circle of its own accord. In a minute it had become solid.

With a new flat spoon he'd pulled from thin air, Mitch

leaned over me and did a quick flip that sent my little pancake circle over onto its other side. It was a warm, golden colour.

"I think it's done," I observed moments later in surprise, and he nodded and took hold of my wrist so that I was the one who did the flip this time. It landed neatly on a waiting plate to the side.

"Yours. Now mine," he plopped some more mix in the pan and trusted me to do all the fun parts. "Perfection, right there, Miss Lili One," he commented, as his landed on a plate next.

He swept all of the white powder off the bench, then swept me up to sit on the bench before I could blink. He handed me my plate and jumped up to sit beside me.

"You look like you'd normally go the fruit topping option," Mitch reflected. "But today you can be a syrupy baby." I blinked down at my plate to find a sticky sugary topping all over my pancake.

"Yep," he grinned again. "Totally authentic."

He watched with satisfaction as my eyes filled with true delight at the first taste.

"I don't think I've ever tasted something so … real," I admitted.

"Not in this lifetime," he agreed, polishing his pancake off in moments.

"I *cooked*," I remarked. "I feel abnormally accomplished."

"There's something to be said for it," Mitch stated, and I noticed he was tucking into a second pancake. He'd cheated. "I cooked in a team, and it was way more fun. Who knew?"

"There's still the dishes to do," I pointed out, finishing mine.

"There's never dishes to do, when you're with the star who made them," Mitch told me, brushing his hands together as if the job was done. Simultaneously, the mess, the plates on our laps and the pan beside me disintegrated into a fine sand that whirled around him and dissolved.

"Almost as good as your pixel effect," he gloated.

"Better," I told him honestly, and I slid down from the bench almost regretfully.

"Where are we off to today?" he followed suit, trailing me towards the door.

"I'm off to be Queenie's guinea pig," I answered. "She and her techies are going to see if I can be used to follow in V's footsteps. But *you* are probably needed to plan for that family outing to collect Evangeline's dreamer."

He followed me to the door of my room, crinkling his nose in distaste. "You should have company. Remember, we're in this whole self-discovery, new me business together?"

I grabbed the bag that was all I'd packed before coming down to the Rogue base. It had my real book in it, and I stowed V's jumper inside – for luck.

"Alright, then," I let the door close behind me. "I bet they'll find some way to make you useful in the lab."

But instead of being useful, Ned and the medics in the lab became suddenly quite dazed as Mitch dawdled in behind me.

One doctor tripped over a surgerybot while trying to appear unphased.

Only Queenie was as unflappable as ever as Mitch sat himself down on a wheelie chair and propelled himself over to her.

"Good morning!" he twirled to a stop at the silver bench I was supposed to be sitting on, under the light. A nearby cleanerbot rolling past him short circuited as he layered on the charm. "I'm here for support."

"You certainly do inspire," Queenie told him. "But make sure you don't distract."

I unzipped my jacket and slid onto the bench under the light, exposing the designs beyond my tank top.

"Lili already told me to be useless," he confided in Queenie, eyeing off my arms, collar bones and shoulders.

"Useful," I corrected him.

Ned had put a hygiene mask over his beard, and appeared to have regained his composure. He lifted one of my arms and started examining some of the newer designs, closer to the surface. I lit them up for him to see more easily.

"There's some more recent entry points here," Ned rumbled into his mask, his gloved fingers probing at skin that was hardly even tender anymore.

"And here," I told him, lifting my hair and tying it into a ponytail.

His touch went across to my neck and then followed around my hair line to my temples. "I can hardly see the resealed lines from where the Master Techy burrowed into your head," Ned commented appreciatively.

"Burrowed? Into your head?" Mitch spluttered.

"Remarkable work," Queenie remarked as she observed the faint incision marks.

A medic lowered a machine covered in prongs and scalpels towards my arm.

"Woah, woah, woah!" Mitch wheeled backward in protest. "You guys know Lili is awake, right?"

"I hate pain blocks," I told him. "They make you dopey."

"Just fine tips, for now," Queenie instructed, and the medic controlled the machine so that a cluster of needles reached for my arm, prickling their way in. Ned, Queenie and the medic watched their screens for visual of what was going on beneath the surface of my skin.

"Ya'll just said how good it was that she was all healed over …" Mitch said weakly.

"A bit deeper," Queenie ordered.

The prongs on the screen inched their way past tissue and surges of light that ran in veins along my arm – my designs.

"Your … your skin is lifting into little skin tents…" Mitch gagged. I glanced away from Ned's screen to the multiple needles digging into my flesh, moving around and tugging at the skin so that it bunched. A prong dedicated to clean up was catching little drizzles of blood as they appeared.

"This has been my life," I reassured him easily. "Those silver lines you can see had to get in there somehow."

"Now there's something we haven't seen before," Ned muttered as a tiny chip came into view. "Let's get a good look at that." The needles moved around to take images.

"You're used to this?" Mitch was mortified, and green.

"Used to it. Was born to it," I promised him.

I felt a tug as one of the prongs jabbed into the new little chip from which my most recent freedom design had sprouted. There was a burning sensation as the prong began to read the data of the chip and download a copy of it. A 3D image of it was immediately projected over the screens so Queenie would be able to take it apart digitally.

Mitch sagged with relief as the needles withdrew at last and new prongs sprang forward to pinch and seal the skin.

"I'm glad that's over," he confided. "I nearly lost my pancakes."

"You won't like the rest of this, then," I warned him.

I leant forward and they began to slice delicately into my neck to play around under the skin there. V had been able to use scanner insertion technology a lot of the time, but before they could do that, Queenie and her team had to see and understand his brilliance, copying it directly.

"Lili is doing this because we need a way to be able to do this for people easily," Queenie explained. "Pain free."

"I feel sick." Mitch was disgusted.

"You don't need to be here. You can start working on your other jobs."

Looking pale, he nodded. "Right. I can go be moral support from over there."

"Useful from over there?"

"Useless from over there," he corrected me, and he wheeled away to a line of high tech desks along the walls.

The medics around him paused their work – dazzled.

"You can read very carefully through the real book I've got in my bag," I called after him, feeling like he still might lose his pancakes. "You need the distraction."

Excerpts from: The Collected Tales of Mythological and Historical Heroes

On the subject of influential early historical figures:

** In this section people, lands and cities that are believed to have existed prior to the unification of World are mentioned.*

Cleopatra *was the last independent pharaoh of Egypt, famed for her charisma, wit and charm. In order to maintain the freedom and independence of her country she made alliances with great Leaders of Rome. It is in fact said that these Roman Leaders, first Julius Caesar and then Mark Antony, especially allied themselves with Egypt because of their adoration for Cleopatra herself.*

However when Egypt's loss of independence became inevitable, it is rumoured that Cleopatra took her own life rather than submit to imposed foreign control. In our World, power struggles are a distant memory, for our Leaders are the only overseers we need.

On the subject of influential early mythological figures:

*The **Crone**, or **Hecate**, had been worshipped in the earliest of times, and women who had possessed similar characteristics of healing or intellect had been admired. However as time, gender expectations and religious belief shifted, worship of Hecate and women who were like her, was condemned. Free or clever women likened to Hecate (or **Lilith**) were accused of witchcraft and were hanged or burned to death in their thousands.*

On the subject of influential early mythological figures:

In some myths, **Helen** of Sparta was cursed by a vain goddess called Aphrodite. Aphrodite was said to have been charged with overseeing the development of love within humanity, however she was herself a jealous creature. When Aphrodite saw Helen's enchanting beauty, the goddess of love cursed the woman to live with a broken heart.

This certainly seemed to be the case, for Helen's beauty led to the King of Sparta's fixation and possessiveness over her. She was forced into a loveless marriage.

When Helen did fall in love, it was with her husband's enemy – prince Paris of Troy. She fled to Troy in the hopes of living happily with her beloved, though her husband followed, along with the Greek armies, to burn Troy down.

The Greek Soldiers famously built a colossal, hollowed out horse, hiding within it, and tricking the Trojans into bringing the seemingly harmless creation within their walls.

It is a great comfort that today modern dating involves no such risks or tension, with compatibility tests and feelings switches readily available.

| 22 |

- The Star -

"Mitch!"

Dora Cate burst into the lab, tugging Theus along after her.

I tore my gaze from where Lili was now being challenged to test the boundaries of her energy. She had already been scanned, observed and also drained of blood for analysis. I could feel that the stars were getting ready to shine over the part of the world that was above us, and she had not had a break all day.

As Dora drew up beside me there was the sound of electrical currents whirring, the smell of smoke, and an echoing crash as Lili was thrown backward into a rack of equipment.

"What on World?" Theus gaped, watching as Lili picked herself up a distance away, electricity still visibly crackling around her body.

"I'm guessing you can only handle that voltage because of the stamina you built from getting all of those designs," Ned was telling Lili. "It did charge you up, but we clearly need a non-lethal way for Ordinaries to boost their power so they can handle running internal tech for themselves."

"Or maybe we should just find a way to allow people to log on or off from a public connection as they please, rather than completely eradicating the Leaders' virtualtree." Lili's voice was slightly strained now, as she was levitating and holding the weight of a lab bench up over her head to see how much and how quickly energy would be burned from physical tasks.

"Either way, normal people would crash after too much exertion if they didn't have some outside support," Queenie mused, observing the unwavering levels on Lili's chart. "But I like the idea that the change could be with how much everyone's tech is controlled."

Dora pulled herself onto the bench beside me. "That looks intense. But Lili's helping. We'll work out how to liberate everyone to have independent choice – without risk of hacking or random combustion."

"True," I tore my eyes from Lili's shoulders, bunching under the bench's weight.

"Plus, it's handy to know she can fly too," Dora smirked.

"What are you alluding to, dear one?" I enquired.

Dora shrugged innocently. "You make a good match, is all."

"Is that a … *book?*" Theus exclaimed, referring to the open, ancient pages of Lili's text, which was resting on my knees.

"It's Lili's," I answered, holding it up and showing them the cover and title. 'The Collected Tales of Mythological and Historical Heroes'.

"Be careful," Theus winced at how frivolously I must have been holding the treasured item.

"Oooh," Dora Cate grinned. "Lili has to have been drawn to an interest in that topic for a reason. And drawn to ancient things, like you."

"Actually Mitch," Theus pushed up his glasses. "We're the ones who have come to find you here for a reason."

"Am I being summoned to help Evangeline find her dreamer?" I asked glumly.

"Not yet," Dora leaned back on the bench. "Evangeline is going through some kind of identity crisis after last night. Jo's been counselling her and getting her faith bolstered up again."

I tried to lower my eyebrows from where they had sky rocketed upwards.

"Evangeline is letting her guard down to someone?" I spluttered.

"I think she actually appreciates how straight talking and completely fair Jo is. I've heard Jo tell Evangeline off a few times since being here, and Evangeline seems to appreciate it."

"This *is* the angel who tries to incinerate essences, right?" I questioned glibly. "The one who prefers to *do* the telling off?"

"I think Evangeline has had to reassess some things. She needs comfort, and there's solace in being attracted to your comforter," Dora remarked. "Just like you were with Lili last night."

This time my elbow slipped off the bench and Theus cried out as I jostled the book.

"Evangeline? Attracted to Jo?" I guffawed. "She's never had enough warmth in her essence to be open to or attracted to anything!"

Dora shrugged. "Times change."

She had me there.

"Can I just …" Theus reached over and carefully took the book from me. "Not that I don't trust you."

"Of course," I said magnanimously. "So what inspired you to seek me out anyway?"

"We're after your long memory, ancient one." Dora tapped my head. "You've been showering us all in the earliest of scenes, but we want to know what you think about the original visions you shared with Theus and I."

I held my hands up. "Butch and Aris really need to help you out if you want specifics," I told them. Then even as I said it, I felt the approach of Gabe's meaty essence. "But you knew that, didn't you?" I grimaced at Theus resignedly. "I can't catch a break."

And a moment later I felt an even fatter, more densely ego coated essence on its way.

"You didn't!" I accused Dora.

"You said we need our stars along for the ride," she answered matter-of-factly, right as the physical beings that accompanied those two pudgy essences arrived at the lab.

"I thought I'd seen enough of you two," I rolled my eyes at Gabe and Aris. Then I held a hand up as they started toward me, downward turned mouths at the ready.

"No. Nothing personal between us today. Just business. A favour to your dreamers."

Aris ground his teeth, having probably planned a real lecture about how I'd deserved everything I'd got so far through-out eternity. But he begrudgingly took a seat, following Butch's lead.

"Right." I thought about it for a moment, and decided that while I knew I could recall images and project them into the open, I wanted to confine the experience rather than be over-whelmed into reliving it again. That was just too much.

I reached forward and touched one of the screens by the bench Dora sat on. I focused hard on the screen and on one particular memory, and immediately the screen flickered to life with the image of Prometheus and Epimetheus working side by side to create the earliest life.

"Clever way to contain it," Dora noted appreciatively. Theus just drank in the image eagerly.

"Gabriel, get a feel for Theus' spirit. Which brother was he?" I asked.

Gabriel's expression became mighty uncertain, but hesi-tantly, he put his hand on Theus' shoulder and peered at him deeply.

"You look like a stern parent," I tried not to snigger.

"Gah!" Gabe threw his hands up and stood in annoyance. "I don't know! I've never done this!"

"Down, Butch," I told him firmly.

Gabe was boiling under the surface, but he lowered him-self back down without erupting into his own heavenly fire on the spot.

"What do you recommend?" he asked bitingly.

I tapped my chin, thinking. Then: "look harder," I supplied wisely.

"Grrrrr!"

"Truly," I said piously. "You can already see Theus' essence, now you want to look *into* it and get a feel for it."

Clenching his jaw rigidly, Gabe turned from me, back to Theus and held his dreamer's shoulder again.

"Concentrate," I said softly. I had to focus carefully myself, and block out the fact that the medics had just brought Lili's Soldier team in to evaluate her changes in combat since having been 'updated'.

"Really? You guys are gonna make me charge at her alone?" Curtis whined on the other side of the lab. "It was bad enough training with the four of us against her before she got stronger."

"Unfortunately, I have to sit myself out," Junior was saying a tad too regretfully. "Remember, I was on death's door only very recently."

On the other hand, Bear and Jana moved forward together without hesitation – ready to get the job done. In seconds, Bear was skidding across the cleared floor like a cannon ball. Jana went flying, but arced and twisted to land like a cat. Curtis still hadn't budged.

I kept watch on Gabe despite all of this, and his eyes were hard. But he was searching, pushing to find out what I meant. What I had felt when connecting with our kind.

"That's it," I encouraged. "Reach out your senses to connect with Theus' true self, beyond the surface and what he can remember. Find the true Theus that has existed for centuries."

Gabe's face became more intent. "I can feel it."

Theus was transfixed.

I kept contact with the screen, for my own sanity, and then took hold of Theus' hand.

A stirring of images, of countless faces, lives, memories from all of Theus' long history started to flash quickly across the screen. Now we were all mesmerised.

The images were quick, they were all of different ages and different eras, but they were all unmistakably Theus. Even as haircuts, clothes, nose size, colouring and settings changed, it was clear that we were seeing Theus' adaptations throughout history being re-wound. With Gabe's help we were scrolling backwards until Theus' essence was ready to reveal his true, original self.

And then …

"*Prometheus,*" Theus whispered the word in awed relief. Recognising himself, and his full potential at last.

Gabe and I drew back from Theus unsteadily, while Dora took Theus' hand.

"Your dream was to protect humanity. To help people to live."

She showed him a page of Lili's book, where Prometheus' story, and his sacrifices were recorded. "You made humanity and you gave humanity light and warmth," Dora said softly.

"Your dream, still, is to give humanity the resources to survive," Gabe added, his voice touched by wonder.

"The Human Resources guy," Theus grinned, tracing the page of the book.

"My turn," Dora stated firmly then. "Because I am almost certain that I was the girl with the box full of Evils."

I gestured for Aris to have his moment in helping his

dreamer. For once we weren't dying for them to have their epiphany.

Aris took Dora's hand in his massive ones, enveloping it, and he turned to Gabe.

But Gabe frowned. "I'm still not sure of exactly how I penetrated so deeply into Theus' psyche and spirit. It was a feeling."

"How do you do it then?" Aris asked me gruffly next.

For Dora's sake I made the effort not to tease. "Just look. Look further than the Dora you see on the outside. Look further even than her spirit as it is now."

"I see her essence."

"Good. Now search for the particles that burn more deeply. They are less bright, but they are strong. They are older."

I saw Aris stiffen, and Dora frowned.

"What is it?" she asked.

He shook his head. "No."

Her face became impatient, and she shook her hand in his. "I need to know."

Aris seemed pained. Then he reached for me, and grabbed hold of my wrist. Quickly I touched the screen again, to save our minds.

At once an image of fire burst across the screen. There was the sound of cursing, of yelling, chanting, and also of women screaming.

The name Hecate was being spat and hissed as the screaming died away and the flames grew higher.

It was a witch hunting era.

A ring of darkly dressed, chaste, pale faced puritans surrounded the pyres where Dora Cate – who they called Hecate – was being burned along with the pagans who had followed her. "The crone is dead!"

All of them were blindly following their strict beliefs in a time where change or difference was terrifying. None of them knew that they had not killed that being's spirit, and how fortunate this was.

Suddenly the screen's picture changed. There was still fire. There were still screams. But now we gazed up at the giant wooden form of the Trojan horse, which had been filled with hidden Spartans, and now all around us there was battle and despair. Dora had not opened a box this time, but she had sought a love filled life and had still unleashed *hell* in that lifetime – and on the screen she, Helen, gazed around herself in horror. Troy was falling.

Helen of Sparta, now Helen of Troy, turned to meet the charging Spartans calmly.

A slash of red, and then a blaze of gold, and we were looking upon a straight backed queen upon a throne. Her dark eyes glittered, and her black hair framed her face. Sunlight poured over her as if Ra himself had become infatuated with Cleopatra's spirit. Caesar already had. And soon Marc Antony would too. Had one of those besotted leaders been Theus? She would not let Egypt fall to Rome. She was strong. She would rather die than see the health of her kingdom fail.

Pandora was screaming as if it was her own soul that was being punished, rather than the world, as the Evils roared past her. The screen shook and whirled with darkness. She had been tasked with the ability to create change, but change before growth was not always pleasant.

Then the image shifted to an earlier time, where Hecate – or Gaea – was known better for her glory, her wisdom, and her farsightedness, not feared for 'witch craft'. When even my kin and I were just new, she had been among the 'gods' and 'goddesses' created to start all of life, and she had been one of the greatest of them, endowed with guardianship over the sea, earth and sky. Her job had been to breathe health and growth into every corner of life. Mother Nature.

As we watched, Hecate was soaring across a star studded sky, her dark hair billowing behind her. But in the image she turned her head … and looked directly at us. She was not one to be fooled, even in memory or from behind a screen.

We were all rattled under her gaze, and the image distorted as we drew back unconsciously before we were released.

I pulled my burning hand from Aris', and saw that Dora Cate was frozen, staring blankly.

Aris quickly rose, hovering over her anxiously, while Theus was still holding Lili's book, gobsmacked.

"Dora?" I asked hesitantly.

Her glittering eyes refocused on me and I felt relief. That had been overwhelming, but she was intact.

"Those women didn't all look like I do, but they were definitely me," she said with almost as much spunk as usual. "And in some lives I was profoundly wise, in others I was floundering. In all of them my fate seemed cursed or isolated. But I can see, in my contrasting roles across lifetimes, some method to the madness."

Theus was nodding, in awe. "You played a crucial part in history."

Dora beamed at him. "I think my dream has always been to find a balance between life and death that leads to growth and change. For nature and humanity."

"*And,*" I sat back in my chair, beyond impressed. "In every life you were totally bad-ass."

Aris was pale and a little incredulous. "Dora, in one life you were created under a curse and then brought on man's greatest, most necessary test. In another life you were associated with witchery – altering people's perceptions. And in your first life you had the potential to be the giver of all healing to the earth." He rubbed his jaw thoughtfully. "Those are all things we need now. We are all being tested in the present time. People are in need of change. And the world needs healing."

"Exactly the kind of dreamer that could help us," Gabe agreed.

"The universe has OCD," I said once more. "It was always going to work it all out. Have everything come full circle."

"Maybe all of us really are being brought together, and recognising our true dreams, for a reason," Theus speculated.

"Well a dream for change, growth and health in the world is relevant. It goes nicely with a dream for giving humanity the resources to survive." I looked over at my dreamer, Lili, again then. "So I guess we do need to work out how all the dreams fit together, and make them come true. Reach a state of Shangri-La in this world, with spiritual awareness and fulfilment leading the way."

I noticed that Lili was shaking with concentration. Her team had limped back to their rooms and she sat on the bench under the light once more. She was hooked up to a cord that dug into her temple.

"I think we need some time to digest all of this," Theus commented tiredly. But he seemed more confident, and more comfortable in his own skin than before.

Dora gave me a warm hug and Theus shook my hand gratefully before they left, but I was distracted by Lili – watching her carefully while her skin drained of colour.

"Michael …" Aris began gruffly.

"Mmm?"

"Thank you." Gabe said sincerely. "You have done a good thing. Many good things."

"No worries," I said. "Break time now, though. Like Theus said."

"I think we should talk," Gabe tried.

"Break time. Now." I disagreed, and they noticed at last that I was watching Lili.

A line of blood traced its way down from her nose and over her lips. Her eyes began to flutter.

Gabe and Aris faded to the background to me as they stepped back almost respectfully, and I rushed forward, running to catch Lili as she swayed where she sat.

"She resisted us for a whole twenty minutes!" one of the medics exclaimed excitedly, taking the cord from her temple to do the readings. "Brainwave can be overcome!"

Lili slumped against me, her forehead on my shoulder and her skin cold as I put my arm around her.

"Just because she's tough doesn't mean it's right to try to

break her!" I scowled at Queenie and her team. They stopped celebrating and became appropriately abashed as I let my cool façade drop momentarily.

"Mitch," Lili lifted her head. She appeared terribly satisfied. "They're helping me. I'm the key, and I need them to do this so we can learn."

"You did great, Lili," Queenie came forward. "We were never able to completely shut you down against your will. But, you're right Mitch." Queenie put her placating hand on my arm.

An image of boundless sand rippled across my mind. The air wavered and danced under the pressure of the sun while a retinue of caravans, servants and laden camels travelled onward. They were carrying gifts of gems, gold, spices, and countless other riches. On a camel herself, rode their leader. Her rivers of black hair were covered by a sheer veil. Her sharp, brown eyes were wise. Knowledge was what she thirsted for. It drove her on. To Solomon. Where she would learn much, and perhaps also teach. Her dream was wisdom, to find the answers.

Sheba …

Queenie took her hand from my arm slowly. Even without the screen, this memory had been contained and nobody else had seen. Our eyes connected, and though she showed awareness of what had just passed, she did not show shock.

"A star knows best," she continued. "Lili should rest now. You have allowed us to collect so much information we could practically clone you, Lili." She smiled. "I know it's outlawed for space reasons, but I *am* a Rogue."

"As long as you've got everything you need to know," Lili's resolve flickered just slightly.

"Right then," I didn't give her a moment to think, but swept her off the table. "You need air."

Excerpts from: The Collected Tales of Mythological and Historical Heroes

On the subject of influential early historical figures:

** In this section people, lands and cities that are believed to have existed prior to the unification of World are mentioned.*

The **Queen of Sheba** *was a woman of great intellect, loveliness and wealth. Her quest was to attain knowledge, and she crossed the desert to meet King Solomon, who was renowned for his wisdom. They spoke as equals, with great admiration for each other as they matched wits.*

Natural intellect is a quality to be admired – though it is of course not a necessity when intelligence can be implanted or your tech can do the thinking for you.

On the subject of influential early historical figures:

Geronimo *was an Apache leader. His tribe was attacked by Mexican Soldiers, which resulted in the murder of his family. He avenged his lost loved ones, and then turned his fury on American settlers who were forcing his people from their own Apache territories. He broke his way free of reservations numerous times, eluded capture and led others to safety. For many years his efforts were focused solely on his wish to preserve his people's free way of life until he was at last forced to surrender. His final words were of regret for having ever given in.*

In our society, we know that giving in and surrendering to the rules is the only thing that makes life peaceful, comfortable and stable.

| 23 |

– The Dreamer –

"I can walk, you know," I told Mitch with some amusement as he launched me right out of the ward before I could change my mind.

His usually overly unbothered act had still not returned.

"Even better, you can fly," he told me. But after a moment he calmed down and set my feet on the corridor floor.

"You noticed," I congratulated him, getting my balance as my body rebooted to systems normal again.

My head was still lurching slightly, but it wasn't as bad as my rebirth day. And I'd done well against all of the technical hijackings, which was extremely promising. It meant that V's work was likely impenetrable to hacks or viruses, so civilians wouldn't be at risk without Leader controlled Brainwaves.

"Where are we going?" I asked with mild curiosity.

"I told you, you need air," he replied deviously.

"How do you propose to get us uncycled air from down here?"

He just shrugged. "We'll find an exit and test my new capabilities outside." He sounded very confident.

"We might both be too valuable for the Rogues to just let us go," I mused, but he waved an unworried hand.

"They're all about freedom and free will down here," he reassured me. "In fact I'm following a very helpful Rogue's essence right now."

"That sounds slightly creepy," I commented.

"He helped me scan out of here once. Just before I met you and your team," Mitch explained. Then we rounded a corner and came across a gentleman with long, white hair plaited down his back. When he saw Mitch he smiled.

"Star-born," he greeted Mitch. "Are you lost once more?"

Mitch grinned. "Oh, not quite so much as I was when I last saw you."

"That's good to hear," the older man replied, his steady eyes reading Mitch's face. "You scarcely knew yourself when we crossed paths."

"You're right," Mitch nodded, and then reached out a hand as if introducing himself. "Michael," he referred to himself by his true name.

When the other man clasped his hand in return, Mitch's eyebrows raised and his lips quirked up again. They both seemed to be seeing something I couldn't.

"Geronimo." Mitch greeted him with intrigue.

I reflected back to different heroic tales in my precious book, and thought that I recognised the name.

"Quite the rebel spirit you have there," Mitch commented with admiration.

Geronimo was smooth with acceptance as he slowly nodded. "May I help a fellow rebel?"

"Actually, my friend, we need a room with a view," Mitch replied. "I'm going to see if I can take it from there."

Geronimo guided us to another level, and left us at a smaller conference room. The room was dark except for the glowing orange light that poured in from a wall sized window.

"I'm getting better at spontaneous revelations from people," Mitch told me as he ushered me into the room. "Will you lock that?" he asked.

Then I started with surprise as I turned from locking the door to find Mitch waiting patiently – standing beside a perfectly made opening in the thick window. Intense heat poured in from the wide opening, but there was not a crack or chip of glass to be seen.

"Glass is made up of sand particles. I can put it all right back," he promised.

"Impressive." I approached him, peering out at the massive drop and burning magma below. "When I laser through glass it's irreversible. But you can just magic it away."

"I'm a magical little star. Twinkle, twinkle," he agreed. Then he grinned and held his hand out. "Want me to do some magic and get you out of the rabbit hole? You did call me a rabbit once."

"You noticed before that I could fly for *myself*," I pointed out.

"Maybe later. You're tired now." He grabbed my hand. "But you can do your own twinkle star impression and turn on your cold designs."

"Have you considered the risks of leaving the burrow

again?" I asked as he drew me closer to the opening in the glass.

Despite my reservations I let my cooling protection designs flare to life to combat the furnace-like waves of air rolling in.

"If the assassins locate you, you and the new form you've taken could be destroyed for good."

"I feel utterly safe," he grinned winsomely. "I have you."

"You just said I was too tired to even fly," I argued dryly.

He chuckled. "Course I did. I wanted to hold your hand."

And then he pulled me through the opening and we were soaring upward, flying away from the heat.

My designs automatically protected me from the overwhelming temperature, and my own flight control kicked in as I peered back to see that the glass we'd exited from had become whole again.

"You know the volcano opening from your memory will be long gone if the Leaders had anything to do with it," I called to him warningly.

"Trust me," I heard Mitch say, and we hurtled toward the oppressive layer of rocky roof, where there was no exit in sight.

But just as we were sure to dash ourselves to oblivion, I felt the air movement changing around us. It was rippling upward in a cloud that Mitch followed, and in moments I saw a kind of split above us. I hardly had a moment to think before we were shooting through an old volcanic side vent – and with a rush of thick, hot air, we burst out into the open. Outside.

I gasped in the crisp freshness of it, panting with the exhilaration. But Mitch continued racing us onward across the dark sky, pulling me along at an incredible pace so that we soared over vast lands and cities. Hours blurred by in what felt like moments as we even passed over enough space to have once been countries.

I wasn't sure if even my new capabilities would allow me to travel that fast or far. But while I was fascinated by the views whirling by, Mitch was instead growing more surprised.

"That was once rainforest and waterfalls. That was once ocean. I think that was once France. That was once desert. That was once Ethiopia." He pointed at clustered cities, and pushed on almost desperately. "The Colosseum is gone. Notre Dame. The Pyramids. I bet there's no more of Michelangelo's art left."

He was becoming increasingly disconcerted until at last he found a towering mountain that had not yet been built too heavily upon – probably being the backyard of a Leader's lofty retreat. Then he pulled me down to land on a rocky ledge, which he paced with a frown.

I took in my surroundings with quiet appreciation, sitting to give him time to process.

"Lili, just then I didn't see any recognisable landmarks, or even many recognisable land masses for that matter," Mitch announced after a few moments. "Why?"

I cocked my head to the side. "The first Leaders got rid of any markers of a disunified past so that old tensions or pride would die. And the second Leaders worked out how to change what your world map would have looked like – bringing old countries closer together for convenience and added togetherness. It caused a lot of tectonic dramas I believe," I crinkled my brow as I tried to remember that far back into my edu-updates.

"They … changed …?" He was stupefied for a moment, becoming still. And then he grimaced, coming to sit beside me.

"What upsets you most?" I asked.

He shook his head, stunned and struggling to decide. "I think I'm upset that this is a world that has been made to forget its history, though history is a lesson. Every dream of the past has been meant to guide the future. And that's all gone." He sighed. "I do know that all things fade. There were so many works of art that I saw painted, celebrated, restored, before fading or flaking to dust. I saw statues carved from rock, being put up, being stolen and then recovered. I saw cracks appear in their marble faces, the sharpness of their features blurring and wearing away under the spreading stains of moss and age until they were unrecognisable. I saw magnificent buildings rise from the ground, ringing with voices, and then gradually breaking away, falling or being overcome by war. But now there are not even diverse accents or features on faces. People look World and speak World. It's like all of the flavours have been sucked out of this once diverse place, and nobody even realises that the vibrancy is gone or what they're missing."

While he spoke I calmly leaned my back against the rocky wall, gazing out at splashes of wild green plants that were springing out of crevices between the rocks around us. I let my fingers brush over completely real, spongey green moss, and I thought about how we were all one streamlined, cohesive World – but that now we were all equal and healthy, perhaps we could go further to achieve something even more beautiful. Create our own vibrancy and mark on time that would leave a legacy for the next generation to build on.

"Maybe you needed air more than I did," I reflected when Mitch stilled.

He took a deep breath and nodded. "At least out here we can watch something real and natural."

He rested his head on my shoulder and I followed his intent gaze outward, noticing now that the sky was lightening.

I saw that it was awash in the softest blues, then touches of pink and strokes of orange that grew outward, intermingling to make stretches of warm colour.

"I don't think I've noticed those colours before," I said quietly after a while, captivated by something I'd hardly noticed on any early shift. "Normally hologram ads stand out more than the rising sun."

The hues became lighter until the upper edge of the sun inched its way over the skyline to fill my vision.

"I feel better already," Mitch replied. "The sun still works."

"And there are digital records and copies of many things from the past, for those who want to look back," I added consolingly. "You haven't completely lost your Michelangelo's works of art."

I didn't mention that the final pieces of the Sistine Chapel's roof had been sold off long before I was made. And they had been too aged to really prove there had ever been any paint on them.

"Michelangelo painted Adam with a naval because I dared him to, you know," Mitch informed me with a touch of nostalgia. "Our little joke."

"Wasn't he labelled as a heretic because of that?" I scoffed. "Adam was meant to have been *made* rather than born."

"Michelangelo was a real independent character. You'd have liked him," Mitch grinned. Then he became quizzical. "Do you have one?"

"One what?"

He poked me in the middle. "A belly button? Miss Rock Hard Abs."

"I was grown and hooked up to different things, so yes," I explained. I gazed at the sun, which was now higher in the sky and its light was touching the tips of our boots.

"That must have been a hard experience," Mitch sympathised.

"It was my version of normal," I answered. "But it must have been harder for you, to face an eternity of death. An eternity of waking to unfamiliarity, knowing nobody properly, and realising that it is pointless to try."

"Oh *this* time has been hardest. It's been a vast leap into a whole new way of being," he agreed. "But I meet great people." He stretched. "You're not so bad. And in the past I bounced around in each era that I visited so much that I had long enough to really immerse myself in the periods. Sometimes I even got to spend great stretches of time with a client, like I did with Michelangelo."

Mitch reached across to entwine my hand in his then, causing a flutter in my stomach.

"Plus, I didn't always have to shock everyone into having their dream come true. Sometimes I just phased out to my next cycle," he said reasonably. "And though dreams are not always safe, or able to guarantee 'happily ever after' and eternal satisfaction – they sate a burning desire of the soul. A need to contribute to the world, or to accomplish that one thing – big or small – before moving on. So my sacrifice is worth it."

I let out a pent up breath of air. "I'm not sure I've ever felt enough emotion in my life to equate to that. Or at least not in this life. V once warned me that it was unlikely I'd even been programmed to feel love when all I needed to feel was loyalty."

"Lili, believe me, I know a powerful, passionate dreamer when I see one. And I see one in *you*," he assured me. "I've taken part in ground shaking, earth changing dreams. Along with small personal ones. And dreams that were only needed for a short time rather than to shape all of time. Once I just helped an ordinary young man dig a well, and another time I was a dying slave beside Spartacus – inspiring him to wage all-out war against slavery." He began listing dreams on his fingers. "There was the time I pushed some of Napoleon's soldiers, who were on duty in Egypt, into 'accidentally' uncovering the Rosetta stone. And there was the time I simply had to make an apple fall in front of a fellow for him to have his Eureka moment. So, clearly, I know what I'm talking about."

"You … inspired Newton's Law of Gravity?" I coughed incredulously.

Mitch snickered. "I always spread the rumour that I dropped that apple on his head," he confided. "Way better story. But," he continued as the sun became warmer. "Never have I seen dreams connect to each other so obviously as they seem to be now. All heading in one direction. And never has it seemed more important for a rebellious dream to come true."

I nudged him with my shoulder. "I saw what you were doing with Dora and Theus – finding their beginning and their true dreams. Perhaps I could have a very old, rebellious spirit and origin dream too."

He lifted his head from my shoulder then.

"Yes, I believe you do," he answered.

I bit the inside of my lip. Nodding.

"The woman who escaped the Utopian garden in the vision you had …"

"I think it was you," Mitch affirmed. "Lilith."

I released a pent up breath. "I've read about Lilith – the queen of darkness and mother of all evil."

"Lilith was one life of yours. She was only seen as a demoness for breaking the rules to be free," Mitch replied seriously. "Her punishment for rebelling was to be portrayed so horribly, because breaking the rules was like breaking everything."

"But you broke the rules to grant her that dream. To grant *me* that dream."

"It was the first dream to ever be realised," Mitch said stoutly. "It started a whole new path for all of the stars when I began granting dreams like yours."

"It also started the whole evolution thing," I remarked dryly. "I'm glad I've got the Biobeauty to do my styling now. Your makeovers turned me into a primate."

"I was new and inexperienced," he defended. "But it did the job and you were free to live your life."

"Evolving painfully slowly, along with the rest of human kind," I scolded lightly.

He reclined against me again. "What I don't know is why you're still here, when your dream was already granted," he admitted.

"I have been thinking about that," I ventured. "And I don't believe I need you to perform any essence tricks to help us understand. Because I think I've seen my past lives in my sleep."

"You dreamed of your soul's past?" he asked in amazement. "What did you see?"

I remembered back to all of the mental perfection checks, where the flawless Lili One model had in fact been rather imperfect, describing dreams that had been diagnosed as glitches.

"For such a blank person – just following Soldier directives in reality, in my dreams I have always been impassioned or fierce."

"You're impassioned and fierce in this day and age too," Mitch protested. "Who else could take all those needles from Queenie, even in the name of progress?"

I smiled, but went on. "In many dreams I was like Dora Cate – or Hecate. I was seen as a demoness, a seductress or witch, blamed for unexplained deaths or happenings."

Mitch grunted in frustration. "Lilith just wanted to be equal. She was a woman who challenged an oppressive system and so she became feared and scorned. I am so sorry that you suffered such defamation, when out of the two of us, I was the first one to be a felon. Hell, I even made a deal with the Devil."

"In one of the dreams, or lives, Satan actually helped me," I speculated. "In that dream a mysterious, shrouded man led me to safety, into a tunnel that seemed to have no end – as if I might have been Persephone, a character from my book."

"So Persephone was not abducted after all," Mitch puzzled over it all.

"She – I – was saved. Given peace for one lifetime."

"But by Satan? Hades? I just can't see it."

"Perhaps he had gained respect for *you*, after you saved him," I told my flummoxed star. "And perhaps he knew what I was to you, and helped me as a way to repay you."

Mitch puffed. "That old Devil."

"But one of the most recent dreams was always of a woman, covered in inked designs, sitting in a cave and waiting," I continued. "The woman had lived a very long, free life, she had evolved, and she now remembered the star-like being who had helped her at the beginning of time."

"Now that's very interesting," Mitch commented.

"In the dream the woman was ready to die, totally fulfilled. But she was waiting for a bright disc of light – wanting to speak to it. Because she had decided her spirit had to stay to help her star-like saviour and others to find freedom as she had."

"You ..." Mitch gasped. "You *chose* to stay? You chose to stay for a new dream ... and for me?" He shook his head in consternation. "But nobody has ever been able to, or wanted to choose to stay when they have been ready."

"I must have been quite strong willed back then," I remarked.

"Strong willed all throughout time, I would say," he spluttered, wide eyed.

"Perhaps I can also be like the rumours of Lilith in other ways," I joked. "Birth rebels like demons for our cause, or steal the children of the surface World to join the Rogues."

Mitch winced uncomfortably. "I'm afraid your soul went through many lonely lifetimes, just to stick around for me."

"Just as you did, for helping me," I countered. "I was the start of all of your problems."

"You were the beginning of the *making* of me," he returned, laying himself out on the rough ledge now. He rested his head on my leg, his eyes skyward to the clouds. "What a divine creation you are," he told me wonderingly.

"And you are utterly flawed," I laughed wryly when I saw that Mitch had lit up a cigarette from nowhere. He pouted as I flicked it from his fingers. "Such vices the angel of justice has."

"I'm a hard worked saint," he argued, already puffing at a new cigarette. But he grinned at my annoyance and only half regretfully let the cigarette burn up into embers and then burst into gold dust. "So what do we need to do? What might be holding your second, even bigger dream back? We'll have to overcome it."

"Well," I pondered. "While there's a lot that you don't recognise in this era, people *are* more unified, and a new kind of beauty is emerging in the blendings of this time. Perhaps if we help it, it will grow," I answered thoughtfully. "But there are grave problems holding us back. The Leaders are the key there."

"The Leaders sound like monarchs," Mitch reflected.

"Yes, they inherit their station. But they are born to a different form of power. They're born to business related wealth and born to World ownership."

"They own the rights to the globe?" Mitch asked in bewilderment.

"And people. People's minds. Their tech. The most powerful family are the Pendragons, who are descended from the big internet and phone companies of the past. They now run the Sciences and tech, and were the ones who designed Brainwave. Another power family own the media, but they have to work with Brainwave to collect metadata and maintain their status and popularity. Lesser families also rose to wealth and power as new problems evolved over time. They profited from inventions to cleanse the air and water, and now they own World resources and dictate space. But the Pendragons are the real Leaders."

"In amongst all the dating adverts, I remember seeing some holograms about the Pendragons," Mitch recalled. "There was some issue about them though."

"Yes, the Pendragons are in a terrible crisis," I explained, visualising the noble but unhappy image of the missing heir. His neat blonde curls always hung a little, as if in defeat, while his mother Uthoria towered over him. "The ultimate Leader believes the Rogues abducted her heir, Cam Pendragon, so control may have to pass over to a new Leader group who is not in the Pendragon line."

"Hmmm. A time of upheaval," Mitch commented. "Perfect time for change, and perfect time for all these dreams, old and new, to come true."

I sat up straighter on the rock. "But we would also want to keep *some* Leader established ways," I reasoned. "Before our systems of power existed, a number of the original cultures had already become almost extinct through war, disease or poverty. Some areas of the planet were near deserted, though the only thing that made those places unliveable was the warring that drove people to flee. I am glad that there is no war, or poverty. And regulation of each person's chemical make-up, genes and cells has also meant that disease, mental health problems, addiction, criminal intent, anger, disabilities … all hardly exist anymore. Ailments can largely be programmed out or catered for."

Mitch stretched his legs out on the ledge. "So they have established comfort for people, and equality – by subduing them into uniformity. Subduing people, stifling nature, none of it's healthy."

"No. It's an improvement, but it's not healthy. And it needs to change," I agreed. "But to change in the right way."

"Alright. We need to make a Camelot," he announced, looking up at me.

"But in the meantime," I glanced at the distant morning sun. "I guess we should find our way back."

"We could make pancakes again," he grinned, helping me up.

"You could teach me something else to cook." I let my designs light up to lift me as he began to rise from the ledge too. "We could try those eggs again."

"I feel happy." He pulled me closer to float beside him.

"We'll probably need to meet with Evangeline when we get back," I teased.

"Unhappy," he grimaced. "I feel decidedly unhappy."

Excerpts from: The Collected Tales of Mythological and Historical Heroes

This is a first edition text, published by the World's third generation of great Leaders. Congratulations – you've purchased one of the last Leader approved hard copy texts!

On the subject of influential early historical figures:
** In this section people, lands and cities that are believed to have existed prior to the unification of World are mentioned.*

Ned Kelly *was an Australian bushranger in a time of early European settler history. He became famous, or infamous, for rebelling against corruption and becoming a bank robbing outlaw. He held great fascination for, and often gar- nered support from all who heard of him, so all Soldiers of the time were intent on his capture.*

Ned Kelly and his gang fashioned themselves protective metal armour that left only the eyes and legs uncovered. They held an epic standoff against Sol- diers in the Australian bush, eventually leading to the capture of the wounded Ned Kelly, who was later sentenced to hang.

It is a relief that our modern Soldiers are programmed to be incorruptible followers, and Ordinaries have no desire to challenge them.

| 24 |

– The Star –

"Have you ever felt the need to wear metal body armour? As a Rogue, you obviously feel at home Down Under. You're also definitely an outlaw and I *know* you've felt the urge to shoot at cops – or Soldiers … *Mister Kelly.*"

I was annoying Ned as he and Queenie checked us over before our mission to find Evangeline's dreamer.

"The universe is not being at all creative with dreamer names, is it?" I eyed off the grumpy medic's bushranger-y beard.

Ned grunted.

"Haven't *you* had variations of the same name throughout all of time?" Will asked me good-naturedly. He had taken to revelations of his backstory with much more enthusiasm than Ned had, having willingly signed up to the online identity search program.

Rogue bases across the globe were now filled with countless numbers of my brethren and their dreamers, and all of the stars were viewing as many Rogue profiles as possible to see if they could have any epiphanies of recognition.

Will had been ecstatic to find out that he had originated from the great Scottish freedom seeker, William Wallace. But Ned on the other hand had taken no interest in complicating his current life. Instead, Ned had been innocently sitting in the background of somebody else's screencast when one of my kin had recognised the surly medic's image – exclaiming excitedly that Ned was in fact *the Ned* who had stood up to corrupt authorities.

Considering the very slim chances that the correct angelic being would be gazing at the same screen as a human they might recognise, Ned had been very lucky in everyone else's opinion.

"Yes, but *our* names are part of our heavenly essence," I told Will demurely. "Our names are the true words for us, and came into being as us angels were born from the brightest parts of the stars."

"Hmf," Ned replied poignantly, flashing his light to check my starry eyed pupils.

Evangeline arrived at that moment, her sharp eyes scanning us and the padded room. But Jo was holding Evangeline's hand supportively, making her slightly more tolerable.

"Lili is, as expected, good to go," Queenie stated.

"Course she is," I interjected. "She's number One."

To stay as covert as possible, only a couple of Rogues were going with Evangeline – Will and the blonde, confident Rogue who Lili had whispered looked like an Arthurian knight from her book.

And it had been decided that I was the best star to go along, instead of Aris and Gabe, because I was so amazingly powerful and we couldn't have too many stars out in the open.

The only plus side was that Lili had refused to leave my precious self unprotected, so she was coming too.

"This one's ready too," Ned jutted his chin toward me.

The knightly Rogue approached as Will finished hooking himself up to open our virtual passage.

"Need any help with co-ordinates?" the knight asked Will, clapping his hands together and eyeing our rag-tag group.

"All sorted," Will replied. "Evangeline is apparently following some kind of gut feeling about where her target last was. She can't get a vibe for an exact current location, as if her target is in hiding or majorly conflicted. So we're just going to have to go up and search for clues."

"Sure, I'm up for some detective work," knight Rogue shrugged easily.

"Good luck," Jo told us, and Evangeline kissed Jo goodbye in the most natural gesture I had ever seen from her.

Then Will was opening the portal in the wall – unleashing the crazy energy currents that sucked us helplessly into the technological tunnel of wires.

I coughed and dusted myself off when the portal doorway closed, leaving us with the faint whirring sounds that belonged to the tunnel world stretching before us.

"I wasn't even knocked off my feet that time," I told Will proudly. "But it feels like my skin is vibrating, and the hairs on my arms are frizzled."

"You're a natural online traveller," Will congratulated me, and even though he only led us a short distance, he stopped at another section of the wired wall that looked the same as any other part.

"This outlet should pop us out at the nearest plug on the site of those co-ordinates you gave us," he told Evangeline. "Let's all be ready in case we turn up somewhere conspicuous."

I braced myself as Will hooked himself up to create a new opening.

And –

I had the distinct sensation of being chewed up and spat out again.

"A real natural online traveller," I wheezed.

My legs were up over my head, and Lili strode over to disentangle me. Of course Evangeline seemed to have been dumped onto a bed. And the Rogues were upright, with Will appearing to be completely fine. However the blonde knight was looking deeply disturbed.

"You've got to be kidding me," he scoffed in disbelief, staring about himself sickly.

"Pretty fancy," Will agreed.

Even though we were in a bedroom, the ceiling was higher than that of the apartment room I had back on base. Everything was pristine, with white and cream colours, gorgeous furniture, and the expansive bed even floated of its own accord under a waterfall of material flowing from the ceiling.

"Wowee," I breathed, checking over my shoulder to find that we had just been shot out of a portal through the biggest screen wall in history, and I actually wasn't too upset to have landed on such luxurious carpet.

"No, it's not the grandeur of the place," the knight grimaced. "It's just that, I don't think you have to look for clues."

"Do you know who lives here?" Will asked in confusion.

Knight sighed. "I did. This was my room."

Knight appeared nauseated.

Will cringed on his friend's behalf. "This is the place you escaped?"

"Why did you want to?" I asked, fascinated that my body had left a snow angel imprint behind.

"This is a loveless place. I never wanted to come back. And I definitely don't want to take the only other person who lives here back to base with us." Knight's voice was extremely pained.

"I can feel there's no one else here at the moment," I told him, even though it was unhelpful. Distress was written all over his face.

"But *I* can feel that I'm being pulled somewhere," Evangeline said, lowering herself off the floating bed.

She crossed the grand room to the door and peered out.

"I'm betting there's surveillance all over this place," Lili warned.

"My face has probably been scanned a thousand times already since we've been here, and movement from all of us would have been picked up," the knight followed Evangeline through the door hesitantly. "We don't have long before security arrives."

Outside the bedroom the house opened up lavishly. We stood four floors up, gazing over a banister that was more like a balcony over a lushly carpeted ballroom. A roof to floor window took up the entire wall opposite us, and there was a view of manicured lawns for as far as the eye could see.

"You said only one other person resides here?" I asked, gaping at the floors below and then up at the arched roof high above us.

"Yes." The response was disgruntled. "Her."

Now my mouth was hanging for a different reason. There was a portrait almost as high as the lofty roof as I turned to the wall behind me. It was an imposing, old style painting of an intimidating business woman and her son – our knight. He was much younger in the picture, and somehow like a shadow fading into the background, in spite of the size of the image. The real man beside us, despite horror written all over his face, appeared healthier and more self-assured. In fact he looked like an entirely different person to the uncomfortable creature in the painting.

"She's known in the business Leaders' sector as the Slayer," the knight said ruefully, glaring at the coldly staring woman that loomed over us. "She's my mother. Uthoria."

"But …" Evangeline was frowning in confusion. "It's not her that I'm being drawn to. It's him, in the painting." She turned to the knight now. "It's you. Or … who you were before, when this picture was done."

"What is your name?" Lili asked the knight, her face changing from consternation to surprise.

I winced. She was bypassing the unwritten law of awkwardly letting someone remain nameless if you've known them too long and not asked.

The knight Rogue hunched as if cornered, becoming

much more similar to the baby-faced, miserable figure in the painting.

"He's Cam," Will spoke up for him. "Cam Pendragon. The Leader heir that everyone's been saying we abducted."

"You are the heir to the World?" Lili's voice was aghast.

It certainly seemed like the weight of the world had just dropped onto knight Cam's shoulders.

Then we were frightened out of our reverie by a new voice.

"Master Cam? And ... *Mitch*?!"

I knew the voice at once, and incredulously peered around Lili, where she'd blurred to stand in front of me in under a second.

"Molly?"

Lili stepped aside when she saw that I recognised the new-comer, who was standing a short distance away.

"What's going on here?" I asked uncertainly.

"We've been found out," Will said urgently. "She must work for Cam's mother."

"Actually, I oversee cleaning for all the major Leaders' properties in the business sector," Molly's face was perplexed. "But I'm only here virtually."

She gazed at Cam and myself questioningly. "You don't seem very abducted Master Pendragon."

"We're just here to get some of my past ... baggage," Cam managed. "You could get in trouble if Uthoria knows you're speaking to us," he added hollowly.

Molly smiled. "What can I do? I'm virtual. I only plugged myself back in because Brainwave sent me an alert that the carpet had been indented, which the Ultimate Leader hates." Then Molly became serious. "But I'm surprised the security team aren't here already. You need to leave."

"Letting us go without raising the alarm yourself will definitely get you into trouble," Will shuddered.

"The alarm sensors would have been going off for a while before I even arrived and stopped them. I really don't know why nobody's rushed in yet," Molly frowned.

"They'll be surrounding the place," Lili commented quietly.

"Yes, you should go," Molly nodded. "I'll distort the sound recorders later and tell them I tried to get Cam to stay to see his sick mother. She's being moved back here tonight to be made more comfortable."

"Thanks for helping us," Will smiled at her, whipping out a cord so he could hook himself into the nearest power.

"I'm happy to help Master Cam. And you too, Mitch," she answered, regarding me warmly. She looked very well. Like a changed person. "Even if you did promise you'd stay out of trouble with the Rogues."

I smiled at her as her image began to pixelate then, before it disappeared.

"Let's go," Lili said, taking hold of my jacket sleeve.

And then the gigantic window across from us exploded inwards.

Daggers of glass fell over us in a deadly blizzard.

I had enough time to feel my eyes boggle in my head, and to think that Molly was going to have her cleaning cut out for her, before I felt an incredible grip around my middle dragging me backward and into Cam's bedroom.

Lili had blurred me out of harm's way even before the glass had reached where I'd been standing.

Her grip released me then, and I didn't see, but rather felt her leave and return; this time catapulting both Evangeline and Will into the room as if they were as light as dolls.

"Get us out of here!" I heard her growl at Will while the first shards of glass started to impact on the floor where we'd previously been standing – as if they were in slow motion and we were on high speed.

I'd hardly taken a breath before Lili reappeared, covering Cam as she ran with him hunched under her grip.

Will was still scuttling to stand up from where she'd thrown him, and ten assassin Soldiers were just bursting through the shattered glass, before Lili slammed the bedroom door closed.

She sent Will trotting toward the giant screenwall, and then hauled the hover bed up to flatten it against the door.

"Hurry!" she ordered, as Will fumbled for his cord again. "There are windows everywhere and that bed is hardly going to help for long!"

She shepherded us all towards Will, and her eyes and designs were literally alight with superhuman energy.

But just as Will got himself organised, the door, doorway, commandeered bed, and parts of the wall all shattered inwards in a burst of splinters. The ten Soldiers moved almost as fast as Lili, sweeping in before Cam had even raised his own laser shooter.

But Lili's fists exploded with light and energy, and she sent out a volatile blast that rocketed into her opponents.

Three of the ten assassins were knocked out, smoking

against the far wall. The others were just dazed and still staggering towards us.

I didn't even see her move, but I did notice an assassin Soldier, who had lunged towards Will and the gateway he was making, suddenly lift and then collide with the floor.

Lili was stationary long enough to be visible as she gripped the Soldier's cranium and sent a pulse from her hand into his skull. Lights out for him; effective immediately.

Then in a blink she was colliding with the rest of the Soldiers and they were all being engulfed in a blinding force field of her light.

Two Soldier bodies hurtled out of the brightness, then there was violent movement churning within the light, and two more thudded away.

Will got the portal open just as Lili reappeared beside us and bodily hustled us all through the gateway.

And then there was abrupt silence as the portal closed on the chaos of Cam's bedroom, with nearly all of us knocked off our feet this time.

For a moment I was stunned, lying on the tunnel floor and gaping like a fish out of water. But when I finally disentangled myself from Evangeline's wild flaming hair, spitting it out, I stood shakily to look for Lili.

My dreamer was bent over, hands on her knees, regaining her breath. She held up a finger, signalling me to wait when I made to approach her.

She did not look up, but I noticed a wisp of sizzling electricity dancing along her slender digit and curling around her fingertip.

She was breathing extremely deeply and slowly. Controlling herself and reining in the adrenalin and power.

When she straightened up at last, leaning her back against the wired wall as the others pulled themselves together, her eyes were still flashing with slowly fading light.

"You blow me away," I told her honestly, and leaned beside her – feeling the buzzing vibes rolling off her even more than from the tunnel itself.

"You blew them *all* away," Will puffed then.

"However," Evangeline began, for once appearing to be evaluating someone to her liking. "None of them were dead."

"They were normal Soldiers a week ago," Lili replied. "Maybe they can be again. Now that we've found out that your dreamer has quite a lot of power and influence."

Cam frowned and turned himself away from us. "I want nothing to do with any of it," he said, and launched himself back down the tunnel.

Excerpts from: The Collected Tales of Mythological and Historical Heroes

This is a first edition text, published by the World's third generation of great Leaders. Congratulations – you've purchased one of the last Leader approved hard copy texts!

On the subject of influential early historical figures:
** In this section people, lands and cities that are believed to have existed prior to the unification of World are mentioned.*

Joan of Arc, *or Jeanne d'Arc, was a French peasant growing up in a time of war between England and France. When Joan heard what she believed to be instructions from the voices of angels, she did not hesitate to inspire and lead the French army to victory against English strongholds within France. She was by the Dauphin's side when he was crowned.*

Her quest was to see the right ruler in power to lead the people.

Yet at nineteen when she was captured by the English she was sentenced to be burned at the stake, accused of being a witch and heretic – lying about the voices of angels.

Now, if a citizen is ever acting questionably, they can simply be re-conditioned in a humane way.

| 25 |

– The Dreamer –

The board room was full to its limits with people crammed onto every perch and leaning against every wall space.

I was snug in V's hoodie and Mitch was tapping a silent tune on my knee, leaving little gold puffs where he tapped.

Cam Pendragon was seated opposite us, looking entirely uncomfortable and quite like his missing person adverts again. It was hard to believe how transformed his happiness as a free man had made him.

"Every Rogue station is now full beyond its capacity," Queenie was reporting to Jo. "We are sheltering the stars who heard Mitch's message, and their targets. But there are also large numbers of Ordinaries getting messages to us and being rescued around World daily. They no longer feel safe in the Leaders' hands above."

In just over a week our own Rogue base had become more like a crowded city.

Rooms had filled up as sometimes entire families or friend groups had been brought down, though nobody dwelling beneath the surface minded and resources did not seem strained. Instead, with such increasing numbers it felt like the Rogues were on the cusp of achieving progress. So many minds had already been changed even without new chips or updates.

"There are great numbers of dreams being brought to light," Queenie continued. "We are hearing of more dreamers who have new or old dreams to offer, and," she peered momentarily at Cam. "We can see a pattern of why all these dreams are surfacing now."

Cam's shoulders dropped, but I saw a number of Rogues with proud or more confident expressions standing taller in the room.

Many Rogues, like Will and even Queenie herself had now been matched up to stars who had arrived, searching for them. Out of my own team, Bear had been stopped in a passageway and told by a star that they knew him. As Beowulf – an ancient fighter for fairness, loyalty and the protection of the weak.

It seemed like Rogues had the right kind of dreams for this stage in time.

"We have gathered dreams of liberation and justice, dreams of rightful leadership, of wisdom – and dreams of a better World," Queenie finished calmly.

"Now, perhaps, we may also find a solution to our problems," Jo spoke up then. "Has research on Lili shown the way for how Ordinary people and Soldiers could survive without being hooked up to Leader power?" she asked Queenie.

Queenie's expression became apologetic then.

"Lili is one of a kind," Queenie explained. "Her creator did invent something that would allow people to think, to access power and knowledge, and to be safe from hacking. But he achieved this with Lili through invasive procedures. We have yet to discover a way that we could liberate people en-masse and without causing mayhem or discomfort." Queenie's eyes flickered to Cam again. "There is hope though, that if the right Leadership can be installed above, then there will be no need to disconnect people from Leader systems. Rather we could simply change the connection slightly so that people become *less* controlled. Then more minds, that do not focus only on Leader advantages, could be brought in on environmental issues."

Cam never made eye contact with anyone for the rest of the meeting, and somehow managed to be one of the first to leave as the packed room was dismissed.

I felt a twinge of worry over his reluctance to try to aid the World, until Mitch drew my focus.

"Let's not dwell on it all for tonight," Mitch pulled me up. "Instead, we'll make stir fry!"

And before long he was helping me to toss sizzling vegetables and to dice meat – the aroma of cooking food surrounding us.

I served the food into his miraculously appearing bowls while he set a miraculously appearing table under the starry roof, which was lighting the room warmly. I could hear him whistling the tune that he had been beating out on my knee earlier.

"Ready!" I called, feeling light hearted.

The bowls I had filled disappeared from the bench and

then reappeared on the table in front of him. The pan and all of the mess we had created had already vanished. "Ready," he agreed.

He pulled out a chair at the table and I crossed to take my seat.

Gazing at the steaming dish with anticipation, he was just about to take his own seat when a knock sounded at his door.

"Not ready." Mitch pouted.

"Michael," I heard Evangeline's snappy voice. "It's us."

"*Never* ready," Mitch slumped glumly. Then he grabbed our bowls and forks irritably. I left the table, which instantly seemed to have never existed, and sat on the couch as the normal lights came on in the room. He gave me my food with an apologetic expression.

"Is Jo with you?" he called out to Evangeline hopefully, spearing some meat on his own fork and not heading to the door.

"No."

Mitch sighed. "Butch or Aris?"

He had the air of one dreading the apocalypse.

"No. Just Cam and I!" she was growing impatient.

"Ok," he said with resignation, and the door opened automatically.

Another sofa appeared across from our couch, and Mitch took his spot beside me as I started to eat.

Evangeline crossed the room and seated herself on the other sofa, with Cam following unhappily behind her. He was even *more* defeated than he'd been in his missing person adverts now.

"We have a problem you can help us with," Evangeline told Mitch bluntly.

Mitch rolled his eyes. "Why don't you get straight to the point?"

"We've got to help Cam realise his dream," Evangeline went on, while the miserable young man sank down into his seat beside her.

"These things are getting more and more forced Eva," Mitch said. "And it may not do him any good. Cam just may not be in a life cycle where his spirit is ready yet."

Evangeline crossed her arms and sat back haughtily. "I've been drawn to him now for a reason."

Cam played with the hem of his jacket morosely. "I know Evangeline is right."

I put my now empty bowl aside to listen.

"It all fits too nicely. We need a legitimate Leader who can be accepted into power and make change happen. I just don't see how I can be it. Being away from the Leader culture has felt like the real dream come true, and following *our* leader down here."

In a surprisingly gentle way, Evangeline put her hand on Cam's.

"It would be up to you to create a *new* Leader culture. And, Jo was never meant to lead in the way a ruler does. Holding power is not in her spirit or journey. She seeks only to find the rightful and best leadership, and then to help it flourish. No matter the cost to herself."

"And this time Jeanne will see the goodness that results

from her actions, and receive only gratitude. Not further trials," Mitch asserted, leaning forward.

Evangeline regarded him thoughtfully, nodding.

"Jeanne?" I asked.

"Or Joan of Arc," Mitch affirmed.

Evangeline sniffed, almost proudly.

"She definitely doesn't want to rule?" Cam asked, disappointed.

"The Rogues don't wish to conquer and revolutionise the world. Just to heal it," Evangeline explained. "Having a rightful Leader who could make changes without first destroying everything is the miracle Jo has been waiting for."

Cam slumped, anguished. "It's all too perfect."

"What's really bothering you?" Mitch questioned.

Cam rubbed his creased brow agitatedly. "I left …" he grimaced up at us. "When I found out my mother, the Slayer, was dying. Precisely because I knew it was soon going to be my turn to step up."

Mitch let the air whistle out from between his teeth.

"Uthoria has depended on experimental technology to keep her alive, but there is only so much it can do. As she has become sicker, her grip on the World has grown tighter, and the World has become sicker too. I did not know that Soldiers were going to lose all free-will, or that stars and dreamers existed and would be hunted down to limit independent dreams," Cam went on. "But I am not surprised at her choices. I knew she wanted control over all things, just not how she would get it, or really why. And now, with her death approaching, the search for me has intensified. Not because she wants to be with me in her dying days – but simply because she wants her power to shift to someone in her bloodline, and to someone she thinks will realise her vision and weakly follow her way of ruling. I don't want to do that."

Mitch regarded him kindly. "Maybe we do need to help you to understand it all. Maybe we need to try to see your mother and connect with her mind, like when I reached out and saw all of the stars to contact them."

Cam was pale, but when Evangeline squeezed his hand, he nodded.

"She won't be aware of us?"

"I'll just try to lightly touch her mind and understand it," Mitch reassured him.

"Shall we join sand again?" Evangeline asked, pursing her lips and flicking her hair.

"No!" Mitch answered hastily, almost jerking back in his seat in case she planned to grab for him. "I should be able to reach out and find the Slayer without support. It's just one person."

When he was certain Evangeline was going to keep her hands to herself, the sand started to swirl about him, and his eyes became intently focused on it.

It became thicker, spinning in the space between our couches, and images began to play across the circling sand as if it were a screen.

We saw the surface World, where streets were sealed off, due to be erased and rebuilt to maximise space. We saw a new Artificial Air plant being built by bots. And hologram adverts for pet updates – a new bark control and toileting regulator on sale.

Then we saw the image of the same grand home that we

had occupied only days ago – the Pendragon mansion, which already appeared spotless again.

Our vision reached a window, and began to surge into a vast bedroom.

We all leaned forward, our eyes trained on the image of a woman resting in the bed in the middle of the sand projected room …

But none of us expected the sudden burst of flames that exploded outward from Mitch's sand, blowing us all back in our chairs.

Shock sucked my breath away, but when Mitch cried out in pain I launched over to try to protect him from whatever was happening. I helplessly watched as his face contorted, and when he opened his eyes – they flashed with flame.

"Hijacked," he wheezed.

I heard Evangeline hiss and I saw that the sand was still swirling between our couches, still burning. But now, instead of the image of Uthoria's bedroom, there was a sharply featured, inhuman face made of flames peering out from the sand at us.

"Who let *you* out?" Mitch half groaned, allowing himself to hang against the arm I had thrown out protectively across his chest. He was panting and his eyes were blazing as he focused on the sinister face. "Your job isn't in the physical world."

"Thanks to you," the voice was smouldering, though not unfriendly in its reply.

I recognised the voice, and I recognised the sharp features.

"Ohhhh wow," Cam gaped.

"And I'm only out here because I'm working toward the task you set me, Michael," the voice demurred. "To test, to push, to make people learn, and choose and grow."

"You don't normally hang out in dying ladies' bedrooms to fulfil your task," Mitch grimaced, passing his hands across his eyes so that the flames died out in them.

"This lady is different." The glittering eyes in the fiery sand narrowed. "She possesses the spirit that has animated some of the top dictators, conquerors and emperors through-out history. She threatens the process and disrupts the natural unfolding of my work. Her dream must be realised so that she stops. And moves on."

"Even so, you're not a star and she's not your dreamer," Evangeline snarled. "Why are you with her?"

"I may not be a star who can force her dream on her. But I am the one who claims all spirits. When they are ready. And with your help, Uthoria's will soon be ready." The face smiled a little. "I've simply been waiting with Uthoria, knowing that in this time you would inevitably seek her out, because you *must* send her soul to me if things are ever to progress."

I held Mitch more tightly — he had been right; an awful lot of dreams were being made to happen lately. Things were coming to a head. But the dream of a woman possessing such a power-hungry soul, may not come true sweetly.

"So you're 'helping' us out?" Mitch coughed, and smoke is-sued from between his lips. "You've burnt me, you know," he added accusingly.

"Nothing your heavenly fire did not already put you through," the voice was velvet. "And I'm so glad you went through that great burning trial. I knew you would find your way. And that the others would see your value."

The sharp eyes shifted to me next. "I also knew *you* would find your way."

I was speechless as the face drew a relishing breath in then.

"Ahhh, Persephone. How I loved you in the age we spent together. You knew me as Hades. I was loath to let your spirit go on to the next cycle when it was time. You would have been comforted and safe with me, for I cradle all spirits that come to me with utmost care."

"Well her spirit has moved on, mister clingy," Mitch said crossly.

"Yes, her spirit has found yours at last," the sharp lips curled. "And I would not have been able to keep her, because a spirit only finds peace in 'Hell', the Underworld, Heaven, the Elysian Fields – Shangri-La – when ready. When enlightened enough. Although," the face paused, stretching its way forward in the sand to peer at Mitch and I more closely. "Now, as I see you both together, I can see I shall not wait another lifetime before I will have the honour of tenderly caring for *both* of your spirits. You have become ready, in this lifetime."

I felt Mitch lean more heavily against my arm, straining forward with curiosity. "You mean …?"

"You have a spirit within you, too, Michael," the voice affirmed. "You have had your own journey, in preparation for the next."

"Return to the issue at hand," Evangeline cut in, demanding her own answers.

The intense gaze released Mitch and I from its power.

"I need Uthoria's soul so that I can continue my work and progressive cycles can resume more naturally. Perhaps Uthoria does not need a star to help her reach fulfilment. Perhaps she simply needs her son to help her realise her dream. He must be here, when she passes. But she has barely weeks left before her current body dies and her soul moves on to begin its destructive patterns again."

"Right. Understood, thank you," Evangeline replied curtly.

There was a pause as the eyes shifted back to Mitch. "I'll be seeing you, my friend."

"Soon?" Mitch asked with interest.

There was banging and shouting at the door to Mitch's apartment then, before Aris and Gabe came crashing in – coming face to face with the fiery projection of Death.

The sharp lips smiled at Mitch again, and then the sand burst into an inferno before disappearing.

I cradled Mitch as he gripped his head in pain.

"What in the blazes was that about?" Aris thundered.

Gabe was gasping, trying to get his breath back.

But Cam stood up resolutely. "I can't ignore my duty. And I certainly cannot ignore the Devil."

"Damned if you do, damned if you don't, some would say," Mitch agreed against my shoulder.

Excerpts from: The Collected Tales of Mythological and Historical Heroes

This is a first edition text, published by the World's third generation of great Leaders. Congratulations – you've purchased one of the last Leader approved hard copy texts!

On the subject of influential early historical figures:
** In this section people, lands and cities that are believed to have existed prior to the unification of World are mentioned.*

*King **Uther Pendragon**, described as being ruthless, 'giant-like', formidable, and supposedly even a dragon slayer, was father to the legendary King **Arthur Pendragon**.*

*Historians believed that Arthur's story was based on the exaggerated exploits of a great Roman commander in Britain. According to the legends, Arthur's reign began when he withdrew a previously immovable magical sword – **Excalibur** – from where it had been buried in stone.*

*Arthur protected his people, treated his knights as equal to himself, and was known as a chivalrous, beloved figure who sought to unite divided tribes in his idyllic kingdom of '**Camelot**'.*

The great kingdom, Camelot, was peaceful and prosperous. A symbol of a utopian, perfect society, and a goal for future societies to work towards. The kind of World our great Leaders surely seek to establish for us.

| 26 |

– The Star –

"This was a great idea," Lili told Dora Cate as she expertly maneuvered her way around the Rogue gymnasium. "I needed this. I'm not used to sitting back, leisurely waiting for scientific breakthroughs."

"Yeah," Curtis puffed and sweated. "Thanks so much for the invite to a 'fun team exercise'."

"You're welcome!" Dora ducked as Lili sent Cam hurtling across the gym then.

"So, Cam," Dora addressed the currently less than elegant flying figure. "Do you see now that if you legitimately take power, it will be quite helpful?"

"Ooof," he replied as he hit the padded wall and bounced off it to the floor.

"Apart from being the picture of roadkill right now," I remarked to Dora as Cam picked himself up. "I think Cam seems rather restored, and resigned to the idea of Leadership. Maybe he's ready to be our knight in shining armour."

Dora nodded in satisfaction and lifted herself up onto the

top of some monkey bars, easily skipping her way over them before coming to a stop over Theus' head.

Theus was sitting cross-legged on some mats, eagerly pouring over Lili's book as Dora now swung down to hang over him.

"Evangeline has talked me into realising –" Cam began to reply, and then dived sideways as Curtis and Junior, who had charged at Lili together, both flew into the wall now too.

Cam dusted himself off again. "– That the reason I joined the Rogues was to help the World. And that I can only really make a great difference if I do inherit the power."

"WAAHHHOOOOAAH!"

Will also landed on the pile that was Curtis and Junior.

"Evangeline's right for once," I grimaced, resting my elbow on a squishy cube and giving up my struggle to get out of a giant foam pit. "You could be the *ultimate* Rogue – breaking free of what's gone before."

"Mitch, you know that pit was designed for endurance and dive training," Dora said as she swung upside down. "You're not meant to stay in it."

I puffed some foam away from my face. "I am enduring it. And it isn't by choice that I'm stuck," I told her primly. "All of my kicking to swim out of these foam chunks has made no difference."

" 'Least we've got the Leader problem sorted," Will panted as he jogged past my pit. "But Ned and Queenie are having no luck finding ways to reverse the past Leaders' control measures." Will paused to duck into a commando crawl to grab a handful of beanbag missiles. "And it sounds like the Slayer's time is running out."

Cam's blonde head appeared as he stuck it up from behind a padded hide-out. "They've got until the death knell, so to speak, to figure it out," he commented a little sickly. "It's only then that she will release her power drive – the Excalibur chip, to pass on her reign. I won't go to her until just before it happens because I'll surely need Evangeline with me, which will draw the assassin Soldiers. And the other Leaders have to be there as witnesses for the transition of power, but because they know Uthoria's like an absolute rock, they'll only gather when they think she really is on the cusp of giving Excalibur up."

"I think the Soldiers will need to be freed, or cured first for things to really work," Dora speculated. "Or the stars will keep being hunted and going up in smoke, and if you and Evangeline are caught then Uthoria will die but she won't be truly gone."

"Not to mention I'll assume Leadership with little actual power if the whole World and all of the Soldiers stay as she's programmed them." Cam scaled and slid down a padded slope. "She always wanted to set things up so all I had to do was be a puppet following already established rules."

"YIPEE!"

I sank further as Curtis belly flopped into the foam pit.

"It'll all happen in the right time," I reassured Cam, clawing foam lumps away from my face.

"Hey …" Curtis whined, only now realising that he wasn't getting anywhere as he tried to scramble out of our soft, lumpy jail. "No, Junior, don't!"

Junior did a spectacular flip into the foam and disappeared beside Curtis, while we both got sucked in a little deeper.

In moments I heard Junior's muffled complaints – and then a very quiet and indignant: "I'm stuck."

"Welcome," I told Curtis. "All we can do is wait for the end with as much dignity as possible."

"Or you could always fly out," Theus remarked helpfully, putting the book aside to join the disjointed group conversation.

"Jo wouldn't be happy to have sand all through her training course," Dora grinned. "There are no high tech drills in here, but she's proud of it."

"You know," Will began, and then dodged a missile bean bag that Cam had pelted at his head. "I've never seen Queenie so frustrated. She's really at a loss. She even told her star to 'shoosh' as he tried to give her a pep talk before."

"I've definitely seen Ned this grumpy," Cam grinned. "But perhaps not so desperate for solutions. His star has happily stayed out of his way on a swivel chair at the back of the lab."

"Ohhhhhhh, I don't know *why* they're so tense," Dora interjected sarcastically. "It's just the *World* counting on them to meet a deadline." She swung down from the bars to land in Theus' lap.

"Beeear," Curtis appealed to the hulking man, who was preoccupied with watching Jana take on the indestructible Lili.

Lili finally seemed more than mildly entertained, rolling up the sleeves of her favourite hoodie – V's.

"Come onnn Bear, help a buddy out."

There had still been no sign of Junior resurfacing, apart from some jostling of the foam above where he'd landed.

"We're trapped like flies," Curtis cried pitifully, and Bear sighed, turning away from the action as Jana began whipping around Lili like a graceful feline; actually managing to send Lili down onto the mats.

Bear obligingly reached into the pit to fish Curtis and myself out of our prison, plucking us free as if we were weightless. Then he came up with the handful that was Junior, who was amusingly disgruntled as he was lowered back onto solid ground by the collar.

"Thanks man," Curtis said, pulling foam bits from his clothes.

And I was just sitting myself out on the sidelines to watch Lili and Jana, when I saw Lili unexpectedly freeze – turning pale and frowning. She squeezed her eyes shut.

My heart stopped.

There was a sudden building of electrical sound that seemed to be coming from Lili herself. As if all of the tech within her body was firing itself up audibly.

"What the f –" Curtis' voice was drowned out by the noise.

"I'm getting a *call*," Lili yelled in both surprise and warning. Because, who would be calling an out of range, and also totally disconnected, number?

Who would be able to?

And why would it be creating such a wild surge in Lili's power?

Totally calm, but without opening her eyes, Lili scooped Jana up and sent her flying to Bear like a spear. He caught

Jana just as Lili's eyes flew open – emitting an explosion of light that also burst from every design on her body, blinding us all.

The light blew outward from Lili with a pulse of energy that threw me back against the padded wall, and my vision budded with fireworks.

Squinting, I saw the globes around the gym flickering erratically, but Lili directed her brilliant line of sight toward a length of the wall that was covered in dance hall style mirrors.

The onslaught of light took form against the mirrors, and I gasped as I realised her gaze was showing a projection of someone else's face.

The person's face was close up, dirty, stubbled and sweaty. Pressure was written across every enlarged feature.

"Lil?" the person whispered in joy. The whisper was so loud that I gritted my teeth, but Lili kept the image steady.

In fact, I had never seen such emotion on Lili's face as she stared at the man, and I felt a momentary pang like a rabbit punch to the chest, similar to what jealousy was meant to be like.

"Lili, my miracle girl," the strained man said hoarsely. "Lucky I know your private number! I've tried for so long, but I don't have much to work with here. They only let me use tools when I'm supervised."

"… V?" Lili breathed – still in disbelief.

"I don't have much time," V's voice sounded more frantic now. "I'm being held at The Centre. The experimental section. I want that lunch you promised me. And that life you promised me. And my hoodie." V; Lili's creator, managed a smile over the fact the she was wearing it. "Lili … I need your help."

"I promise, this time you'll get it," Lili answered so fiercely that the transmission crackled. "We need you down here. I'm coming to get you back."

V nodded. "Knew you'd say that. See you soon." His eyes darted to the side, and the image cut out.

The mirrors were mirrors once more, the lights sputtered and then stopped flickering, and Lili blinked while we all remained stunned.

"Your team is behind you, Lil," Curtis at last announced. His hair was blown back as if he'd been in a wind tunnel.

"If we have the Grand Techie to help Queenie," Dora began excitedly, "then we may have just found the elusive second part to our solution." She crawled out of the shell-shocked Theus' lap.

I shakily made my way over to Lili, and when I put my arm around her I felt a trace of static emanating between us.

"He's alive," she remarked with wonder.

"Remember what I said about Virgil?" I grinned. "How his dream was for a wholesome world? Well that's alive too."

She gave me an energised hug before she turned to the others, who were scraping themselves off the walls.

"How soon until we're all ready?" she asked. "I've got an idea."

Excerpts from: The Collected Tales of Mythological and Historical Heroes

This is a first edition text, published by the World's third generation of great Leaders. Congratulations – you've purchased one of the last Leader approved hard copy texts!

On the subject of influential early historical figures:

** In this section people, lands and cities that are believed to have existed prior to the unification of World are mentioned.*

Beowulf *possessed the strength of a bear. He saved King Hrothgar's Scandinavian kingdom from the murderous attacks of a creature called the Grendel. The Grendel was a bitter creature who hated joy and had long attacked King Hrothgar's people to keep them from happiness. Beowulf strove against the Grendel until the creature was so miserable itself, that it died. Beowulf's strength of spirit allowed him to overcome this challenge, just as our great Leaders strive every day to rid our modern World of any 'Grendels' that may jeopardise our carefully regulated happiness.*

| 27 |

– The Dreamer –

"Seriously, I want that jacket," Curtis whispered from where he and Junior were waiting.

"I know," Junior groaned. "You've been fawning over it for weeks."

"It's not practical attire for action," Evangeline disapproved, glaring from a short distance away where she waited with her own team.

I glanced over my shoulder at Mitch, but the jacket had vanished, and he was smiling at Evangeline innocently.

"You look fit and ready," I said, and he grinned, his face lit with the dim red tunnel light.

"I've been blessed aesthetically," he told me, his grin not faltering as I swatted a suddenly appearing cigarette out of his fingers. He was only doing it to annoy the other stars.

"But *only* aesthetically," Evangeline muttered, her voice almost blending with the humming of the wires in the tunnel.

Bear and Jana adjusted the sights on their lasers beside me as our team waited for Will to ready our portal. Will's star, Raph, watched on, visibly nervous to be playing even a small role in our venture after having only recently escaped the World above.

"I just can't believe that after all these years of being a holy presence, a muse, a classical entity of enlightenment…" Raph jiggled from one leg to the other with jitters. "In this century I'm only good for bait."

"You get used to feeling like a target," Mitch comforted him with overdone warmth, and Raph stopped bouncing on the balls of his feet, assuming an awkward expression.

I observed Dora Cate's team, with Aris, Curtis, Junior and Ned waiting behind her as she readied her portal.

Cam was feeling the pressure as Evangeline watched over his shoulder with Jo, Gabriel and the Rogue that Mitch had called Geronimo waiting to go.

We were all only small distances away from each other in the tunnel, but the portals we would be using were mostly going to be spaced out around the outside of the base V was being held in.

Dora and Aris would be letting their team pop up on the outside perimeter of the base to stage an attack, but they would be keeping the portal open for a speedy escape, and Cam and Evangeline would do the same for the other 'attacking' team. The noise making, the open portals, as well as the stars, would all serve as assassin distractions from my team and the real action.

We would be surfacing in the interior part of the base. Will and Raph would be letting us out in the corridors we'd estimated V would most likely be being kept in, but then they would shut the portal and create a new one beyond the base to await our escape.

"Good to go," Dora called.

"Ready," Cam agreed.

"Let's do it!" Will affirmed.

And three portals opened simultaneously.

I grabbed hold of Bear, Jana and Mitch to keep them upright, before we were sucked out into surface existence.

"Good luck!" I heard Will's snatched whisper before the gateway into the virtualtree sealed shut and he and Raph disappeared.

We were now in the middle of a long, grey corridor, lined with sterile, cool lights and endless doors and rooms. It was silent and deserted in the early morning hours, but security would pick up on us soon enough.

Jana nodded to me, her eyes glittering, before she and Bear quickly turned to check their side of the long corridor. She ran swiftly while Bear loped along beside her like his animal namesake and they quickly scanned each room with a device that Queenie had given them to compensate for their Brainwaves.

If Bear and Jana found nothing in their wing, they were to move further through the complex, create a disturbance away from us, and then make their way out to the neighbouring building where Will's portal would be open and waiting.

I pulled Mitch along beside me, running the opposite way and using my own internal scanners without issue.

"Every door's the same," Mitch whispered. "None of them look like a holding bay."

"Tricky," I agreed, scanning yet another empty office as we moved by quickly.

Keeping up our pace, we passed into a new corridor and found more deserted rooms.

"Duck!" I warned when we rounded on a window in one wall; a surveillance office manned by two Soldiers.

Mitch was still running and registering my warning, so I pulled him to land forward on his chest and sent him sliding along the shiny floor past the window counter.

I instead lifted off to shoot soundlessly over the window, but I registered one of the Soldiers asking: "What's that outside the north wing?"

I checked my internal clock in the corner of my vision. That would be Junior, Curtis and Ned, rigging up some serious techsplosives to breach one of the walls outside the complex.

Any moment now Jo, Gabriel and Geronimo would also be making all hell break loose outside the front gates.

I landed beside Mitch in time to pick him up as he finished sliding along the corridor. I sent a pulse of power through the digi-lock of one automatic office door, and pulled him inside the empty room, just as a tremendous explosion sounded from the direction that Jana and Bear had taken.

Bear had promised that he'd rigged up something spectacular to really make everyone at The Centre's lives miserable, and he'd definitely succeeded in making the very foundations of the unsavoury building shake.

Instantly an ear-splitting alarm sounded and a vibration of what would normally be intruder-crippling lasers rippled in an invisible wave throughout all of the corridors.

I felt the wave travelling outwards like aftershock quakes, spreading onward to disable anyone not registered to be in the building. However none of my team would be affected without a full Brainwave line.

Stunned, but on high alert, the Soldiers down our hall burst out of their office, barking transmissions to every other Soldier in the vicinity while the building shook and the alarms continued as if World War Seven had begun.

The sterile white lights had turned to angry, urgent amber, throbbing on and off while the Soldiers now dashed past our office.

"Oh my Lord, that sound," Mitch tried to block his ears. "And those fissure lines weren't there before," he eyed the plaster.

"Bear said he had something good planned," I replied, and grabbed Mitch by the elbow to drag him back out and down the corridor, scanning the rooms we passed hurriedly.

I pushed him against the wall when we rushed into the next corridor, right into the path of five new Soldiers jogging our way. But with five blasts they found themselves dropping into unconsciousness and I tugged Mitch to get moving again.

"Made it to Curtis," Bear rumbled, risking a transmission now that secrecy was pointless. "About fifty Soldiers on our tails."

"We've convinced ours that we're trying to break in," Junior added, panting his own transmission. "I've counted twenty here. We won't last long."

"Assassins converging on the gates too!" Curtis reported what he could see of Jo's team in the distance.

"Don't wait," I warned quietly. "Get back to the portals before they're attacked and have to be closed."

Then Mitch and I skidded to a halt. The corridor had opened up to a massive, glass wall that looked into a laboratory.

Lines of Soldiers stood guard around the inside of the lab, with its other three walls made of concrete.

An impenetrable door of steel, like the entrance to a vault, was barred off at the end of the room.

"Seriously," Mitch gaped. "He's in there, isn't he?"

"I'll take the Soldiers, you take the doors."

" 'K," he answered weakly. "First door looks easier."

The first door was built into the glassed wall. Hesitantly, Mitch reached out and pushed, hardly daring to hope.

And it swung open without resistance.

Mitch's eyebrows shot up. "Very eas– "

All of the Soldiers moved toward us as one.

"Right." Mitch's eyebrows were straight back down.

And then we were both sprinting into the room.

Mitch ducked, dodged, and even flew his way past snatching hands, tearing through the crowd.

I caught the wrist of one Soldier who seized at Mitch's white T-shirt. I pulled the Soldier's arm in a circle so that the Soldier whirled off his feet in a somersault. But I didn't wait for him to hit the polished concrete, reaching for the next opponent and sending that one flipping backwards with a jab to the collarbone.

It only took a moment for me to be swimming in hard, unyielding Soldier bodies as they swarmed me, and life became a blurred demonstration of offensive combat.

Whirling, blocking, thrusting, jabbing, breaking, jarring; I threw them off one by one, and one by one they came back to converge again.

My own body burned with the power of my designs, and I was scorching my opponents, but their overwhelming numbers made it hard to see. Even hard to breathe.

I'd lost sense of where Mitch and the vault door were, and could only risk releasing contained explosions to stun the teeming Soldiers for fear of hitting my star with anything bigger.

I broke away from a strangle hold but felt the fast stab of pain as a swipe got under my guard to hit the soft skin between my ribs. I twisted to keep that superhuman hand from delving deeper, but my breath sucked in and I was slower to punch a launching Soldier out of the air as she came at my face. Her boot hit me in the cheek and my eye felt as if it was going to pop free of its socket.

Blinking in pain, I was tackled to the ground by a handful of charging opponents and we skidded backwards until my head cracked against a massive glass tank – a roof height, aquarium-like chamber in the corner of the room.

I kicked two opponents off me and propelled the others back momentarily with a stronger shock of power. Then I scrambled up against the tank, pausing in surprise at how freezing the surface of the glass was. The watery substance inside glowed oddly blue and sent shivery chills along my arm, despite the thickness of the glass.

"Mitch!" I yelled desperately. "You need lift off!"

I hoped he'd heard me as I hurriedly lit my fists up like electrified boxing gloves.

And even as I punched through the thick vat, feeling the glass smash inwards around my knuckles, I was seized around the middle, by my shoulders, my arms, and ankles – weight landing on my back and dragging me down.

As my bloody fists were wrenched free of the glass the water immediately surged outward, shattering the rest of the tank and engulfing me in a freezing wipe out.

I had not expected the severity of the cold of that startling, glowing substance, but my chest constricted and my head pounded as the bursting wave slammed over my body and stole my air.

The Soldiers gripping me were dashed away like dolls but I pushed myself upright, and dragged my way forward, seeing a gushing pipe at the back of the tank.

Staggering, I took hold of the pipe and wrenched it from its socket, unleashing a violently surging fount of shooting, icy water that blasted over my opponents.

I choked on a bitter mouthful of fluid myself, feeling its exact journey as it ran down my throat and chilled my lungs. My fingers purpled and I shook my head clear, turning to duck under the spouting jet but nearly stumbling with how agonisingly stiff my frozen legs were.

Taking gulping breaths, I noticed that the 'easy' first door had swung shut, and it was now as if we were all in some kind of nightmarish winter themed fishbowl.

I felt my heat regulation tech sputtering almost uselessly as the water level fast rose to my calves, covering the concrete floor like a glowing pool of toxic nuclear spill. Lying in that toxic spill were the sprawled bodies of the Soldiers, all thrown about the room as if a tech grenade had gone off.

They were twitching and shuddering with the cold, and I slowly lowered my hands into the water, ignoring the way that they curled into throbbing claws at the iciness.

I set my fists alight again and sent torrents of electrical currents through the water. They snaked outward from where I knelt like electric eels, speeding toward each weakly splashing Soldier.

There was thrashing and there were cries of pain, before all of my former comrades laid still; stunned.

Gnashing my teeth together with the effort just to move, I rose and turned back to the remains of the gushing pipe. I grabbed a bloody hold of the jagged, broken spout and twisted it closed.

"Bravo!" Mitch's voice brought me back to the moment, and I turned to find that he was hovering, completely dry, beside the door.

The door had gold bursts and black scorch marks all over it.

"I had this thing glowing red-hot, but when the water touched it, the whole lot steamed and froze. I think one good smash now and we'll break through!"

I nodded, shivering as I registered the desperate yells of my team in the back of my mind. First Jana, then Curtis. There were the sounds of ammo rounds, techsplosions and running feet. They were all pulling out. All of the teams had made it back to the portals – just. But they couldn't wait for us any longer. We would have to get our own way out, and find shelter until they could track us and come back.

"You're a mess," Mitch said with concern.

I waded my way toward him, moving through glowing

blue liquid and floating, still bodies – and pulling up Soldiers in danger of drowning to drape them over any available perch.

Gathering my strength, I slammed my icy boot into the imposing door, and was relieved as it cracked and disintegrated into nothingness.

The water lapped its way into the large, unlit holding-room beyond the doorway, and sitting on a bed against the far wall was a dark figure with goggly eyes.

"About time!" V crowed excitedly. He was gripping a sheet from the bed that he'd made into a knapsack full of odds and ends, and he at once made to jump up for escape.

"Wait," I warned him. "Don't touch the water."

V seemed to register the water in the darkness for the first time, and the smile lessened on his face. "You shouldn't be touching that water either!" he scolded. "It's an experimental crippling agent for preserving Leader bodies – stopping all cells and organs from decaying, or working. The Slayer ordered its design, but it was a failure, and so strong that I accidentally corrupted all of the water in this wing."

"Lucky I gave all my attackers an electric shock of energy then," I grimaced and stepped aside so that V could see the Soldier bodies strewn everywhere in the lab as the water ebbed away.

"You will have saved their lives," V told me, standing up on his bed in readiness. "But this is dangerous even for you."

"I'll heat myself back up when we get out of here and my designs dry off," I leaned in the doorway, shivering. "But we have to get out of here first. The other teams have had to retreat, so all of the previously distracted Soldiers out there will soon be in here."

I looked to Mitch then. "Will you do the honours?"

Mitch left the shadows to levitate his way to V, who gaped at him in admiration as he saw my companion clearly.

"Star boy," V stated in wonder and in greeting, taking Mitch's proffered hand enthusiastically.

I splashed back to the door in the glass wall and peered into the corridor.

The lights had returned to normal and the alarm was off. But with the external problem resolved, the Soldiers I'd forced offline in the lab would not go unnoticed. We would be being hunted soon.

I gestured for Mitch and V to touch down when we reached dry floor beyond the lab, and they followed as I led us quickly down the hall, straining my stinging ears for sound and searching frantically for an out.

We had to leave the heart of the building and move toward where there would be windows overlooking the city.

I winced at the tightness in my chest as we rushed onward, but at last managed a throbbing, chapped smile as we rounded another corner.

"Thank your lucky stars," I gasped to Mitch as we spotted a window at the end of the corridor, which offered a view of a still dark morning sky.

Moving faster, I stripped off my jacket, which was somehow stiffening, and wrapped it around my damaged hands as we reached the glass separating us from freedom.

"I'll do it," Mitch quickly cut in, getting ready to magic the window away.

"As soon as you do anything to this glass, the alarms and the chase will be back on," I told Mitch, my teeth chattering and my energy visibly flickering in my designs.

"You're shaking," Mitch commented uneasily. "Want me to get my non-appropriate jacket to reappear?"

"I'll be fine. You two fly together as soon as the window's open, and I'll follow. We have to get a few streets away at the very least."

I *was* trembling, but I didn't give myself a chance to think about it. I nodded at Mitch.

He obediently turned the window to a falling sheet of sand, and the siren at once screeched back to life as if this time signalling World War Eight.

I dropped my jacket, which had now hardened completely, while Mitch obediently pulled V out with him and began hurtling across the dark sky.

I jumped so my saturated boots were on the sill, but put a hand out to catch at the frame while my breath wheezed in my chest and my heart ached.

Then I heard a laser blast – before it hit the back of my shoulder with a thud, like a shove in the back. And I cursed myself loudly as I toppled forward in a freefall, half skidding and half sliding down the smooth building until my frozen fingers found a hold on one of the gigantic robotic window cleaners.

The massive arm was slowly running down the length of the building, and I winced as I jerked to a stop with a grunt.

It felt like shards of ice had pierced my lungs as I caught

my breath and pushed off from the complex, and my designs sputtered to life to catch me mid-air.

My vision flickered and then refocused as I glanced back to see that Soldiers were sprinting down the hall and clamouring towards the window, but they got smaller as I got further away.

I caught up to Mitch and V as I'd promised, and we swooped down to get lost amongst the dark streets – jogging across stretches of fancy Ordinary apartment block lawns while my limbs began to deaden and I fought desperately to stay upright.

Just stay up, I told myself.

Up.

Excerpts from: The Collected Tales of Mythological and Historical Heroes

This is a first edition text, published by the World's third generation of great Leaders. Congratulations – you've purchased one of the last Leader approved hard copy texts!

On the subject of influential early historical figures:
** In this section people, lands and cities that are believed to have existed prior to the unification of World are mentioned.*

Sir Isaac Newton *was an English scientist of great brilliance. He gave the World an understanding of motion and gravity, and is rumoured to have had an epiphany about these things while watching an apple fall from the tree he was seated under. In some accounts he was hit on the head by this apple, though these accounts seem like wild exaggeration for the purpose of telling a more engaging story.*

Sir Isaac Newton made it clear that what goes up must come down.

| 28 |

- The Star -

My heart jolted in my chest as Lili went down.

I cried out as she dropped to the grass and V and I skidded to a halt beside her.

"This is bad!" V moaned. "That stuff was entirely experimental. Meant to suspend life."

"She's frozen," I whispered as I sat her up.

Her skin was so pale as to be almost blue in the silvery moonlight.

"We've got to heat her up!" V replied urgently. "And we have to get her inside somewhere before we're spotted."

I threw her chilled arm around my neck and scooped my own arm under her legs to lift her, hurrying toward the dark outline of the nearest building.

"I can't get us into this skyscraper without setting off any alarms or being scanned," V whispered anxiously. "I don't have the right tools."

"I can magic away some glass?" I offered, thinking rapidly.

V shook his head. "Sensors."

"Right. Well I'll fly us around the apartments. There's

bound to be an open balcony door," I suggested quickly. "And I can send anyone inside into deep dreams."

"Go," V nodded worriedly, squinting up at the building's great height. "Come back for me as quick as you can."

There was a sound similar to the humming of drones or jets, and we both pressed ourselves fearfully against the wall and into the shadows. An arrowhead formation of Soldiers pelted across the slowly lightening clouds – for now assuming we were still flying, and searching for us above ground level.

"Wish me luck," I grunted to V the moment they had passed – quickly launching Lili and I upwards to soar past level after level of closed balcony doors.

Lili wasn't even moving with faint shivers anymore and I held her close, frantically circling the building now for any doors I had missed.

"Please God, Goddess, Allah, Buddha, Biame, Breged, HaShem, Yahweh, Raab, Jupiter, Zeus, Ra, Shiva, Vishnu, and Brahma, Fate, Powers that Be, Universe … Please, please, please under any name …"

I zipped past it in a whiz, but my heart jumped and I jolted us to a stop before reversing us back.

"Yes! Thankyouthankyouthankyou!"

I rushed us to the one balcony with an open door and quickly, gently lowered Lili onto the ledge.

"Geeze!" V nearly jumped out of his skin as I zoomed back down to him and hoisted both him and his bed sheet full of goodies up to the ledge.

We had barely touched down beside our fallen Soldier before I heard the disbelieving intake of breath from the room inside.

"What in the World…" a female's voice came from a dark bedroom adjoining the balcony.

I was just getting a good handful of sandyman dust ready, when a young, immaculately groomed – despite having just been woken – woman peered out at us from the door.

A beautifully manicured hand flew to perfectly glossed lips as she gazed at her balcony floor in horror.

"Is that … *Lili?*" she asked with wide mascara-d eyes. "Bring her in!"

We didn't wait to be told twice, and I swiftly lifted Lili again, carrying her through an expansive bedroom to a luxurious chaise lounge.

"You know Lili?" V asked sharply, pulling the gossamer curtains across the balcony doors as the sun started to break over the horizon.

Then I recognised the young woman as if from another time. I'd seen this woman with Lili on the first day I'd laid eyes on my fateful new dreamer in a café.

"I was Lili's Regular buddy … before she disappeared. I'm Tiff." Our host pulled a lace trimmed kimono about herself, eyeing us more closely.

Her face flared prettily with shock again as she recognised me. "You're the superstar from the café!" she gushed, flapping a hand at me excitedly. "I should've known you'd be trouble. You've made her go Rogue!"

V pressed a hand to Lili's forehead, and then put his fingers to her pulse, looking sick as he did so.

"Her lips are blue," Tiff said, coming closer to Lili. "And … is that blood?"

I rushed to lever Lili up on an angle, and V cursed as we saw a palm sized, rent open blast in her shoulder. She was so cold that the blood flowed from it only sluggishly.

"Oh wow," Tiff sank down to the plush carpet shakily. "I don't have any second-skin patches for something that nasty."

"Grab whatever you've got, it'll do until we leave," V told her, positioning Lili on her side. Tiff scuttled out of the bedroom to find her 'second skins'.

I turned in search of a blanket for Lili, but stopped short when I found two gorgeous Adonis's asleep in the middle of the bed, with a small space between them for where Tiff had been. I quickly threw some sand at the sleeping beauties to keep them that way.

"Don't mind them," Tiff rushed back in with a few packets of gauze. "They're heavy sleepers."

"Heavier now," I commented.

V hurried to tear open the packets, and one by one pressed each piece of skin coloured gauze to Lili's shoulder, overlapping them to cover all of the torn flesh. I watched as the material seemed to attach to her skin as if it were real scar tissue sealing the wound.

"I'm glad you haven't woken them, actually," Tiff told me then. "Drew has a real thing for delicious people. And frankly, I'm finding you overwhelmingly delicious myself."

I sidled awkwardly back to Lili, who looked no better.

"The bleeding wasn't our real worry," V said tensely. "She's being frozen to death. Her organs will start to shut down soon."

"I thought the liquid was meant to suspend life and pause death," I winced.

"The liquid was too good at suspending life," he replied flatly.

"Well you should get her out of those frozen clothes," Tiff cut in. "And put her in hot water and steam. Get her into my Biobeauty."

"She's literally out cold, that would drown her," V rejected the idea, shaking his head.

Tiff put a perfect hand on her gorgeous hip. "*I am a specialist.* There will be no drowning under this technician's control."

Obeying the petite lemon-blonde commander's assertive gaze, I quickly lifted Lili again, and brought her to a modern bathroom.

In seconds Tiff was hustling me back out. "I'll take it from here."

The automatic door slid shut on my nose, cutting me off from my dreamer.

I heard some technological sounds and movements, before a perfumed aroma and a cloud of steam issued from under the door.

I paced the hallway while V hugged himself comfortingly and leaned against the wall to wait.

Precious minutes passed before the door opened and Tiff leaned out of the sweetly smelling room.

"Alright, she's warm and dry. But I don't think it was strong enough," Tiff stepped aside to let us in, and I found Lili laying on the bench of a machine that reminded me of a large, old style solarium.

Despite the bruises across her cheekbone and eye, she

looked like heaven – wearing fresh combat clothes, and even her hair and nails were now styled. It was as if she was just sleeping.

"She's still too cold. The heat couldn't reach deeply enough," V agreed, rushing to check her signs of life. "She's not breathing," he gulped tensely. And then: "her heart has stopped."

"No!" Tiff's long-lashed eyes were horrified. "Please, let me alert the life saver bots. They arrive in seconds. No one dies like this anymore."

"We're all dead if she's scanned and found," V had drained of colour.

I wasn't paying attention to them anymore. Something inside me was burning, and I determinedly stepped around them, pressing V out of the way.

"Woah," he said when he saw me, quickly falling back to clear the space.

"Heavenly fire," I told him with a frown of focus.

I could feel the heat sparking in my core, igniting in my blood, colouring my vision and lashing at my airways.

I thanked the universe as the agonising fire grew to rage in every capillary, and danced through every cell – my molecular makeup becoming flames that roared and tore beneath the surface.

And then I knelt down, placed my lips on Lili's, and gave her the kiss of life.

Something likely unheard of in this technological age.

I allowed golden, healing heat to pour from my soul and into hers. Spreading the burning warmth into her core and outward to her extremities.

"What in the World ..." Tiff whispered once more in uncertainty.

Then I put the heel of my palm on Lili's chest, my other hand on top with interlocked fingers. And I didn't just use my body weight to compress her chest, I used the golden heat in my hands to enfold her heart in warmth.

Her body shifted with my motions – and every part of her radiated with blinding light that ran through each of her designs.

I felt it.

I felt the beat beneath my hands as I jolted her back to life.

I heard her draw in a massive breath of air.

And I pulled her into my arms as her eyes flashed open.

They glanced about wildly until they took in my face. Then the tension left her body and she slumped into me. She reached an arm up to hug around my neck in grateful relief, still gulping in oxygen.

"You're ok," I told her softly. "I've got you."

I leaned my forehead against hers as she closed her eyes in shocked exhaustion.

Excerpts from: The Collected Tales of Mythological and Historical Heroes

This is a first edition text, published by the World's third generation of great Leaders. Congratulations – you've purchased one of the last Leader approved hard copy texts!

On the subject of influential discoveries:

It was found long ago that radiation from overexposure to our daily technology, like our microwaves, holograms and screens, can cause headaches, depression, anxiety, memory issues, sleeplessness and cancers.

However a World referendum in 3034 proved that humanity could not accept life without risky technologies. It was decided that a life without tech was no life at all, and risking side effects was worth it.

As a result, the Sciences put their focus into finding positive solutions to either protect against or use radiation waves constructively. One solution was for radio-waves to become a way of transmitting healing or numbing vibes or messages to combat mental health problems usually caused by the same waves.

Leaders have found this development to be very effective for helping all people to remain calm and tranquil.

| 29 |

– The Dreamer–

"Lili?"

I woke in a dark room, laying on a strange bed, and aching all over.

I pressed a hand to my eyes and squeezed them closed for a moment, trying to work out what had woken me.

I drew a shuddering breath and propped myself up on my elbows, wincing at the tightness in my chest and the ripping feeling in my shoulder.

I could vaguely remember having seen Tiff. She'd been kicking two terribly sleepy men out of her bed on my behalf, and I'd groggily realised that one was the headphones guy from our Soldiers and Regulars course.

Then I hadn't woken again until …

"Lil," the voice came again, more insistently.

"I'm here," I rasped.

"I can't see you," Curtis scolded. "And I've been trying to reach you. You ok?"

"Alive," I answered honestly. "Just no mirror handy."

"Alright, can you send co-ordinates through?"

"Give us half an hour," I managed. "Then I'll send some. We'll have to move so the person hiding us doesn't get hurt."

"Half an hour it is," he replied amiably. And I was relieved by his vibrant tones. Nobody else could have been too badly hurt.

"Thanks." I cut the transmission and forced myself to sit up completely. I felt like I'd been to hell and back.

Wincing, I limped my way from the bed to the door, leaning against the frame to get my breath.

"Oh Lili!" Tiff gushed at once, looking resplendent in her sleepwear as she perched on a cushy couch. Then she turned to beam at Mitch. "You sure are one angelic defibrillator. I've never seen someone literally get kissed better before."

"You finally nabbed Drew." I managed a smile.

"And yet I kicked him out for you!" she teased. "Davey too. What a true friend I am."

I grimaced in return. "But allowing me to be here is putting you at risk. I'm sorry not to be a better friend, or protector, myself."

Tiff waved a hand at me. "I knew what I was doing when I took you in. I've seen your face on nearly every screen I've come across." Then she took on the more dreamy expression I was used to. "And Drew and Davey aren't just good for sleeping with – they've opened my mind. Honestly, Drew's not Rogue, but he's definitely anti Leader and invasive technology. Drew actually convinced me to reprogram my Biobeauty machines at work to be mostly manual and limited in Brainwave control. Now my clients are the least brainwashed people I know. They walk out saying their heads feel clearer. Turns out Leaders have stepped up using all Biobeauties – in salons and homes – to emit Leader commissioned additives and emotions. Even screenwalls and holograms are doing it full time as people pass them. It's got worse ever since more of us civvies have gone Rogue."

"That's interesting," V tapped his chin thoughtfully – reclining amongst the cushions of his chair. "Lili is the key to all my lost data. Now we just need to spread it to everyone else. Perhaps I could use the Leaders' strategy against them. Use already existing emissions to influence the already existing files within people. I could undo all of the Slayer's control – using surface tech to send out messages and change mechanisms in everyone's Brainwaves."

"They wouldn't feel a thing?" Mitch asked.

"It wouldn't be a total overhaul like Lili was. They would just be switched from complete public control to a more private, individual mindset," he answered. "But it would be a mass conversion."

"And it would be a mass dream granting with so many goals met at once," Mitch mused.

"Right," Tiff chipped in. "This is fun."

I checked the time inwardly and pushed myself up from the doorframe.

"No more fun. I'm not putting you in any more danger," I told Tiff firmly. "We have fifteen minutes to get clear of Tiff's rooms before Curtis makes contact again and we make a noticeable ex –"

I paused as my acute hearing picked up on a humming noise.

"Get down!" I hissed, ducking and pressing myself against the door frame.

V and Mitch both dived behind the sofas they'd been sitting on just before a Soldier circled slowly into view through the sheer curtains.

He was peering into each room of the apartment building with sharp eyes, but from outside it looked like Tiff was alone in her living room, pondering life, so the Soldier moved on to spy into the next apartment.

I let out a pent up breath. "If they're searching buildings then they've finished checking the streets and they'll come in soon. And now we have twelve minutes to be gone."

"There's a virtual hub a couple of floors down," Tiff supplied helpfully, and the three of us made for her front door, V clutching his bed-sheet full of tricks again.

"It's the kind of hub where everyone goes to sit in the one dingy room in their tracksuits, but when they hook up they're in a fancy bar," she explained. "Very exclusive."

"Tiff, I can hardly thank you …" I began, but didn't expect her sudden hug.

"You're welcome," she beamed. "I *knew* you'd be trying to fix everything."

I hugged her back.

"Goodbye and good luck, my buddy," she said warmly.

Excerpts from: The Collected Tales of Mythological and Historical Heroes

This is a first edition text, published by the World's third generation of great Leaders. Congratulations – you've purchased one of the last Leader approved hard copy texts!

On the subject of influential discoveries:

During the time of the second generation of great Leaders, commissioned human beings began to be grown in laboratories. These people could be made to serve whatever purpose was most necessary at that time.

It was not clear if these people had what is commonly referred to as a 'soul' or real emotions of love, and for a while the ethics of creating people without families and perhaps without real feelings was debated strongly.

However it was decided that creating people with purpose, to be put to use, was worthwhile so that other humans could benefit from the experiments and labour that these people could be used for.

The creation of these people has of course been limited due to overpopulation, but there is hope that one day in the future a perfect model can be invented, which will lead the way to great progress for all of humankind.

| 30 |

– The Star –

Lili was sitting on the ward bed, and under the pale light, around her crop top, I could see the blooming purple of a bruise that coloured her entire side.

It spread out from beyond the support patch Ned had put on her ribs, to cover half of her front and all the way to her spine.

I could also see the marks where my own hands had pressed into her chest.

She winced as I helped her get an arm through her zip-up top, and I guided her slice-covered fingers through the sleeve.

Lili had defied all medic orders to stay in the ward another night after she'd spent one night under observation.

Her heart had stopped and she had been lifeless the day before, but today she was just stiff and irritable. There wasn't much they could say as she rejuvenated so speedily, and as she insisted on staying firmly in the middle of the action.

"Ouch?" I asked as she stood and stretched; testing her muscles.

"Ouch," she agreed. "But a good ouch. Let's visit V."

I shrugged at the medics helplessly as I followed her out of the ward and down a little further to the lab where Queenie was working with V.

I nearly did a double take as a completely realistic 3D image of Lili stood in front of them, before V tapped some buttons and the image became that of a memory chip.

"You've done a remarkable job Queenie," V told her admiringly. "You have been so thorough that it's like I've got most of my past work here."

Queenie and V appeared to have been coyly enjoying each other's flattery for a while. Queenie seemed alight with the fun of matching wits with someone on her intellectual level. Meanwhile her star, Raziel – the great and wise, mystery resolving angel – was swivelling his chair in slow circles in the distance, the picture of boredom.

"Any luck?" Lili asked, examining the hologram.

"Queenie has all of your information," V said happily. "So I feel right at home, and quite confident that I can find a way of going virtual and transmitting signals or waves through the technology above ground."

"Cam, Jo and Evangeline have done some spying," Queenie also informed us. "They think we may have just a day left before they have to confront the Slayer. Maybe less. Everyone's on high alert."

"I always meet my deadlines," V wasn't worried. "We'll give this Pendragon a World he can actually make changes in."

"So we're not needed yet," I told Lili, taking her hand and pulling her gently away with me. "We've got time to make breakfast."

She smiled a little at that, and allowed me to drag her to our quarters.

"Lili! You're up and about!" Curtis came bounding from the room he shared with Junior.

Peering into their room, I saw that Theus and Dora were draped over Curtis' bunk, and Will was in one of their chairs. They'd all been playing some kind of hologram game where the figures strutted around on the floor challenging each other.

"Still kicking," she confirmed.

"What are you two up to?" Junior asked from inside.

"Breakfast," I answered cheerfully.

"Oh great!" Curtis grabbed a jumper from inside the door. "That'll beat a rec room breakfast!"

"How nice," Dora grinned at us, pulling Theus up and skipping ahead to my room. The others emptied out to follow them, with Curtis even banging on Bear's door so that he and Jana appeared.

I raised my eyebrows at Lili, at a loss for words.

"Want to try the eggs thing again?" she said in a daring tone. "We're more practiced this time."

I created a long table for the guests crowding my apartment, and together we cooked load after load of miraculously appearing eggs in every possible style of egg creation imaginable.

We maneuvered around each other naturally, and the noise on the other side of our bench was incredible. As if I had suddenly acquired a loud, and *real* family.

Lili was smiling and her cheeks were flushed as we fed the

demanding masses. And all of us, especially Lili, forgot our worries or our pain for a moment, in that frenzy of food.

Finally the two of us were sitting down with the 'family' too, amongst the yelling and joking and heckling and jostling.

When Lili had finished eating – at what was now closer to lunch time, she rested the un-bruised side of her face on my shoulder contentedly.

And in that instant I felt like the summer sun was rising in the pit of my stomach, with its soft yellow rays lighting up my core.

I realised that I'd witnessed others going through that exact hazy, soft, filled up, weightless feeling since the dawn of time.

Lili lifted her head from my shoulder then, making me blink and notice that everyone at the table had stopped moving. Cutlery had stopped clattering and voices had paused as our guests paid attention to some kind of internal message.

"Meeting room, now," Dora filled Lili and I in, and I regretfully watched Lili's face become serious again.

I let the table and all breakfast materials disappear as if they'd never been while the room emptied as fast as it had filled up.

Lili waited for me, and I knew I couldn't resist.

"Hey Lil?"

She regarded me quizzically.

"You look cold again."

I reached for her, circling one arm around her so that our bodies swept together. And I pressed my lips to hers.

Another kiss of life, with both of us warming right up.

Her hands rested on my hips and mine pressed against her back.

And when I drew back Lili smiled like the summer sun was rising in the pit of her stomach, with its soft yellow rays lighting up her core too.

Excerpts from: The Collected Tales of Mythological and Historical Heroes

This is a first edition text, published by the World's third generation of great Leaders. Congratulations – you've purchased one of the last Leader approved hard copy texts!

On the subject of places, events, conflicts and movements:
** Note, in this section, lands that are believed to have existed prior to the unification of World are mentioned.*

The Greek Spartans *were raised to be fierce warriors. As young children they faced trials, such as surviving in the wilderness alone. If they died it was seen as fair, because only superior warriors were successful citizens of Sparta.*

Some myths say that when a force of millions of Persians attempted to invade Greece, three hundred Spartans and their leader Leonidas held off the advance of the Persians until a united Greek navy could be gathered, sacrificing themselves to block the Persians' path on a narrow pass.

A tale to remember when you feel outnumbered or are facing impossible odds.

| 31 |

– The Dreamer –

Mitch and I ran to catch up to the others, slipping into the bursting meeting room where two chairs had been kept for us near Jo and Cam.

My stomach was doing little flips, my skin was prickling with heat and I was breathless, though none of it was from the quick jog. And none of it was usual for me.

"The Slayer has run out of time," Jo informed the crowd, and Mitch took my hand, inspiring new tingles as we turned to listen.

"The Leaders are all being summoned to Uthoria's bedside to be ready for her to pass power," Jo added, and turned to Cam, who drew in a deep breath.

"Though my mother is no longer conscious," he began. "She only has to feel the touch of the person she has chosen as preferred candidate, and her Brainwave will do the rest. Her Brainwave has a program called Excalibur that can withdraw identity files of control from one person and transfer them to another."

Evangeline cut in then. "So obviously we have to get Cam

there first, as she may have felt forced to select a second preference."

Cam's face was pinched, and for once I also felt a faint desire for things to stay the same for just a short while longer. If only we could stay down here, without a revolution to worry about, for just one more night.

Very un-Soldier-like, my focus wandered from the World-changing briefing as I glanced at Mitch.

He was already watching me from the corner of his eye. He gave a wink and squeezed my hand.

"I'll try to go in undetected," Cam said. "I'll take Evangeline, and would appreciate Mitch's help along with Lili's strength."

I nodded, making an effort to keep my gaze forward rather than on my star.

What if we lost each other in all of this? Death had said this was our last lifetime.

"We must hope that the strength of Mitch and Evangeline will be able to enlighten Uthoria, and somehow help her realise her dream without having her own star there," Cam added grimly. "We have no choice but to do this now, even though we don't yet have the ability to make a fresh start or any real changes."

"WAITWAITWAIT!" V came flying towards the doors from down the corridor. "I can help with that!" he stooped over to catch his breath, looking up at his startled audience with a triumphant expression. "Well ..." he gasped and lifted his green goggles. "I can nearly help with that. But we'll need more than just a small team."

"That's more like it," Dora clapped her hands together enthusiastically. "That's the way it should be."

V wove his way between people and clutched the back of Will's chair. "I've worked out how to utilise mass produced tech above ground – like adverts and Biobeauty machines. And I can use these to gradually reverse any emissions that have been conditioning people in the past. But for a faster change, I am going to need every Rogue and dreamer to make their way above ground. To storm the streets, and to open a portal from every source they would usually use to go virtual. With so many ports open, I'll be able to send my energy waves out en-masse. Then I'll also have enough connections established Worldwide, that I'll be able to spread my influence through the digital veins connecting *everything* up – reaching into all tech in existence. It'll be like flipping a switch toward enlightenment and free choice."

"That could cause widespread confusion," Jo commented with concern. "We don't want to put our own objectives before the wellbeing of all citizens, thrusting them into something new before they're ready. That's what the current Leaders would do."

"You're right," V agreed. "That's where the stars come in."

"What can we do to help?" Gabe asked.

V grinned. "Well, you angelic beings contain the power to open people's eyes up to the truth in a healthy way. This is your exact purpose; to reveal to people what they truly need and desire. So we're going to need every star we can get to spread their influence so that the surface citizens can embrace the change, can embrace their liberty without descending into mayhem, so that they can easily break through the mental shackles that have been programmed into them."

"We're going to need an awful lot of sand," Mitch commented beside me.

"Yes! A global sandstorm," V danced on the spot with glee. "With all of your kind rising from every Rogue base across the planet, giving it everything you've got."

"I can get the message out while you go," Jo told Cam. "We'll wait to give you a chance before it all starts. And then every able bodied person will be playing their part to make this incredible dream happen."

"Let's do this," Cam nodded resolutely.

Within the short time it took us to prep, the whole station was already buzzing. The nervous tension was practically sizzling in the air as word spread across our base, and presumably to every other Rogue base under the earth. The corridors were erupting with action.

Mitch, Evangeline and I went with Cam to the padded landing room, which would soon be teeming with people – all preparing to flood into the virtual and then real World.

"Uthoria would have wanted her privacy, so her many Soldier guards should be stationed *outside* her bedroom," Cam was telling V.

"I'll be able to turn the power off in the Slayer's house for a split second and no alarms or Soldiers should register your arrival in her bedroom," V nodded. Then he gave me a slap on my good shoulder before he quickly exited the padded room.

With hardly a pause we were being sucked into the tunnel

of wires – and we at once rushed onward to find the right point in the wall.

Adrenalin pumping, I kept my team upright as we were hurtled out into Cam's house – finding ourselves right in the middle of the Slayer's room, with no alarms going off.

Cam cautiously followed Evangeline and Mitch towards the bed, but the hard faced sleeper did not stir when Evangeline and Mitch tried to communicate with her.

I paced the room, listening for any movement from the guards outside as precious time passed.

"She really is like a rock!" Evangeline hissed, becoming increasingly frustrated, and Mitch's forehead even beaded with sweat as they both tried to touch the Slayer's mind.

"What's wrong?" Cam at last whispered edgily.

"She's too deeply unconscious for us to get through to her," Evangeline answered agitatedly.

"There are no realisations happening here," Mitch admitted tersely. "We aren't in tune with her because we weren't meant to be her stars, and she definitely isn't responding to us."

"Should I just touch her hand anyway?" Cam fretted. "The Leaders are guaranteed to be arriving soon. All jostling to see who she's chosen to draw Excalibur."

"No, you can't. The problems won't end for the World if we don't get it right and make her move on," Evangeline scowled.

But then both Evangeline and Mitch gasped, staring at each other in horror.

My heart jumped up to get wedged in my throat as I practically blurred forward, fearing that one of them had somehow been hurt – or that Uthoria had just suddenly died.

"What is it?" Cam whispered nervously.

"It's Tien!" Evangeline answered in shock. "Being reborn close to here!"

Mitch turned toward the window. "And she has no idea what's going on."

"Michael, we can't go to her now!" Evangeline hissed.

"She's been killed by them before," Mitch frowned. "Who knows if she'll be able to survive and come back if they get her again."

"That's the same for you," Cam echoed what I was thinking.

Evangeline gripped Mitch's arm desperately. "If we go to help her, we could jeopardise everything here."

For once he didn't pull away from her.

"I know what it's like to be left to die by your family," Mitch answered quietly. "And I know the universe has a reason for bringing Tien back to us, within our reach, at this exact moment."

Evangeline stood back from him, gaping.

I hurriedly strained my mind to find the last traces of V's final contact to me from before his rescue.

"OUUUUCH!" V's voice seared my mind. "Whhaat??" he moaned.

"Power off again. Now," I ordered, walking over to the vast window, lighting my fighter designs.

The moment the power was off, I ran my hands around the window in a rectangular shape; using laser heat to slice a glass doorway free. I lowered the glass rectangle to the side just as the power came back on, and Mitch pulled me to himself for a second.

"Did you know …" he whispered beside my ear. "That you are the first person I ever loved?" he drew back and grinned at me before flying out in a golden haze.

"Well," Cam gulped as he joined me at the window – though his gaze was downward. "The Leaders are here."

Excerpts from: The Collected Tales of Mythological and Historical Heroes

This is a first edition text, published by the World's third generation of great Leaders. Congratulations – you've purchased one of the last Leader approved hard copy texts!

On the subject of places and people of interest:

** Note, in this section, lands that are believed to have existed prior to the unification of World are mentioned.*

Arthur Pendragon *built his kingdom of* **Camelot** *as a place of fairness, where people could aspire to be the greatest version of themselves. It was a place of heroes and growth, where resolutions were reached diplomatically, change was achieved through learning and forethought, and poverty was combatted with shared wealth and care.*

Arthur and Camelot represented the need for morality and for people to see that they could be greater than their station or even than their own belief in themselves.

However, legends say that such an idealistic place could not survive in such a young, inexperienced World, and that that is why inner turmoil and outer threats from other armies were able to cause Camelot's fall.

The legends also described how, when the time was right for the World to reach new heights and to embrace a better way of being, a state of 'Camelot' would arise again. In a sense, Arthur would return: the once and future king.

| 32 |

– The Star –

The assassin Soldiers were on my tail at once.

They had been on the perimeter of the Slayer's house, and they had seen me.

I could feel how close Tien was, and how afraid she was.

They had felt her too.

I wasn't the only one closing in on her.

My speed was incredible, but time stretched until I saw her from above – running for her life as five of them chased her down, aiming their poison weapons.

I swooped down to land so that she ran into my arms, and I engulfed us in a whirling sandstorm to blind both my pursuers and hers.

Tien knew me immediately, and buried her face in my chest. I pushed up and carried us away, feeling a rain of darts penetrate and poison the sand I'd left behind.

I dodged us around buildings and under a bridge, hearing the darts piercing holes in the structures as we passed. Despite my speed, they were now coming from everywhere –

drawn to me like magnets – and I had no idea how to lose our hunters.

"Michael!" a voice suddenly roared both inside my mind and outside my physical body.

And I saw Aris leaning out of an abandoned workshop below, reaching out to us recklessly.

Careening at top speed, I angled us towards Aris and we hurtled down.

I let Tien go so she pelted in through the open warehouse door and into Aris' arms. He pulled her straight into the portal Dora had opened, and I dodged a stream of blasts as I was swallowed up by the portal after them.

The darts were embedded in the wiry wall nearby and my pulse was racing as I laid breathlessly on the tunnel floor, while Aris hugged the fairy-like star, Tien, as if she was actually *his* angel.

The tunnel rang with voices, and I pushed my head up to see that the passage was filled for as far the eye could see with people and stars. They were waiting to spill out into reality.

Then I felt two mighty fists drag me to my feet before I was smothered and wrapped nearly out of existence by Aris' embrace.

"Thank you," the lion husked.

"Gah," I managed, before Tien put a hand on Aris' arm and I tapped out for release.

The Rogues around us were staring at Tien for her exotic, dark skinned beauty, and at Aris – for his completely out of character lack of grumpiness.

"We have to get back," Tien told Aris calmly. She turned to me then. "You were where I needed to be."

"I knew it!" I rounded on Dora. "Can you get us back to the Slayer?"

"No …" Aris moaned.

"Easy," Dora said. She plugged right back in, and gave me a light shove. "See ya!"

I poured back out into the Slayer's bedroom, Tien toppling after me. We landed safely on the carpet – which happened to place us very unsafely in the middle of a tense standoff.

I blinked up at the hostile ring of Soldiers encircling Evangeline, Lili, Cam, the occupied bed, Tien and I … and a group of flummoxed, terrified Leaders. But the Soldiers weren't attacking.

They were frozen because Lili had her hands around the throats of two of the Leaders – threatening to kill them if any Soldier made a move.

There was also a momentary advantage from everyone's surprise at us two little stars popping into existence in their midst.

"Go!" I told Tien, hurriedly throwing a thick curtain of sand up around our encircled group, shutting the Soldiers out. Gritting my teeth, I turned my sand to fire – a twisting wall of heavenly flame to shield us.

Tien ran to the Slayer, crouching over the prone woman, and I felt a hailstorm of poison bullets try to penetrate my inferno of sand and burning power.

I cried out as the darts turned to ash, but left scars of spreading grey across my whirling sand. I could feel the poison kill each golden particle, which had been part of my own self.

Lili dropped her hostages and let her lightning energy blaze alive so that it twisted around her arms and flared in her eyes. The Leaders whimpered and scrambled back from her as she lifted her electrified hands to my whirling sheet of sand, sending out her own crackling power to join with mine.

There were shouts of consternation on the other side of our shield, but this time their darts all bounced back as if hitting a force field and I felt no pain.

I sensed two Soldiers try to run at our tornado and be flung backward too.

"Why on earth didn't we think of this before we both died at different points in recent history?!" I called to Lili over the noise of the sizzling hurricane.

She shook her head with raised brows and a grin, before glancing over her shoulder at the gathering around the bed.

The Leaders cowered together now like good witnesses as Tien took the Slayer's hand, and the Slayer's eyes flashed open.

"Use Michael's sand," Evangeline told Tien briskly.

"And look as deeply at your dreamer's essence as you can. Beyond their current, surface experiences," I called.

Evangeline reached for both Tien's shoulder and for Cam's while Tien stretched her free hand out to brush her fingertips against my sand.

At once the image of what Tien wanted to show her dreamer was cast across my sand like a fast revolving cinema screen.

It was an image of Uthoria, glaring at one of the 'missing' holograms of Cam.

"For this World to survive, we must have strict order. One step out of place will be too much, and the balance will be lost," the memory of Uthoria was growling.

Then, just as I had seen Theus and Dora's many faces changing throughout time, Uthoria's image shifted, at times becoming masculine.

"Hitler," I muttered in distaste, seeing the dictator shouting to the masses about a need for racial purity. "And Napoleon?" The leader was scowling and driving his soldiers on in an effort to take England.

I recognised Queen Mary I – Bloody Mary, who had ordered the deaths of thousands of protestants. And possibly Ghengis Khan, who had united Mongolia by drowning it in blood. There were many others, all similar in their tyrannical natures when it came to getting what they wanted.

Satan had not been exaggerating about Uthoria's soul. It had to move on.

Finally there was an image of a man we had not seen before, in a time that appeared medieval. He wore a crown, and glared down at his son.

"King Uther Pendragon, and Arthur," Tien murmured.

"For this world to survive such a dark age, we must have strict order. One step out of place will be too much, and the balance will be lost," Uther was growling.

Evangeline added her own hand to my screen of sand now, while keeping hold of Cam.

Cam's images were different to the others I had seen so

far. They did not begin in more modern times. They went straight back to Uthor's son – Arthur.

Arthur sat at a round table. He was about to face his final conflict as he addressed his followers.

"My ideals, and all of the most beautiful ideals of humanity, are represented here, in our Camelot. The dream of Camelot is for a world that is healthy, and just. Camelot will never truly fall, but will rise again when the world most needs peace, and a chance for life."

Beyond us, in the streets outside of our torn apart bedroom, there were crashes and the sounds of voices being raised. The Rogues were flooding out into the real world, and soon V would unleash change.

Tien was speaking now, leaning over Uthoria and urging the dying Slayer to hear her words.

"Your dream for ultimate organisation and for a functioning world is coming true through your own son, through Cam. He can restore balance to people and the environment without controlling or hurting them, but by guiding them to health."

More and more voices were echoing from outside. It felt like the world was throbbing. People were waking up and wondering.

"Your soul has been willing to resort to any means to accomplish your wish," Tien went on. "Sometimes you have created what can be seen as order. But in your willingness to destroy, you have also brought pain. *You* have caused imbalance."

Evangeline's face was blanched with shock as realisation

dawned on her features. "Your son is not just Arthur returned," she said to the Slayer. "He is Arthur's ideals and Camelot's ideals all in one. He represents the idyllic world. A world restored, and a world that will survive. Grant him the power to do as you have wished. To save this world. Grant him the power to do this in his own way."

Then the ground shook beneath us, not just in that building, but in all of them. I heard lightbulbs burst and screens shatter. I felt a tsunami of vibrations rattle up, out of the earth, consuming all technology as V flicked the switch so that the world would never be the same.

Time seemed to pause for a moment, as the sand and electricity blurred around us, and as we watched on.

We all saw the slight movement of Uthoria's lips as she smiled a thin, hard smile. And we all saw the fingers of her hand shakily open.

Cam slid his hand into hers, and she held him as she allowed the Excalibur file to transfer its data to her son.

She died with that smile still on her face, her soul at last satisfied enough to rest.

Cam slumped, having lost a mother who had finally understood him. But his tears were glad ones – that he had been given the freedom to do things right, as he'd always wished.

"I'm sorry, but this isn't over!" Lili raised her voice over the sound of the whirling sand. "Curtis and Junior say the others need help!"

The Soldiers outside my sand were still unleashing charge after charge of poison bullets into my protective wall.

So maybe not *everything* had changed yet.

"The stars are still targets," Lili yelled, "and the Soldiers are not waking up! V thinks we need bait, to draw them closer to a place full of enough technology – radiating with enough of the transmission that they'll be converted back to free thinkers!"

That's when she looked at me.

"Great," I sighed.

Excerpts from: The Collected Tales of Mythological and Historical Heroes

This is a first edition text, published by the World's third generation of great Leaders. Congratulations – you've purchased one of the last Leader approved hard copy texts!

On the subject of places, events, conflicts and movements:
** Note, in this section, lands that are believed to have existed prior to the unification of World are mentioned.*

Ancient Asia produced many incredible inventions, and Ancient India developed architectural wonders.

The Middle Eastern Golden Age was a time of medical and mathematical advancement in history, and the European Renaissance was a time of wonder. People began to be curious and to learn about the physical World rather than focusing on superstition.

Surprisingly, these times of progression and beauty came about when people were given the opportunity to think more freely.

It is a relief that these times are past and we can now reap the rewards without having to go through the disorder of change or having to puzzle through too much ourselves.

| **33** |

– The Dreamer –

"When Lili and I lift off, our shield will come with us and everyone will need to duck," Mitch was telling the group. "The Soldiers will follow us out, but there are guaranteed to be bullets flying."

One of the Leaders came towards me then. One who particularly needed to redeem himself, in my eyes.

"You could take them to the updates centre in the hospital," Soldier Leader Con suggested gruffly, making an effort to look me in the eye.

I nodded. He was right. It was the place where all Soldiers had been created to be as they now were, and it was also a facility oozing in up to date tech. V's waves would be radiating from the place.

As the others got down behind the bed, pressing against the carpet, I saw both Tien and Evangeline stand firmly with Mitch. Tien took one of his hands, and Evangeline took Tien's so that they could fly with us. They added their sand; another layer of armour, to Mitch's.

He regarded them for a moment, before he held out his other hand to me.

I withdrew my touch from the spinning wall of sand, but I kept my fighter designs alight, and the voltages pumping through the sand did not fade. I took his hand in mine.

Feeling like we were carrying the colossal weight of the whole World on our shoulders, we hauled ourselves upward, forcing our feet to lift off so that the sand shifted upwards with us.

We crashed our way through the remains of the window, and out into free air, struggling to maintain height.

I felt the sting of each bullet that hit the sand as if it had pounded into me physically. The Soldiers in the Slayer's room had followed as Mitch had said.

"Can we hold this?!" Evangeline shrieked under the pressure of our swirling sphere, as Mitch tried to angle us upward.

My internal maps showed that we were mere minutes from the hospital, but my teeth were already gritting with the weight of the sand and the effort of keeping it electrified as it spun.

There was crack after crack of rounds being fired, and we all felt the winding impact as each shot collided with our shield.

"Is it working?" I yelled across my line to V. "Are they following?"

"You've probably got all the Soldiers for miles following you," his strained voice answered quickly. "But it needs to be bigger to get more attention!"

"We can't manage anything bigger!" I groaned – labouring as if trying to run through water.

"They need to feel it from all over the World!" V insisted.

"How?!" I groaned back.

"Wait … Gabriel here has an idea. He's speaking to Jana."

"Oh sure," I panted. "I'll wait." At least I could count on Jana to be extremely helpful.

We were edging our way across the sky in an agonisingly slow procession.

Tien and Evangeline were beginning to pale as the attacks on our shield – our bait – grew to be an onslaught. Surely we had managed to get the attention of every Soldier alive. Surely we were feeling the fire power of every poisoned gun to have ever been issued.

Then I felt Mitch jolt in surprise, and I peered through the rushing air in astonishment myself.

Aris and Gabe had burst into our midst, air-borne and adding their own sand to the mix – helping us to hold it all. They were wearing the tech survival packs that my team, and all normal Soldiers had used for flying or driving before the latest updates had changed everything.

"We portalled into the Soldier bases. They had rooms full of these," Gabe yelled.

"They didn't just portal us two though," Aris called. "Stars from all over the world are on their way."

"We're behind you, Michael," Gabriel shouted.

And our sphere widened suddenly to embrace an influx of stars I had never even seen before. With every minute more stars appeared beside us and the sand globe extended but grew easier to bear. I let the electricity ebb outward from me freely, though I was sure we hardly needed it anymore with so much buzzing power.

Soon I wondered if every star on the planet had portalled over and found their way to us. I could hardly see them all in the distance and the haze.

"YES YES YES!" V was cheering. "The sky is TEEMING with Soldiers on your tail! You can't even see the clouds for sand and Soldiers! Keep going, you're nearly there!"

"Will you be ready to hit them with everything you've got?" I asked through gasps.

"Baby, the place is jumping it's that full of my waves! And the waves will spread outward through the crowds like the best explosion you've ever seen."

"One we'll survive," I grunted. "Right?"

"You're there, X marks the spot!" I heard Curtis bellowing his own transmission.

"We're here," I yelled to Mitch. "The waves should flow outward and keep on rolling over us."

"*Should* ..." Mitch's voice was strained. "I would prefer to know that you and I will get to come out of this and live happily ever after ..."

"But just in case," I called. "Did you know ... that you're the first person I ever loved?"

Then I released his hand and descended through the sand, dropping fast.

I let my entire body become ablaze with electricity. Every strand of hair, every inch of skin.

And with one bone shaking detonation, I blasted the roof of the hospital to nothingness.

Excerpts from: The New Histories

The first New Year of the New Age actually started with an event that many had thought was the end of all days.

Rogue forces emerged from thin air to rally in the streets, the entire sky turned to golden light and fire, and technology began to pulse with energy World-wide.

Yet this was actually the start of all things for many people, with reports of a sense of awakening and hope spreading faster than old time pandemics ever supposedly spread.

People at the time described it as a moment of true clear headedness and re-lief.

Now this occasion is marked each year with displays of gold and glorious lights. Like heaven on earth.

– The Star –

I screamed Lili's name as she disappeared like a mirage.

An explosion of heat, air and light rippled up from under us, jostling our great load, and I knew she had done something crazy – possibly burned herself out entirely, to let V's waves crash out freely into the world.

I was ready to drop it all – every bit of my sandstorm could snuff out for all I cared in that moment.

But Evangeline caught at me as she saw me desperately dipping downward.

Aris and Gabe put their hands on my shoulders.

Evangeline placed her palm on my chest.

Once upon a time their eyes had burned with betrayed hate and their grip had forced me down.

Her fingers had sliced into my heart.

They had thought I cared nothing for what people really needed.

Now she simply felt the hammering of my heart, her fierce eyes pleading. Now they simply gazed at me with sympathy, and hope.

"She's my dreamer," I cried out. "My dream!"

"Let her dream come true," Aris told me, a husk in his voice. "Send our sand out to every person in this world so that they can all be free."

Gabe supported me in the air as I felt myself slump in helplessness.

He held me like a brother and I felt a sob claw from my throat as I forced Evangeline into Gabe's arms, and guided Tien to Aris.

"Get away from me," I told them, and they hesitated. "Get away!" I roared, and my voice pricked the mind of every star who had joined with me.

I would need their sand but not their lives.

"Go," I added, pleading, as the heavenly fire started to burn up my vision and bite at my fingers and clothes.

One by one they sank down out of the sky and I turned my focus inward. Focusing with every part of my own soul, and with every ounce of heavenly power in my being.

Lili would not be the only one to risk her all. I would do anything to make her dream for the world, for all people, come true.

Everything seemed to slow as I built up my storm.

It was rebounding within and around me like a wailing furnace. It was thundering, spearing, multiplying in my chest.

And then I let it all burst out in fireworks of flashing gold so bright that they would light up the entire globe.

Excerpts from: The New Histories

When Uthoria Pendragon, the last Leader of the old Leadership passed, a new order was established.

Uthoria's heir, Cam Pendragon established his council of knights to minister different jobs and be part of the round office.

Knights from then on were to achieve their position by demonstrating exemplary behaviours and by commendable actions. Knights could come from any part of the World hierarchy, and could be put forward as champions by their communities. Or they could put their own names forward for consideration after completing humanitarian trials with enough efficiency, wit and empathy to be commendable.

Each knight was to be in charge of caretaking key areas of life, though each knight also had to have their own sub council of citizen advisors with specific experience, personal interest and research into that area.

Cam Pendragon himself determined that ultimate Leadership was to be a thing of the past, and that after serving five year terms, the most highly commended and provably capable knights could put forward their intentions to be the new overseer. The candidate with the greatest results when undergoing ethics and intelligence measures would have their turn as the World's new guide.

Most importantly, the Camelot Constitution was written to set out rules on how the internal tech of any human being can be used, in what ways it can be used, and how far legal control is allowed to go. A dedicated taskforce was set up in dedication to anti-corruption, anti-virus and anti-hacking protections.

The Constitution also included set rules on the limits to progress that can be made based on environmental impact. For progress is only progress if it does not contribute to the death of our World.

| 35 |

– The Star –

Lili was asleep, dreaming peacefully against me.

I was lightly tracing gold patterns across her palm, which rested against my knee.

The once silvery lines beneath her skin were faintly blue – still healing after all this time. But the gold feather-line veins hadn't faded in my own skin either – where over exertion had made heavenly fire blur through my body to become permanently part of my skin. Like smudged water colours that shone.

"Happy New Year!" Junior burst into the apartment I shared with Lili, and there were happy greetings as he flopped straight in on a couch to watch the screenwall along with the others.

"Happy New Year man," Curtis beamed, and generously waved his bowl of Meteorites under Junior's nose.

"It's starting," Jana purred, ignoring the offensively bright snacks as they passed by her face.

"I am speaking to Cam Pendragon a year on from the day that thousands of Soldiers rained down from our skies." The reporter's lavender eyes were bright as she introduced her New Year story. "A year on from when the Slayer affair came to an end."

The screen split to show Cam, who was standing in the middle of a real meadow.

"Overseer Pendragon, in one year alone you have fulfilled many promises and reformed not only the old Leadership systems, but our way of life," the reporter continued. "You have done it with the support of your people, when normally great change is accompanied by great resistance. However, what, would *you* say, are some of your proudest achievements?"

"*Ooooooh!*" Curtis gushed excitedly. "Do you think he'll say my name? I've been such a good rehab Soldier mentor."

"You're hardly his proudest achievement," Junior told him wryly, reaching across the couch for another handful of orange Meteorbites.

"Besides, our team had enough screen time back when our mugshots were on display," Bear snickered.

"Only Jana's mugshot was worth looking at," Curtis sulked. Jana simply nodded.

On the news update Cam gestured behind himself happily. "Because of the hard work of our above ground teams, I am standing in a real field. Our teams are committed to restoring natural hubs around the whole World."

"*Curtis* … It's an easy name. *Cuuuuuuuuurtiiiiiiiiiiiiiis.*"

"And," Cam went on. "I'm also pleased to say that space will no longer be an issue as World class underlandscapers are currently transforming what were once Rogue bases into entirely new cities. These cities can expand into naturally formed underground cavities, and will be completely sustainable."

The fairy floss haired reporter nodded from her side of the screen thoughtfully. "The knight of Sustainability has recently begun plans to alter our sun filter. Could that put us at risk of global warming once again?"

"I really don't think he's going to say it," Curtis gaped in disbelief.

"Our main goal is simply to absorb some of the sun's energy, which is currently being blocked," Cam explained. "Just harnessing a few second's worth of the sun's energy could power our World sustainably for years."

"You have already put in place programs to nurture nature, and now it seems nature is giving back," the reporter commented. "Mineral springs have been found near all the underground city centres. And this year we had the stories of the first natural born, completely wild species of marine life to be produced in this age."

"That's correct," Cam smiled, looking genuinely ecstatic. "In fact there are talks among scientists that many species of animals may begin to exist more readily without human design, if we keep working on their habitats. And something to watch out for in coming weeks is the opening of the first rainforest of the modern era, with more real sapling trees than anyone in this generation has ever seen."

The reporter leaned back, pleased. "Cam Pendragon, I sincerely look forward to doing the New Year story with you again this time next year," she told him optimistically. "Thank you," she nodded at the screen to sign off. "This has been KimLe reporting."

"Wow," Curtis said flatly.

"Very disappointing," Jana gingerly patted Curtis' orange stained hand as he sat back dejectedly.

"You're late," I grinned as Dora ushered Theus, V and Will in ahead of her.

"Tell me about it," Dora rolled her eyes. "I'm a week over-due already. I've told Ned and Queenie to be on round the clock standby. They'll be dropping their new glitzy jobs to bring me every bit of delivery tech in existence so I won't feel a thing." She sank into the couch that had miraculously appeared for the new arrivals.

"Queenie?" V asked keenly as he reached for a fizz pack. "How's she doing?"

Lili stretched and yawned against my side.

"I was having such a good dream," she said, opening one eye to squint up at me. "But it sounds like I missed the start of your party for our home getting warmed."

"You didn't miss much of the *house warming*," I told her teasingly. "My new family and my new home feels warmer than anything I've ever had."

"Oh, but I'm glad you did make peace with your real fam-ily," Dora cut in. "Before they moved on."

Junior shivered. "Everyone but Jo was probably relieved when Evangeline moved on though. I'd have been terrified if she'd popped up to make my dreams come true."

"I wouldn't say that too loud," I warned. "Stars bounce around in an era for a long while. So you could bump into Eva in your lifetime. In fact, the universe might think it's funny to reunite us all."

The toothpick Junior had started chewing on sagged downward on his lip.

"Well I'm glad that *one* rock star in particular stuck around. And I'm especially glad it's the rock star who can fix lunch," Lili declared, pulling me up from the couch.

"I LOVE that Mitch has stuck around to fix the lunch!" Curtis cheered, perking up as Lili disappeared into the next room.

"You know, you two are probably the only ones on this entire planet who have a real kitchen," V chuckled.

"We're a very retro couple," I agreed, following my dreamer into the kitchen.

She was reaching for a salad bowl as I stepped close behind her to engulf her in my arms.

"I'm happy," I told her honestly, and she leaned her head back to press her cheek against mine.

"I'm *very* happy," she responded.

"Is it because the world didn't end?" I asked.

"Hmmm," she drew it out. "I think it's because my life's finally started. And because I'm sharing it with you."

"Ah. Yes," I nodded. "What a dream come true."

Enjoy a free taste of the new action-romance series: 'Raze Warfare.'
A gritty urban backdrop, gang warfare, a vigilante hero, a corrupt sys-
tem, and a bisexual awakening. Join the action, enjoy the ride.

**RECEIVE YOUR EXTRA RAZE WARFARE
CHAPTER WHEN YOU SIGN UP FOR
SHELLEY CASS' VIP LIST. GET YOUR
BONUS HERE:**

shelleycass.com/coming-soon-02

LINK TO YOUR FREE VIP READER GIFT

OTHER BOOKS BY SHELLEY CASS

'Raze Warfare' New Adult Series:
Action and LGBTQ+ Romance

'A Fairy's Tale' Epic Fantasy Series:
Book One – 'The Last Larnaeradee'
Book Two – 'The Raiden'
Book Three – 'The Army for the World'

Dystopian Future:
'Awaken Dreamer'

Modern Action/Fantasy/Erotica:
'Darkling'

The Sleep Sweet Series for children:
Book One – 'Little Pixie's Christmas'
Book Two – 'The case of the bored baby Ace'
Book Three – 'Mum and Me'
Book Four – 'The Cloud and the Flower'
Book Five – 'Hush'

Dear reader,
I would love to hear your feedback!
Please leave a review and feel free to visit my author Facebook page
or website (shelleycass.com).

ABOUT THE AUTHOR

I was an awkward, reserved year 8 student – totally in love with the escape and comfort offered by the novels I read. I could hear the voices of the authors' characters, I could tune out my stresses and uncertainties as I journeyed with each protagonist through their own troubles. And then one day I could hear the voices of characters who hadn't been written yet, in places that hadn't been created, and I decided to write my own world.

It took a quest of over fifteen years to get that world perfected in three novels – because of course the real world kept getting in the way.

In the real world I became a high school teacher, and still face the epic battle of staying afloat in all the papers I must assess. And in the real world the magic has also sometimes been hard to find. Stress and disunity surface like cancer – making the nightly news too hard to watch on most days.

But in the real world there has also been inspiration – incredible students, loved ones, golden memories, growing up, warm hugs, big laughs and good people.

So I wrote of the things that threaten the world, and of the things that save it. I wish for a real world where the air is clean, the trees can grow without concrete borders, the darkness can be cured with the switch of a light, and the people can all have long days and happy lives.

ACKNOWLEDGMENTS

I am so thankful for the friends who understand me and embrace who I am.

I am so appreciative of my work family, for being my silver lining even on the most stressful days.

I am so appreciative of Wendy – the greatest neighbour to have ever lived, and Linda – the greatest mother to have ever lived. Your patience with reading my novels when they are still rough, clunky, colossal things is indescribably helpful.

I am so grateful for an extended family of extensive love: the bubbly and boisterous Brittinghams, Burkes and Rigbys, and the gracious, gorgeous Tangees, Lennens and Plants. My grandparents too, though lost, are such a special part of me.

I am so thankful for Linda (mum) and Robert (dad), who would move heaven and earth to make us happy.

For my sisters and best friends, Melissa and Leigh.

For my brother (in law), Andrew, and the lights of my life – Jack and Elyssia.

For the love of my life, my sunshine, Jarryd.

And for the little year eight version of me, who first picked up that pen to write.

www.ingramcontent.com/pod-product-compliance
Lightning Source LLC
Chambersburg PA
CBHW070203120726
47909CB00001B/226